Mike Resnick

HAZARDS

The Chronicles of Lucifer Jones
1934–1938

[Being a Romantic Chronicle of Intrigue, High Adventure, Danger, Spectacle, and Thrilling Triumphs Over Wicked Villains, Evil Scientists, Fierce Beasts and Fiercer Men in the Sinful Cities, Primitive Jungles, and Exotic Lost Empires of South America, as Recounted by the Daring, Handsome, Resourceful and Modest Christian Gentleman Who Experienced Them]

Mike Resnick

SUBTERRANEAN PRESS 2009

First Edition

ISBN
978-1-59606-230-6

Subterranean Press
PO Box 190106
Burton, MI 48519

www.subterraneanpress.com

Portions of this novel appeared in *Argosy, Subterranean, Adventure,* and *Son of Retro Pulp Tales*.

Contents

CAST OF CHARACTERS

Erich von Horst, a con man's con man.

Major Theodore Dobbins, late of His Majesty's Armed Forces, and more recently wanted in nine African nations for dealing in certain perishable commodities.

Baroness Schimmelmetz, whose inheritance of $800 million does tend to offset some of her less desirable features, such as her face, her body, and her personality.

Jasper McCorkle, who has modest plans to become the Emperor of Machu Picchu.

Rupert Cornwall, who doesn't travel quite as much as our hero, but is currently wanted by the police of three different continents.

Rama, the Bird Girl.

Bella, the Other Bird Girl.

Dr. Mirbeau, who has found a profitable new use for science on his secret island.

Valeria, a high priestess who is dressed for extremely warm weather.

Henry, formerly of New Jersey, presently the god of a thoroughly lost continent.

Merry Bunta, a charming girl who has perhaps unfairly high standards for her suitors' intelligence.

José Alvarez, one of many San Palmero presidential aspirants.

Culamara, who is either a naked goddess or a naked lady of the evening, or possibly both.

Capturin' Clyde Calhoun, famed the world over for bringing 'em back alive. Not intact, but alive.

The Scorpion Lady, an Oriental criminal mastermind with a truly exceptional pair of lungs.

Bubbles, an anaconda with an attitude.

And our narrator, The Right Reverend Honorable Doctor Lucifer Jones, a handsome, noble and resourceful Christian gentlemen who has certain unresolved disagreements with nine separate South American governments over the finer points of the law.

To Carol, as always

And to B. J. Galler-Smith,
a fine writer and a finer friend

EL PRESIDENTE

My first impression of South America back in 1934 wasn't a whole lot different from my strongest memories of North America, Africa, Asia and Europe: a six-by-eight-foot room, a canvas cot along one wall, steel bars on the windows, and lousy grub.

There are some things that are the same the world over. Most people are friendly and trusting folks, they're approachable even when you don't speak the lingo, and they all love an honest game of chance. They also tend to get ornery as all get-out when you trifle with the laws of statistical probability by gently inserting an extra couple of aces into the game, which I did about ten minutes after stepping off the boat from Spain, and they tend to have the same disheartening way of demonstrating their displeasure.

Which is how I wound up in the calaboose in Ferdinand, the capital city of San Palmero. Over the years I had become quite a connoisseur of jails. This one didn't have the quality of cuisine I found in the jails of Europe, but on the other hand it wasn't anywhere near as crowded as the jails in China or as run-down and badly in need of repair as the jails of Mozambique and South Africa. The guards weren't bad sorts, and as they happily confided, they belonged to the one sector of a sluggish economy that had always boasted full employment during the reigns of the last few rulers.

It was on my third morning there, while I was still awaiting a hearing before the local magistrate (which the guards assured me might well take place in something less than five years, especially — and here they kind of reached into their pockets and jingled their coins — if I could find some way to encourage them to bring my situation to his attention), when I suddenly got a roommate.

He was tall and lean and kind of swarthy, with a bushy black moustache, and he looked like he'd been roughly handled along the way.

"Good morning, Señor," he said as the door was locked behind him. "I am sorry to intrude upon your privacy."

"Truth to tell, I could use a bit of company," I replied. "It gets a little lonely in here from time to time with nothing to comfort me except my copy of the Good Book. What's your name, friend?"

"José Juan Domingo Garcia de Alvarez," he said.

"That's quite a mouthful," I said. "You got any problem if I just call you Joe?"

"No," he said. "But why not José?"

"Because so far, counting poker players and constables and prison guards, I've met thirteen citizens of your fair country and eleven of 'em have been named José."

"It is a popular name," he agreed. "Not as popular as Maria, but still..."

"You got a lot of guys called Maria, do you?" I asked.

"Women, senor. Hardly any men are called Maria."

"Good," I said. "I got enough problems as it is."

"And what is your own name?"

"I'm the Right Reverend Honorable Doctor Lucifer Jones," I told him, "formerly of Moline, Illinois, and currently a citizen of the world." Which was officially true, and certainly sounded better than saying that I had been banished from 33 separate countries due to our different interpretations of the finer points of the law, and had been forcibly requested to leave the last four continents I'd visited. Truth to tell, I was fast running out of major land masses that would tolerate my presence, which is why I wasn't in no hurry to walk into the local magistrate's courtroom.

"Of what church are you a minister?" asked Joe.

"The Tabernacle of Saint Luke," I said. "Donations gladly accepted."

"I have never heard of it."

"Well, it ain't quite got itself built yet," I admitted. "I'm still scouting out locations."

"How long have you been looking?" he asked.

"Oh, maybe ten or twelve years," I said. "You can't just rush into these things."

"I don't believe I've ever heard of Saint Luke," he said.

"You're talking to him," I said. "You'd be surprised how calling it the Tabernacle of Saint Lucifer puts contributors off their feed."

"Forgive an impertinence," said Joe, "but just what religion is it that you practice?"

"A little something me and the Lord worked out betwixt ourselves of a Sunday afternoon back in Moline," I said. "It ain't got no name yet, though I been toying with calling it Lukeism after myself since I'm the guy who thunk it up."

"So God really had nothing to do with it," he said with a smile.

"Of course He did," I shot back. "But He's got a ton of religions named after Him already, and when all is said and done He's a pretty modest critter."

"I understand completely, Doctor Jones," he said. "How did a man of the cloth come to be put in jail?"

"A simple misunderstanding, nothing more," I said.

"You don't seem too distressed about it."

"I view it as an occupational hazard," I answered. "It happens all the time."

"I never realized that preaching was such a dangerous profession," said Joe.

"It all depends on how you go about collecting donations for the poorbox," I explained. "And how about you, Brother Alvarez? What are you in for?"

"I tried to assassinate El Presidente."

"El Presidente?" I repeated. "Ain't that a racehorse?"

"It is Ferdinand Salivar, the President of the Republic of San Palmero."

"Now that's a curious coincidence," I said. "Your president is toting around the same name as the city we're in."

"It's no coincidence at all," answered Joe. "He renamed it Ferdinand when he overthrew the last dictator. It used to be Roberto."

"Is that an old and honored tradition here — naming the capital city after yourself once you get to be the president?"

"Only for the past seven months."

"So it's already been Roberto and Ferdinand in just seven months?" I asked.

He shook his head. "It's been Roberto, Ferdinand, Gabriel, Antonio, Luis, and six Josés."

"I can see you practice a swift and vigorous game of politics in San Palmero," I said. "Back where I come from they told us that any boy could grow up to become president, but mighty few of us were encouraged to do so without the benefit of an election."

"You were not faced by a government that suspends all civil rights, taxes the people at an astronomical rate, executes its opposition without benefit of trial, and allows the president to loot the treasury at will."

"Well, it does go a long way toward explaining why so many of your countrymen want to be president," I allowed. "Were you another candidate?"

"Certainly not," said Joe with all the dignity he could muster on the spur of the moment. "All I want to do is rid the country of its current tyrant. I have no desire whatsoever to rule San Palmero. I would remain in power only for a brief transition period, and would hold democratic elections and reinstate the constitution as soon as possible."

"That's right noble of you, Brother Alvarez," I said. "How long do you figure this here brief transition period will last?" I asked.

"No more than twelve or fifteen years," he said thoughtfully. "Perhaps twenty." Then he paused and added, "Thirty at the outside."

Well, I could see right off that I was in with a deep political thinker who planned far ahead and didn't believe in rushing changes. I didn't know exactly where he stood on the political spectrum, but I finally decided that he was a new type of conservative who wanted to conserve just about everything except maybe the president's hide.

In midafternoon we heard a bunch of yelling and shooting outside, and about half an hour later the guards pulled a bunch of us out of our cells and marched us to the prison workshop, where they handed us a bucket of black paint and a bunch of brushes. Then still another guard brung over a pile of wooden boards and laid 'em down on a work table.

"Start painting," he said.

"You want all them boards painted black?" I said.

"No," he said. "I want you to paint '*Welcome to Umberto, Capital of San Palmero*' on each of them. Have them done by dinner."

He left, and I turned to Joe. "I guess that's good news, Brother Alvarez," I said. "It looks like they replaced old Ferdinand after all."

"It is bad news, my friend," said Joe. "I know Umberto Morales. He will be an even worse despot."

"Maybe he'll have a change of heart now that he's got the top spot," I said.

Well, maybe he would have had a change of heart and maybe he wouldn't have, but as it happened, Fate didn't give him no time to change more than his clothes. The next morning, right after breakfast, we were taken back to the workshop, where we painted up a few dozen signs announcing that the town was now Jesus, which at least gave the place a nice religious tone. We got to take the night off when it became José again, and they pulled out a bunch of old signs from some garage or attic.

By noon of the next day it was Riccardo, and that evening, before poor Riccardo even had time to eat his first meal in office, he was forcibly retired and Joe and I painted a few dozen more signs telling everyone that they were now entering the friendly city of Miguel, and I found myself starting to wonder why San Palmero didn't produce more painters of worldwide renown, given how much free training they were supplied.

"I can see why you guys have given up on elections," I said as Joe and I were chowing down our dinner. "The country could go broke just printing up the ballots."

"I know you are just trying to cheer me up, my friend," he answered, "but the situation is dire."

"Miguel ain't no better than Riccardo and the others, huh?"

"Worse," he said. "I am forced to the conclusion that I am the only man fit to lead San Palmero out of the wilderness, and here I am, locked away in durance vile."

"Try to look at the bright side, Brother Alvarez," I said. "At least your current position ain't such that people are lining up to take it away from you."

"But the situation grows more desperate by the day," he said unhappily. "The people are suffering, the trains are not running, the mines are not producing, and worst of all, the treasury is growing smaller with each passing moment."

"Yeah, I can see where that makes being the president a little less desirable," I said sympathetically.

"True," he agreed. "Yet it is my sacred duty to save my country from this unending string of petty dictators."

"I'm right favorably impressed with you, Brother Alvarez," I said. "Especially given how little might be left in the treasury."

"When Destiny calls, a man of honor must answer," said Joe. "Besides, after the tax rate reaches 100%, I can always confiscate the better farms and factories."

"It's comforting to know that a man of vision will find a way," I said.

"I owe it to my country," he said humbly.

About two hours later we heard more shots, and then still more, and it kept on all night, which made sleeping kind of difficult, and then, just after sunrise, all the shooting stopped and it was suddenly so quiet you could have heard a pin drop if there'd been anyone around to drop one.

José — the guard, not my cellmate — came over a few minutes later and unlocked the door.

"More painting?" I said.

"No, Senor," he said. "You are free to go."

"I am?"

He nodded. "The magistrate was killed last night. In fact, the whole government was killed last night. There's no sense keeping you here any longer."

"Well, be sure to thank the new government for me," I said, stepping out of the cell.

"I can't," said José.

"You ain't on speaking terms with them?"

"It is difficult to speak to the dead, Senor."

"I thought you told me the *old* government was dead."

"They are *all* dead," said José.

"Then I am free, too?" said Joe.

"I suppose so," said José with a shrug. "My wife is the prison cook. I am taking her to the seashore, so there will be no one left to feed you."

Joe joined me, and we walked out the front door of the jail-house together and out into the street. Suddenly a single shot rang out, and Joe dropped in his tracks like a ton of bricks.

"Death to all tyrants!" cried a pretty young woman, stepping out of the shadows with a smoking pistol in her hands.

"He wasn't no tyrant, ma'am," I said. "At least not yet, anyway."

"Well, he would almost certainly have been a tyrant if he'd gotten the chance," she said without much show of regret. Suddenly she began eyeing me suspiciously. "And who are you?"

"I'm the Right Reverend Doctor Lucifer Jones at your service, ma'am," I said. "Weddings done cheap, and given the circumstances in these here parts, I'm willing to make a group rate for funerals. Who have I got the pleasure of speaking to?"

"I am Consuela Fransicsa Diego," she said. "Whose side are you on?"

"From what little I been able to learn, neither side's got a lot to recommend it these days, what with all of them being dead and such," I said reasonably. "You got any other side I can choose?"

"Maria!" she hollered. "Raquel! Did you hear?"

Two more good-looking women stepped out into the street, each carrying a rifle.

"What do you think?" said the one that answered to Maria.

"He doesn't carry a weapon," said Raquel. "That's a step in the right direction."

"He looks like a simpleton to me," said Maria.

"I don't know," said Raquel, studying my face. "He's got a sly, shifty look about his eyes, and his weakness of character shines through like a beacon."

"What do you think, Consuela?"

"I am trying to make up my mind," she said. Suddenly she turned to me. "What do you think of San Palmero, Señor Jones?"

"Well, truth to tell, I ain't seen an awful lot of it, except through the jailhouse window," I admitted. "But you seem like pleasant sorts, at least when you ain't blowing each other to Kingdom Come, which is just about all the time now that I come to mull on it."

"But you like the country?"

"I like it just fine, except for all the bullets flying through the air," I said.

"And you would be willing to stay here?"

"Sure," I answered. "Though preferably not the same way Ferdinand and Umberto and Riccardo and all them Josés are staying here."

Well, they put their heads together and started whispering up a storm, and finally they broke up their little pow-wow and Consuela walked up to me.

"Señor Jones," she said, "I have...we have a proposition for you."

"All three of you?" I asked. "It's a little out of the ordinary, but I suppose me and the Lord could bend the rules a bit for three such lovely ladies."

"You misunderstand," she said. "We want you to become the president."

"From what I seen, being president ain't a job what comes equipped with much of a future — or even much of a present, when you get right down to it. Why me?"

"You'd be perfect for it," said Raquel.

"We could tell right off that you were a man of distinction," added Maria.

"Besides, you're all that's left," said Consuela. "All the other men are dead or have fled to neighboring countries."

"You are not on either side, so as the people begin returning to the city they will have no reason to distrust you," said Raquel.

I walked over to Joe's body. "This here was one of Nature's noblemen," I said. "By rights he should have been your next president, and I want it understood that if I take the job, it's just as his stand-in. I'll run the country exactly the way he would have run it, and I wouldn't dream of doing nothing as president that he wouldn't have done. Anyone got a problem with that?"

"No, Señor Jones," said Consuela. "Or should we call you Doctor Jones?"

"A simple El Presidente should do the trick," I said. "Where's the presidential palace from here?"

"Three blocks north, Presidente," said Consuela. "We will take you there right now."

We had to step around an awful lot of unsuccessful candidates for the office along the way, and I decided that my very first official act had better be to hire a small army of street cleaners. After about ten minutes we walked up to this stately-looking mansion which probably had four or five less windows than Buckingham Palace and maybe a little shorter driveway than the Taj Mahal.

"Where's the treasury from here?" I asked.

"It's in the east wing," said Consuela.

"You mean it's part of the palace?"

"The last 27 presidents didn't want to let it out of their sight," she said.

"Why don't we mosey over to it and see what all the fuss was about?" I said, and a couple of minutes later we were in this big underground vault that had piles of money everywhere.

I felt an urge to put it in neat orderly stacks and admire it for a while, but first I figured I'd better spend a few days counting it, just to see how much I could borrow in times of need. But before I could start, Consuela grabbed my arm and began leading me away.

"You can do the bookkeeping later, Presidente," she said. "Right now you have more important tasks awaiting you."

"What's more important than counting money?" I said as I fell into step beside her, and Raquel closed and locked the vault behind us.

"I realize that the money looks impressive today," explained Consuela, "but it won't last. Between inflation and the debt your predecessors ran up, the treasury will be empty in less than two months. We must do something about that."

"Don't forget that we also have to make plans to hold free elections," added Maria.

I thunk on it for a bit, and suddenly a great big Heavenly revelation hit me smack between the eyes.

"I do believe I got the solution to both problems," I announced.

"Free elections *and* the treasury?" asked Consuela.

"Who says they have to be *free* elections?" I said. "We'll make 'em *expensive* elections and charge anyone who wants to vote a million dollars, or whatever our currency is, and that'll put money in the treasury at the same time we're holding an election."

"And what will become of you, Presidente?" said Maria. "What if some very wealthy men covet your job?"

"I'll just pop into the vault the night before and borrow as much as I need to vote early and often."

"You know," said Raquel, "he's already more resourceful than Ferdinand or Umberto."

"And he's cuter than Riccardo," added Maria.

"Riccardo was a hunchback with a clubfoot and steel teeth," Raquel pointed out.

"*You* found him attractive enough," said Maria.

"It was the uniform," said Raquel defensively. "It blinded me to his true nature."

While they were arguing about whether Ferdinand was brighter than a potted plant and Riccardo was more attractive than a moldering corpse, we finally reached my office. It was about the size of a football field, with a huge, hand-carved mahogany desk at one end. There was a box of foot-long cigars sitting atop it, and I lit one up, sat down on the chair, and put my feet up on the desk.

"You know, ladies," I said, "I got a feeling that I'm going to like the president business."

"Don't like it too much," warned Consuela. "You're only El Presidente until we can reinstate the constitution and live in freedom and harmony."

"Absolutely," I said. "I ain't looking for no lifetime job. I figure twenty years ought to do it. Thirty at the outside."

"I don't think you fully understand your situation," she replied.

"What little tidbit am I missing?" I asked.

"It was a lifetime job for the last 35 presidents."

"Yeah, well, when you put it that way, I can see where we might move the schedule up a mite," I said. "In the meantime, I suppose we got to change the name of the town again."

"To Lucifer?"

I was about to agree, but then it occurred to me that calling it Lucifer would tell anyone aspiring to high office just who stood between them and their goal, and suddenly slapping my name on all them signs didn't seem like such a good idea to me.

Which is how the capital of San Palmero came to be called Bubbles La Tour.

"Bubbles La Tour?" repeated Consuela, frowning. "What is a Bubbles La Tour?"

"An entertainer whose skills and artistry I came to admire on Saturday nights back when I was growing up in Moline, Illinois," I said.

"An ecdysiast?" said Raquel.

"Gesundheit," I said. "Now, what's on the presidential agenda for the rest of the day?"

"We haven't had electricity for the past 48 hours," said Consuela. "I think getting the power on again is the first order of business."

"Yes," added Maria. "It is especially bad on the west side of town, where they haven't had any lights for weeks now."

"What's on the west side of town?" I asked.

"The worst and most dangerous slums in all of San Palmero," she answered.

This problem wasn't quite as easy as the last one, but I mulled on it while I was puffing away at my cigar, and in about five minutes the answer came to me.

"Okay," I announced. "I got this here conundrum solved too."

"What are your orders, Presidente?" asked Consuela.

"Set fire to the slums," I said. "We'll get rid of an eyesore and give the people something to read by, all at the same time."

"That will only last for one night," she pointed out.

"One night's all it should take to get the power on again," I said.

"I don't understand."

"Find the richest folks what ain't left town yet," I told her, "and tomorrow morning spread the word that people can read their evening papers by the light of their blazing houses if someone don't pony up enough money to get the electricity running again."

"You know," said Maria, "it's not a bad idea at that."

"And it would get rid of the slums," agreed Raquel.

Consuela stared long and hard at me. "I'm beginning to know how Baron von Frankenstein felt," she said.

"If he felt anything but hungry, I ain't got much in common with him," I said. "When do they serve dinner around here?"

We moseyed over to the dining room, which wasn't much smaller than the office and was set up to accommodate small intimate groups of two hundred or so, and Raquel went off to see if any servants were left or if they'd all high-tailed it to the hills. She came back a few minutes later and announced that the men were all dead or run off, but that we still had a passel of employees of the female persuasion, and she'd told some of 'em to put some grub on the fire.

Well, truth to tell, I don't know which looked more appetizing, the food or the young ladies what brung it out and served it. In fact, there was so much of it that I invited them all to join us, and after dinner I sent a couple of 'em off to the presidential wine cellar to bring back a few gallons of San Palmero's finest drinkin' stuff, and somewhere around midnight it occurred to me that Bubbles La Tour wasn't actually a resident of the country, and that I had an even better notion for naming the city, depending on who I woke up with each morning.

I stood up, waited for silence (which can be a long time coming when you're keeping company with forty or fifty women) and then issued a Presidential Proclamation concerning the daily re-naming of the city.

"But Presidente!" protested a particularly lovely young maiden with long black hair. "We are all married!"

"Just so long as you ain't fanatics about it," I said.

"It would be a sin," she said.

"I talk to the Lord all the time," I assured her, "and He tells me that it ain't no mortal sin, but just one of them little venereal ones that He don't pay much attention to."

"We could not consider it."

"Just because you're married?" I said.

"Yes."

"Okay," I said. "That don't pose no lasting problem."

"It doesn't?" said another. "Why not?"

I snapped my fingers. "Presto!" I said. "You're all legally divorced by Presidential Decree."

"You can't do that!" protested Consuela.

"A president's got more powers than the captain of a ship, don't he?" I said. "And if a captain can marry folks, then I don't see why I can't un-marry them."

"It's not in the constitution."

"The constitution's in the repair shop, remember?" I said. Then I looked around the table. "Okay, who's interested in having a whole city named after her first thing in the morning?"

I could see each of them was giving serious consideration to cementing her place in San Palmero's history. Finally one of them said, "Well, he's not quite as ugly as Riccardo."

A sizeable portion of the assemblage took issue with that remark and began arguing it. I thunk the two sides was going to come to blows for a while there, but then suddenly some gunshots rang out and a couple of windows shattered and one of the chandeliers got shot down.

"I thought you told me all the husbands were dead or hiding!" I hollered as I dove under the table.

Raquel and Maria ran to the busted windows and started shooting back, while a number of the young ladies joined me. It struck me as a propitious time to get to know the hired help a bit better, which I was in the process of doing when Consuela finally stuck her head under the table.

"You can come out now, Presidente," she said.

"I'm comfortable right where I am," I answered.

"But it's safe now," said Consuela.

"It's safer down here," I said as one of my new acquaintances proved to be more ticklish than I expected and began giggling, "to say nothing of friendlier."

But then the young ladies started climbing to their feet, and I figured I might as well stand up too, just to set a brave example. I wandered over to the window and looked down on the front lawn, where I saw a bunch of corpses in dresses sprawled across the grass.

"Either we got some women campaigning for the presidency," I announced, "or you ladies are married to the most peculiar batch of husbands I ever did see."

"They are women," said one of the young ladies. "They are sick and tired of the mess men have made of this country and have decided to take it over themselves."

"Can't they think of nothing better to do with their time than storm the presidential palace?" I complained.

"Such as?" she said.

"Cooking. Sewing. Cleaning. Having babies. All the things women are good at."

"So you think women are not good at anything but house-work?" said Consuela ominously.

"Now don't you go putting words in my mouth," I said angrily. "I think Bubbles La Tour was one of the most remarkable women I ever met, and I'll lay plenty of eight-to-five that she didn't know one end of a broom from another." Which wasn't exactly true, as I was in the front row of the 5-Star Rialto Burlesque the night they arrested her precisely because she proved she *did* know one end from the other, but I didn't see no reason to be so nit-picky.

"I have the distinct impression that you don't appreciate the members of my sex," said Consuela.

"That's a lie!" I said hotly. "No matter where I am I visit the local red light district and appreciate the bejabbers out of 'em every time I got a couple of extra dollars in my pocket!"

I noticed a kind of angry murmuring starting to gain steam among the other women.

"This was your doing, Consuela," said one of them accusingly.

"Right," said another. "You were the one who chose him."

"What could I do?" said Consuela. "He's all that was left. All the rest of the men have fled."

"Maybe that's not the worst of all possible worlds, given the quality of the male presidents San Palmero has had lately," suggested Maria.

"Now that I see him clearly," added Raquel, "he's really much uglier than Riccardo."

"Now just hold your horses a minute!" I said. "I'm El Presidente, and I don't take kindly to grumbling in the ranks! If I hear any more of it you risk running head-on into my righteous executive wrath."

Suddenly I was staring down the barrel of Consuela's pistol.

"And you risk running head-on into a bullet," she said.

I looked around the room, and found to my surprise that I was facing maybe forty or fifty guns and rifles.

"I got another Presidential Decree," I announced. "Anyone who drops her gun and leaves the room gets a ten percent raise in pay, effective a week from next Tuesday."

Nobody moved.

"Tax free," I added.

Still no one moved.

"Okay," I said. "I ain't nothing if not magnanimous. We'll let bygones be bygones. Now, who wants the city to bear her name starting tomorrow morning?"

One young lady tentatively raised her hand, but the one standing next to her slapped her on the wrist and she promptly took it down.

"Well, it's been an interesting and educational evening," I said after another couple of minutes had passed and no one had lowered their guns, "but I think it's time for me to go out and inspect the troops."

"There aren't any troops to inspect," said Consuela.

"I'll find some," I said.

"You can go looking for them," said Consuela. "But I strongly advise you not to come back."

"You mean tonight?" I asked.

"I mean ever."

"And here I thought we were all getting along so well," I said.

"You are no better than our own men," said Maria.

"Worse," said Raquel.

"Okay," I said. "I know when I ain't wanted. I'll just stop off at the treasury and pick up a little cash to see me through to the next few years, and I'll be on my lonely way."

There was an audible click as Consuela cocked her gun.

"I suppose you wouldn't take an I.O.U. in exchange for it?" I said.

"Get out of here," said Consuela. "I'm giving the orders now."

"Just a minute," said Raquel. "Why you?"

"Because I'm the leader," said Consuela.

"I don't remember voting for you," said Maria.

Consuela turned her pistol on Maria. "I've got six votes right here."

Suddenly one of the young ladies shoved the business end of a shotgun in Consuela's back. "And I've got a point of parliamentary procedure."

"That doesn't compare to my point of personal privilege," said Raquel, aiming her rifle at the pair of them.

Well, pretty soon the room was filled to overflowing with undeclared candidates all making points of order, so I kind of gently stepped out into the hall and had almost made it to the front door when the shooting started in earnest. A minute later I was walking around a bunch of bodies that was spread across the presidential lawn, and preparing to high-tail it out of San Palermo, the only president on record to leave office while still alive.

I heard a couple of weeks later that the town had changed names again, from Consuela to Carmen to Bonita to Rosa, and I think there were a couple of Marias tossed in there somewhere.

It just reinforced my conviction that of all the things in this world I don't understand, most of 'em are women.

THE ISLAND OF ANNOYED SOULS

T here are a lot of pleasant ways to see the world — but footslogging through the Amazon jungle without a compass ain't one of them. After being gently asked at gunpoint to leave San Palmero I'd been three days and three nights without seeing nothing but an endless parade of mosquitoes and other six-legged critters with a few eight-legged ones tossed in for good measure, and I'd pretty much reached the point where I'd have welcomed the presence of a headhunter or two just to have a little company.

Of course, that was before I ran smack dab into one. I heard him before I could see him, and he was making such a racket as would have woke such dead as weren't otherwise occupied at the moment. He kept crashing through the underbrush, of which there was an awful lot, and suddenly out he burst, maybe ten feet from me. He was carrying a bow and a bunch of little arrows, but he was in such a hurry that he seemed to have plumb forgot about them. He bumped into me, let out a scream, and stared at me kind of like a cow stares at a butcher.

"Howdy, Brother," I greeted him. "The Right Reverend Lucifer Jones at your service. What's the quickest route back to civilization?"

He jabbered something I couldn't understand, and kept looking back the way he had come, so I figured he was telling me he'd just been to the big city and hadn't found it all that congenial to a guy who was inclined to wander around stark naked and had a tendency to shrink the local citizenry's heads. I thanked him for pointing it out to me and started marching off, but he grabbed my arm and began jabbering again, more urgently this time.

"I can appreciate your distaste for the vices of city life," I said. "But if I'm going to save folks from the wages of sin, I got to go to where all the sinning gets itself done."

He began screaming and pointing to where he'd been and pulling me in the direction he was going.

"I'm touched by your concern, Brother," I told him. "But there ain't no need for you to worry. The Lord is my shepherd. Him and me'll get along fine, once we get out of this here jungle."

He just stared at me for a minute, and then took off like a bat out of hell, and it belatedly occurred to me that probably he and one of the local young ladies and maybe her parents had totally different notions of what constituted a bonafide proposal of marriage.

I started walking, dead certain that I'd be stumbling across a city any minute, but not much happened except that I finally caught sight of the Amazon, or at least one of its tributaries. I tried to remember if sharks hung out in rivers, but in the end I was so thirsty I didn't much care, so I wandered over to the water's edge, knelt down, and took a long swallow, and except for some waterbugs and a couple of tadpoles and a minnow or two it didn't taste all that bad.

Then I looked up, and strike me dead if I didn't see a city after all. It wasn't much of a city, just ten or twelve buildings on an island in the middle of the river about half a mile downstream, but after all that time in the bush it was city enough for me, and I moseyed over until I was standing on the bank just opposite it. I was about to swim across to it when I saw an alligator with a lean and hungry look cruising the surface between me and the island, and decided to just keep on walking until I came to a city, or even a suburb, on my side of the river, but then I saw an old beat-up boat tied on the shore, so I borrowed it and rowed across to the island.

As I was pulling the boat out of the water I heard a noise behind me, and when I turned to see what had caused it I found a great big dog watching me curiously. He looked friendly enough, so I reached out to pet him.

"You touch me, Gringo, and I'll bite your hand off," he said.

I jumped back real sudden-like.

"What are you staring at?" he continued. "Haven't you ever seen a dog before?"

"Man and boy, I seen a lot of dogs," I told him, "but up until this minute I ain't never had a conversation with one." I looked around. "Are there a lot of you?"

The dog kind of frowned. "How many of me do you see?"

"I mean, are there a lot of talking dogs in these here parts?"

"I hardly see that that's any of your business," said the dog. "What are you doing on this island?"

"Right at the moment I'm wondering what my chances are of getting back off it real quick," I said truthfully. "I don't want to upset you none, but I find that talking dogs put me off my feed."

"You're not going anywhere," said the dog. "I think I'd better take you to the doctor."

"I don't need no doctor," I said. "I feel as fit as a bull moose."

"I resent that," said a low voice behind me, and when I turned to see who'd said it, sure enough I was facing a moose with beady little eyes and a huge spread of antlers. "Now go along with Ramon before I lose my temper."

"You're Ramon?" I asked the dog.

"Have you got a problem with that?" said the dog, baring his teeth.

"Not a bit," I said quickly. "Ramon is my very favorite name."

"Come along with us, Miguel," said Ramon to the moose. "Just in case he tries to escape."

"Miguel is my favorite name too," I said as the moose joined us.

"What do you think of Felicity?" said a feminine voice that seemed to have a little more timber to it than most.

I looked off to my left and found myself facing about five tons worth of elephant.

"You're Felicity?" I asked.

"I am," replied the elephant.

"I think it's a name of rare gossamer gaiety," I said. "I've fallen eternally in love with maybe thirty women in my life, and five or six of 'em was named Felicity." Then a thought occurred to me, and I said, "Just what kind of animal is this here doctor you're taking me to?"

"He's a man, the same as you," said Felicity.

"He's a man, anyway," muttered Ramon.

"Before we go any farther," said Felicity, "you must promise not to harm him."

"He must be a nice man to have such loving, devoted pets," I remarked.

"He is a fiend!" growled Ramon.

"A monster!" said Felicity.

"And we are *not* his pets," added Miguel bitterly.

"Well, he must at least be one hell of an animal trainer," I said. "After all, he taught you to speak."

"He most certainly did not!" said Felicity.

"You all just learned spontaneously?" I asked.

"I'm sure the doctor will explain it to you," said Miguel.

"Just keep out of his laboratory," said Felicity.

"I take it he don't like visitors messing with his equipment?" I said.

"I have no idea," said Felicity. "Just keep out of it — and don't accept any food or drink from him unless he partakes of it first."

"And remember," said Miguel, "he is not to be harmed."

"I'm a little confused here," I admitted. "You say this doctor is a fiend and a monster and I shouldn't eat or drink nothing he offers, and at the same time you seem dead set against anyone hurting him."

"That's right," said Ramon.

"And you don't see no inconsistency in that position?" I asked.

"After you talk to him everything will become clear."

We walked for a few minutes and began approaching one of the buildings. A couple of chimpanzees wandered over and introduced themselves, and overhead a bald eagle swooped down and told me that if I so much as touched the doctor he'd peck my eyes out, and then one of the chimps warned me not to drink anything, and I began thinking that if the next thing I saw was a white rabbit checking his watch I'd feel mighty relieved and start trying to wake up, but I didn't see no more animals and pretty soon we were at the door. One of the chimps knocked on it, and then they all stood back and waited for it to open, and when it did I found myself facing a small, pudgy man with thinning white hair, steel-rimmed spectacles, and three or four chins, depending on which way he held his head.

He looked me up and down and finally kind of grimaced.

"You're not at all what I was expecting," he said at last.

"I hear that a lot, though usually from disgruntled women," I said.

"You simply don't look like the killer of twenty-eight men, women and children," he continued, staring at me. "Still, appearances can be deceiving, which is our guiding motto here."

"I don't want to put a damper on your enthusiasm," I said, "but I ain't never killed anyone."

"You're not Juan Pedro Vasquez?" he said.

"I'm the Right Reverend Honorable Doctor Lucifer Jones," I told him.

"What are you doing on my island?"

"Well, for the past hour or so I've mostly been concentrating on being lost," I admitted.

"Then you shall be an honored visitor," he said. "Come right in."

He kind of pulled me in by the arm and shut the door behind me before I could decide whether or not to make a dash for the river.

"May I offer you a drink?" he asked, leading me to the living room, which had a dozen diplomas on the wall instead of the usual animal heads and tasteful paintings of naked ladies striking friendly poses.

"That's right generous of you," I said, "but I ain't thirsty just now."

"You've been listening to the animals," he said knowingly. "Don't worry, Doctor Jones. The drink is perfectly safe. You must not pay attention to a bunch of felons."

"I ain't been talking to no felons, present company possibly excepted," I said. "Just a bunch of the strangest animals I've ever run into."

He walked to a cabinet, pulled out a bottle, and poured two glasses. He took a swallow from one and then handed it to me.

"Will that assuage your fears?" he said.

"Well, under these circumstances, I suppose I can overcome my natural aversion to liquid," I allowed, downing the rest of the glass and holding it out for a refill. As he poured it, I asked him if he had any serious intention of telling me just what felons he thought I'd been talking to.

"Ramon and Felicity and the others," he said.

"I don't want to seem to ignorant," I said, "but just what kind of felony can an elephant commit on an island in the middle of the jungle?"

"I shall be happy to explain it all to you, Doctor Jones," he said, sitting down on a big leather chair. "Let me begin by asking if you are acquainted with the work of Doctor Septimus Mirbeau, who is unquestionably the world's most brilliant doctor and scientist?"

"Sounds like an interesting guy," I said. "I'd sure like to run into him someday."

"You're talking to him," he said. "Can it be that you've really never heard of me?"

"Not unless you played third base for the St. Louis Browns about fifteen years ago," I replied.

His face fell. "That's the price of genius. I have to work in obscurity until I can announce my findings to the world."

"Well, you can't get much more obscure than a nameless island in the middle of the Amazon," I said.

"It has a name," replied Doctor Mirbeau. "I call it the Island of Lost Souls."

"As far as I can tell, the only soul what's lost around here is me," I said.

"The name is a poetic metaphor," he said, lighting up a big cigar. "If I was being literal, I would call it the Island of Lost Bodies."

"It strikes me as a pretty small island to misplace a whole graveyard," I said.

He smiled. I'm sure he meant it to be a tolerant, fatherly smile, but it came across as something out of one of them movies what got people called Bela and Boris and a lot of other names beginning with a B acting in 'em.

"The bodies are still here, Doctor Jones," he assured me.

"You just forgot where?"

"You have just been in their company."

"That's funny," I said. "I didn't notice nothing except a bunch of animals with an unlikely way of expressing themselves."

"That was them."

"I know the vertical rays of the tropical sun can have a funny effect on some folk," I allowed, "but I'm pretty sure those were animals and not men."

"They are animals who used to be men!" he said triumphantly.

"Now why in the world would a normal woman want to turn into a lady elephant?" I said. "Unless of course you're the only man on the island, and there are a mess of good-looking male elephants out there that I ain't encountered yet."

"I have learned how to surgically transform men and women into animals," he said. "Didn't you think it was peculiar that a moose and an elephant could converse with you?"

"Not as peculiar as a doctor who claims they used to be a man and a woman called Miguel and Felicity," I said.

"But they were!" he insisted. "This has been my life's work! I am only a few years from going public with it. There won't be enough Nobel Prizes to honor me. They'll have to create a newer, more prestigious award."

"Just how private can it be even now?" I said. "Some hospital or college must know about your work, or you couldn't have gotten funding for all this."

"My funding comes from my patients, who pay me to transform them," said Doctor Mirbeau.

"I don't want to seem unduly skeptical," I said, "buy why in tarnation would a bunch of perfectly normal human beings pay good money to be turned into animals?"

"Because every last one of them is a wanted criminal," he answered. "What better way to avoid detection than to become an animal?"

Well, I could think of a lot of better ways, or at least less painful ones, but I didn't want to argue with my host, especially since I had a feeling anyone who lost an argument with him was likely to be turned into a koala bear or an iguana or some such thing.

"That's mighty interesting, Brother Mirbeau," I said at last, "and I sure wish you the best of luck with all your Nobel Prizes, but now that we've had a friendly visit and I've drunk my fill, I think it's time I was on my way, if you'll just point me toward the nearest city."

"I'm afraid I can't let you leave the island, Doctor Jones," he said.

"Why not?" I said.

"You might reveal what I'm doing here before I'm ready to tell the world."

"I give you my solemn word as a man of the cloth who ain't never told a lie in his whole blameless life that I wouldn't even think of doing such a thing," I said. "Besides, if I did, they'd probably just lock me up in the drunk tank."

"I can't take the chance," he said. "You may have free run of the island until I'm ready."

"Ready for what?" I asked.

"You'll find out," he said with a strange smile.

Suddenly it started raining, which it does a lot of in the rain forest, and pretty soon we could hardly hear ourselves over the thunder.

"You ain't going to make a fellow white man sleep outside in this weather, are you?" I said, looking out the window.

"That was never my intention," said Doctor Mirbeau. "I'll have a bed prepared for you next door in the House of Agony."

"The House of Agony?"

"That's right," he said.

"You know, I think the rain's lightening up already," I said quickly as it continued to pour. "Maybe I'll just spend the night on the beach."

"I won't hear of it," he said. "You can't be too careful with your health."

Those were my sentiments exactly, but no matter how much I protested, he insisted that I accept his hospitality. Finally he got up, put an arm around my shoulders, and walked me over to the front door.

"Your boat has been moved to a safe place," he said. "You really don't want to leave the island without it, as the water is infested with alligators."

I couldn't see that a river being infested with alligators was all that much worse than an island being infested with a mad scientist, but I kept my opinion to myself.

"Dinner is at eight o'clock," he said as he opened the door for me. "Promptness is appreciated." He stared at me. "I don't suppose you brought a dinner jacket?"

"I could go back to San Palmero right now and get one," I suggested hopefully.

"No," he said. "We'll simply have to rough it."

"What's on the menu?" I asked as I remembered that I hadn't had nothing to eat all day and decided that I might as well make the best of my situation.

"Raoul," he said.

Suddenly a handful of nuts and berries started looking mighty good to me. I walked out the door, and found Ramon, Miguel and Felicity waiting for me out there in the rain.

"I'm surprised to see you," said Felicity. "Most men who enter the doctor's house never come out."

"At least, not as men," added Ramon.

"Do you guys mind if we walk while we're talking?" I said, heading off into the jungle.

"What's your rush?" asked Miguel. "It's raining at the far end of the island too."

"Yeah, but that's a lot farther from the House of Agony than we are now," I pointed out.

"True," he agreed. "On the other hand, it's a lot closer to the House of Pain."

I came to a stop. "Has Doctor Mirbeau got any other houses I should know about?"

"No," said Felicity. "But he has five others you probably shouldn't know about."

"If I ever get off this here island," I vowed to nobody in particular, "the very first thing I'm going to do is never think about it again."

"You will never leave the island," said Ramon. "I am surprised he didn't tell you that."

"Well, he did kind of hint at it," I allowed. "But I was hoping he said it with a kindly twinkle in his eye."

"That was a cataract, and there's nothing kindly about it," said Miguel. "You're stuck here."

"I've run through thirty-four countries looking for the right spot to build the Tabernacle of Saint Luke," I said. "Who'd have thunk I'd wind up having to build it here, with nothing in my flock except a bunch of godless animals?"

"I resent that!" said Felicity.

"The godless part or the animal part?" I asked.

"Both!"

"Then I apologize," I said. "I sure don't want no god-fearing five-ton lady mad at me."

"Leave my weight out of this!" she snapped.

"It's nothing to be ashamed of, ma'am," I told her. "I ain't never seen a ten-thousand-pounder, human or otherwise, what was so feminine and delicate-looking and light on her feet."

She made a sound that was a cross between a tuba hitting M over high C and a trolly car skidding downhill on some rusty tracks.

"Now see what you've done?" said Miguel. "She's crying!"

Her body was wracked by sobs, which made it pretty hazardous for anyone standing in her immediately vicinity, like especially me, so I spoke up and said, "I don't want to be presumptuous, Miss Felicity, ma'am, but if you're that unhappy about being an elephant, why not just have Doctor Mirbeau change you back into the charming lady bank-robber or mad bomber you were to begin with?"

Felicity began crying even harder and louder.

"You simply do not understand our situation," said Ramon.

"Sure I do," I said. "You're a bunch of worthless lawbreaking scum, meaning no offense, what probably committed a passel of crimes against the laws of Man and God, and came here to avoid the just and righteous punishment of an outraged citizenry." Ramon snarled, and Miguel glared at me and began pawing the damp ground, but I held up a hand. "This is your lucky day," I said. "Your troubles are solved. I just happen to be in the salvation business. And as an introductory offer, I'll forgive any five heinous sins for the price of four."

"Our biggest sin is stupidity," sniffled Felicity.

"I absolve you!" I said. "That'll be $1.83 in cash."

"Do you see pockets on any of us?" said Miguel.

"Okay, we'll put it on the cuff," I said. "Just be sure you pay me before you leave the island or I may have to tell God to strike you dead, and He's such a busy critter that I really hate to bother Him unless it's absolutely necessary."

"We're never leaving the island again," muttered Ramon unhappily.

"Why not?" I asked. "I mean, you've got your ready-made disguises, so why ain't you and Miss Felicity out in polite canine and pachyderm society?"

"We were," said Miguel. "Well, some of us were."

"And some of us have never left the island," said Felicity. "You'd be surprised how few places in South America an elephant can go without drawing undue attention."

"Yeah, I can see where it's difficult to hide out in a crowd if there ain't no crowd on hand," I said. "Maybe you should have hitched a ride to Africa."

"I don't *want* to go to Africa!" she wailed. "I just want to be a woman again."

"Our transformations were completed a decade ago," said Ramon. "The police are no longer hunting for us. Our case files are closed. We have returned to the island to be changed back into human beings."

"Well, that seems reasonable," I allowed.

"It's reasonable," said Ramon. "It's just not likely."

"Oh?" I said. "Why not?"

"Because that foul fiend has raised his prices!" growled Ramon.

"It's extortion!" chimed in Miguel. "Where is a moose going to get fifty thousand dollars — especially in these difficult economic times?"

"And there's no sense threatening him," added Felicity. "He knows that we don't dare risk hurting the one man who can turn us back into men and women."

"So you figure you're going to be a full-time long-term elephant?" I asked her.

She began crying again. "I used to be so beautiful! I never wanted to be an elephant! I wanted to be something sleek and feline. And thin. Do you know what it's like for someone who counted calories all her life to eat five hundred pounds of grass and shrubs a day on a minimum maintenance diet?"

"There there," said Miguel, trying to comfort her. "There there."

"And the worse part of it is Cedric!" she continued.

"Cedric? Who's Cedric?" I asked.

"My partner," said Felicity. "Doctor Mirbeau turned him into a mouse, and now I'm scared to death of him!"

"What did you two do before you came here?" I asked.

"Hardly anything at all," said Felicity. "We didn't kill anywhere near as many of my husbands as they claimed. Just nine or ten." She paused. "Maybe twelve at the outside."

"You don't know how many husbands you killed?"

"Some of them died from natural causes," she said defensively.

I didn't see no sense in arguing with her, because it was certainly natural for a heart to stop beating after someone had pumped half a dozen bullets into it.

"At least Cedric is alive and wandering around the island somewhere," said Ramon. "Not like poor Omar."

"Omar was *your* partner?"

"Yes."

"What happened to him?" I asked. "Did he die on Doctor Mirbeau's operating table?"

"No," said Ramon. "Doctor Mirbeau turned him into a rabbit." A tear came to his eye. "I ate him."

"You ate your own partner?"

"It was instinct," said Ramon. "He shouldn't have run. Ever since the operation I have this compulsion to chase things."

"How about you?" I said, turning to Miguel. "You got a partner too?"

"No," said Miguel. Then: "Well, not anymore, anyway."

"But you did have one?"

"I had four," he said. "A father, two sisters, and a brother. It was a family business."

"And are they wandering around the island too?" I asked.

"No," said Miguel. "I turned them all in for the reward years ago."

"So here we are on the Island of Lost Souls," said Ramon, "just a few hundred yards from the man who could transform us back into human beings but refuses to do so."

"Sometimes I get so frustrated I could just sit on him," said Felicity.

"I know you're having dinner with him tonight, Doctor Jones," said Miguel. "Could you intercede with him on our behalf?"

"Well, actually, I was kind of planning to intercede with him on *my* behalf," I replied.

They begged and cajoled and Ramon started growling and I was afraid Felicity was going to start crying again, so finally I gave in and promised to speak to him at dinnertime.

"Thank you, Doctor Jones," said Miguel, who I decided wasn't a bad guy for a moose. "Our prayers go with you."

Suddenly Felicity trumpeted in terror and raced off screaming into the jungle, knocking down trees right and left as she went.

"What was that all about?" I asked.

"She probably saw Cedric again," said Ramon in a bored voice. "It happens all the time."

"Poor baby," said Miguel. "What a comedown."

"Was she really that pretty before the operation?" I asked.

"Compared to what?" said Ramon.

"She was much prettier then than she is now," said Miguel. He stopped and mulled on it for a minute. "Well, a bit prettier, anyway." He thunk a little more. "If not prettier, at least smaller."

"And she smelled better," added Ramon.

"Well, this has been a fascinating conversation," I said, "but I think it's probably time for me to head back over to Doctor Mirbeau's house for dinner."

"Good luck, Doctor Jones," said Ramon.

I started traipsing back through the jungle, and after a while the rain let up and pretty soon I found myself at the front door. I was going to open it when something big and shaggy opened it from the inside.

"You are expected," he said, stepping back to let me pass.

"*You* sure ain't," I said, staring at him.

"Have you got something against gorillas?" he asked me.

"Not a thing," I said quickly. "Some of my best friends are gorillas, or so close to 'em as makes no difference. I just ain't never encountered one working as a doorman before."

"I hope you don't think I enjoy being a house servant," said the gorilla.

"It ain't never occurred to me to seriously consider whether a gorilla would be happy as a butler," I admitted. "But if you don't like it, what are you doing here?"

"I'm hiding from the police."

"Back up a minute here," I said. "I thunk you got turned into a gorilla so you wouldn't have to hide no more."

"I should have saved my money and taken my chances," he said bitterly.

"But you look exactly like a gorilla."

"I used to be a professional wrestler," he said. "The police saw through the surgery instantly."

"You looked like *this* when you rassled?" I asked.

He opened a cabinet and produced two photographs.

"Before and after," he said, and sure enough I couldn't tell one from the other.

He led me into the dining room, where Doctor Mirbeau, dressed in a sweat-stained white tropical suit and a dirty tie, was already sitting at one end of the table, and the gorilla motioned that I was to sit at the other end.

"What do you think of my island now that you've had a little time to explore it?" asked Doctor Mirbeau.

"I suppose it's one of the nicer islands I've ever encountered," I said.

His face brightened. "So you like it?"

"Except for the heat, and the bugs, and the mud, and the rain, and the talking animals, and the fact that you won't let me leave," I answered.

"I can't control the other things, but I'll order the animals to leave you alone."

"Actually, they asked me to speak to you on their behalf," I said.

He made a face. "I thought as much."

"Mighty few animals can lay their hands, or whatever passes for their hands, on fifty thousand dollars," I said. "Why don't you turn 'em back into men and woman and let 'em pay you afterward?"

"I can't," he said.

"Why not?" I asked. "Ain't a delayed payment better than no payment at all?"

"It's out of the question," he said.

"That don't make no sense," I protested. "You need money to continue your work. These animals ain't got two cents to rub together. If you don't operate on 'em, they won't never have no money, but if you do operate then maybe they'll be able to get some."

"Forget it."

"Why are you being so stubborn?" I said.

"Because I don't know how to turn then back!" he bellowed. "That's what I need the money for — to pay my expenses until I learn how!"

There was an angry trumpeting outside the building, and Doctor Mirbeau suddenly turned even whiter than his suit.

"What was that?" he asked in a shaky voice.

"If I was a betting man," I said, "I'd lay plenty of eight-to-five that Felicity heard every word you just said with them oversized ears of hers, and that she is more than a little bit displeased with you."

"Oh my God!" he whispered.

"I got a feeling God's otherwise occupied at the moment," I answered as a couple of lions began roaring, "but I'll be sure to tell Him you called."

Pretty soon some monkeys began screaming, and then a few eagles and leopards chimed in, and Ramon began howling, and it was pretty clear that it wasn't so much an island of lost souls as deeply annoyed and exceptionally noisy ones.

"Save me, Doctor Jones!" he cried.

"I thought I was your prisoner," I said.

"Don't quibble over technicalities," he said. "Save me and everything I have is yours!"

"As far as I can tell, everything you have is an island a trillion miles from anywhere and a bunch of angry animals that want your scalp," I said. "Somehow it don't seem like much of an inducement."

He held up his right hand. "See this ring? That's a six-carat diamond! Save me and it's yours!"

"It's a mighty pretty bauble," I said. "But I could just sit back and pick it up when they finish dismembering you."

"What kind of Christian are you?" he demanded.

"A live one," I said as a jaguar leaped onto the roof and began pacing back and forth. "I'll ask you the same question thirty minutes from now."

"All right," he said. "There's five thousand dollars in my safe. You can have half."

"Half?"

"Surely you don't insist on all of it?" he said.

"I don't insist on any of it," I told him. "I think I'll just watch them hunt you down and rip you to shreds like a naked mole rat, except for the mole rat part."

"All right!" he said. "It's all yours! Just save me!"

"It's a deal," I said. "Though officially and for tax purposes you're giving the money to the Lord; I'm just holding it for Him until Him and me can build our Tabernacle. Now go hunt up the money while I run a couple of plans past Him and see which one He prefers."

As soon as he left the room the gorilla walked up to me.

"Are you really going to save him?" he asked.

"It's the only way to make sure all you animals get turned back into people," I said.

"I'm not going under the knife again!" he said. "Why suffer the pain when I wouldn't look one bit different when it was all over?"

I looked at the gorilla, and thunk about what he said, and then my Silent Partner smacked me right betwixt the eyes with one of His heavenly revelations.

"You've got a strange and inscrutable expression on your face, Doctor Jones," said the gorilla.

"You got a name?" I asked him suddenly.

"Horace," he said. It was the first time I ever saw a gorilla look embarrassed.

"What city are you wanted in, Horace?" I said.

"It's not so much a city as a country," he said. "Things are different here than in the States."

"Okay," I said. "What country can't you show your face in?"

"Brazil," he said.

"All right," I said. "That's no problem."

"Peru," he continued. "Uruguay. Paraguay. Argentina. Chile."

"You been a busy boy, Horace," I said.

"And Iceland."

"Iceland?" I said.

"I have relatives in Iceland," he explained. "I visited them."

"That must be a mighty strict country," I said. "Most places don't usually issue arrest warrants for visiting relatives."

"It was a very pleasant visit," said Horace. "We spent a lot of time together, they showed me the sights, we ate at some wonderful restaurants." He paused. "Robbing those seven banks was just an afterthought. I didn't even need the money from the last five. It's just that once you start, it's...well...habit-forming."

"It's a tragic and touching story, but let's get back to the subject at hand and see if I got this straight," I said. "There ain't no warrants out for you in Venezuela or Columbia or Ecuador, right?"

"And Bolivia," he said as Doctor Mirbeau came back with the cash. "Don't forget Bolivia."

I took the money and the ring and then walked to the front door and opened it. Damned near every animal on the island was lined up there facing it, except for the jaguar that was looking down from the roof. Doctor Mirbeau kind of cowered behind me.

"I suppose you're wondering why I've called you all here," I said.

"Cut the crap and give us Mirbeau!" said Ramon.

"What'll you do with him?" I asked.

"We haven't decided yet," said Miguel. "But it'll be grotesque."

"I got a better idea," I said. "How'd you all like to be turned back into men and women again?"

"He doesn't know how!" said Felicity. "I heard him admit it to you!"

"He doesn't know how *yet*," I said. "He needs some more time and money to work on it."

"Where's he going to get money?" said Miguel. "You can't bleed a turnip, or pick the pocket of a bunch of animals who aren't wearing any pants."

"*You're* going to earn it," I said, "and it'll be credited to your accounts against the day when he can actually change you back."

"Earn it?" repeated Ramon. "How?"

"Felicity," I said. "Tell me again why you stay here on the island."

"Because I'm the only elephant for thousands of miles around," she said. "I'd draw attention wherever I go."

"I agree," I said.

"So she stands out in a crowd," said Ramon. "What's your point?"

"It seems to me that as long as elephants and lions and talking animals are going to draw all that attention, there ain't no reason why they should draw it for free," I said. "You got a whole continent full of people what'll pay good money to see what you been hiding instead of flaunting. You can turn this island into the most popular zoo and tourist destination in South America."

"That's an interesting notion," said Ramon. "But how will we get word out to the public?"

"You'll start with word of mouth in Venezuela, Columbia, Ecuador and Bolivia, and work up from there," I said. "You just happen to have a spokesman and travel agent in your midst — at least as long as he sticks to rasslin' arenas and maybe soccer stadiums what feature riots during halftime."

Doctor Mirbeau stepped forward and promised to stay if they agreed to the plan, since all he wanted was the money and privacy he needed to finish his research. The animals took a vote, and it passed unanimously, and that's how the island became The Mirbeau 5-Star Spa, Resort, Menagerie, Circus and Petting Zoo.

As for me, I had five thousand dollars and a diamond ring tucked away in my pocket, so I bade them all a fond farewell and headed to the river. Once I got there I remembered that Doctor Mirbeau had taken my boat away, and I was about to go hunting for it when a big alligator glided up to the shore. I took a couple of steps back, ready to run if it came after me.

"Don't be afraid, Doctor Jones," it said. "My name is Victor Montez. I'll ride shotgun for you while you swim across."

"Since you're one of Doctor Mirbeau's critters, how come you didn't say nothing to me when I got here earlier today?"

"I wasn't myself this morning," said Victor.

"Mighty few folks around here are," I agreed.

"You misunderstand," he said. "Something I ate last night disagreed with me."

I resisted the urge to ask whether that was before or after he ate it, and just started swimming. A minute later there was a splash, followed by a loud crunching noise.

"Piranha," explained Victor.

"Gesundheit," I said.

"I hope it wasn't anyone I know," he added.

I made it to the far shore, climbed up onto dry land, thanked Victor for his help, took one last look at the island, and headed off to find some congenial spot where the sinners and scarlet women all congregated and I could finally settle down to the serious business of building my Tabernacle.

CHARTREUSE MANSIONS

I wandered through the wilderness for a few days after leaving Dr. Mirbeau and his Island of Annoyed Souls. I figgered any minute now a great big city would break into view, but you'd be surprised how few of them there are down in South America, and especially in the middle of the jungle.

They'd told me that the Amazon Basin was filled with Indians, but I never saw no basin, just a bunch of swamps and rivers. Finally, when I'd been on my own for five days, I ran head-first into a couple of little bitty fellers, maybe an inch or two over five feet, and dressed for exactly the kind of warm humid weather what we was having a lot of, which is to say they wore loincloths and matching headbands, and if they had on a third thing I never saw it.

Well, these wasn't like no Indians I'd ever seen back in the States, before the government guv me my walking papers, but I figgered what the hell, how different can one Indian be from another, so I held up my hand and said "How!"

The one on the right jumped back, and the one on the left looked like he might faint dead away, so I figured I better keep talking while I still had an audience.

"I have traveled many moons," I said. "Seek city of the palefaces. Especially interested in wampum."

They just looked at me like I was some kind of foreigner who was too stupid to speak Indian, and even when I tapped myself on the chest and explained that I was their Kemosabee they just kind of stood there like a couple of potted plants, and I decided that I'd been the victim of false doctrine and whatever these two was, it wasn't Indians.

After a while they stopped looking scared and started looking bored, and finally they just kind of wandered off into the jungle. I suppose I could have followed 'em, but I couldn't see no sense winding up in some little village where I was the only one who spoke Indian, so instead I just started walking again, trusting to the good Lord to direct me to some city that was suitable for building my tabernacle.

I walked another day and night, and it occurred to me that being lost was mighty hungry work and I hadn't et a real meal in close to a week now, living on fruits and berries and the like. I'd found a clutch of eggs one morning and figured to make an omelet, but even before I could remember that I didn't have nothing to cook 'em in, they each hatched out a little alligator. Most of 'em took one look at me and high-tailed it the other direction, but there was one who must've thunk I was his mother, because he kept rubbing against me, and when I started walking he fell into step behind me, and I was thinking that if he stuck around for another three or four years and I didn't come on no city by then maybe I could train him to hunt dinner for us each day, but then he saw a boa constrictor and decided *that* was his mama, and he gave me a look that said I wasn't the only one who'd been betrayed by false doctrine, and then he headed off with the snake and that was the last I saw of him.

I was just trying to figger out whether to keep going in the same direction, or maybe follow one of these hundreds of streams and rivers I kept passing and hope maybe it'd lead me to this Amazon Basin I'd heard about, when the decision was tooken out of my hands, because suddenly, standing not two hundred feet ahead of me, was the most beautiful golden-haired lady I ever did see. Her hair hung down almost to her waist, and I could see even from this distance that her eyes were the deepest, prettiest shade of blue. As for the rest of her, there wasn't nobody ever going to mistake her for a boy, even at five hundred yards. She wore a tattered dress what had seen better days, and certainly longer ones.

"Howdy, ma'am!" I yelled, waving my hand at her.

She turned, saw me, gave me the kind of smile that made me wish it was night out so I could bay at the moon, and waved back.

"I don't want to intrude on your privacy, ma'am," I said, "but for the past week I mostly been concentrating on being lost, and I was wondering if you could lead me to civilization, or at least point me in the right direction."

She smiled again, showing off the whitest teeth you can imagine, and began walking toward me. I didn't hear no music, but she moved her hips exactly like she was dancing to a slow rhumba, and I knew that I had fallen hopelessly and eternally in love again.

"Ma'am," I said when she reached me, "I got to tell you that in all my experience I ain't never seen a looker like you, and I'm ready here and now to plight my trough." I didn't actually know what plighting a trough meant — on the face of it, it seems kind of like digging a trench in an open field — but it sounded like the kind of thing beautiful young damsels what were seriously underdressed would want to hear from a suitor.

She smiled at me again.

"Can I take this here radiant smile as a sign that you return my affection, ma'am?" I said.

She nodded her head.

"Good!" I said. "For a minute there I was scared that you didn't speak my lingo. A couple of days back I ran into some guys in the forest that didn't speak American *or* Indian, and I know that back in San Palmero, where I served as President for close to a full day before we had a little misunderstanding, everyone was called José and Juanita and didn't speak no known language."

I laughed to show her how relieved I was, and she laughed too.

"And here I am forgetting my manners, ma'am," I continued. "I'm the Right Reverend Honorable Doctor Lucifer Jones at your service, but since we seem to be planning to spend the rest of our lives together, you can call me Lucifer. And who do I have the honor of falling in love with?"

"Cluck," she said.

"I didn't quite catch that," I said.

"Cluck," she repeated.

"I beg your pardon, ma'am," I said, "but it sounds like you said 'cluck' like unto a chicken."

"Cluck cluck cluck," she said.

"So are them other two clucks your middle and last names?" I asked.

"Cluck cluck cluck cluck cluck," she said, and suddenly she didn't look quite as beautiful as she had about forty seconds ago.

"You got something caught in your throat, ma'am?" I asked.

She laughed and slapped me on the shoulder, like I'd just made some kind of joke. "Cluck cluck cluck cluck cluck cluck," she said.

"You live around here, ma'am?" I asked, because I figgered I'd better see if anyone in her family spoke any better before I got too all-fired committed to this here relationship.

She nodded her head, reached out and took me by the hand, and began leading me down a winding jungle path.

I asked her about her family, and what country we were in, and how long she'd been here, and maybe a couple of dozen other things, and all she said was "Cluck cluck cluck", and while I enjoyed holding such a beautiful and dainty hand, I got to say that man and boy that was the dullest conversation I ever did have.

Finally we came to a clearing by still another river, and right in the middle of it were two huge chartreuse houses, each with a couple of dozen rooms and a big veranda out front, and sitting in a rocking chair on one of the verandas was a grizzled old gray-haired guy who obviously wasn't on speaking terms with the local barber, because his hair was almost as long as the girl's, and he had it growing out of his chin, too. I noticed that he also had a mighty wicked-looking shotgun laying across his lap.

"Cluck cluck!" said the girl.

"Welcome back, Rama!" said the old guy. "So you finally caught one! Good for you, girl!"

"Howdy, neighbor," I said. "I'm the Right Reverend Lucifer Jones, weddings and baptisms done cheap, with a group rate for funerals."

"I'm mighty pleased to meet you, Reverend Jones," said the old guy, coming over and shaking my hand. "My name is Cornelius MacNamarra, and this here's my daughter, Rama. What brings you to my humble domicile?"

"Hunger, thirst, and mostly Rama," I said. "You got any grub I could borrow?"

"I won't hear of your borrowing anything!" announced MacNamarra firmly. "Everything I have is yours."

"Well, I call that mighty Christian of you, Brother MacNamarra," I said.

"Call me Corny," said MacNamarra. "Especially now that you're going to become a member of the family."

"Actually, I been meaning to talk to you about that, Brother Corny," I began.

"No need for talk!" he cried. "She's all yours, with my blessing!"

"Just the same, I got a few questions before I cart her off to the altar," I said.

"Beautiful girl!" he said. "The apple of her father's eye." He frowned. "Or is it the grapefruit? I've been in this damned jungle so long I plumb forget."

"I don't want to be intrusive, Brother Corny," I continued, trying to get back to the subject at hand, "but when was the last time you sat down and had a chat with Rama?"

"This morning, at breakfast," he said.

"And you didn't notice nothing peculiar about her lingo?"

"Same as always," he assured me.

"I think that's what I meant," I said. "In my travels on five continents, I've met folks with limited vocabularies, but I got to say hers is a little more limited than most."

"You noticed," he said unhappily.

"Kind of hard to miss in the middle of a hour-long conversation like we had on the way over here," I said.

"Damn!" he muttered. "What's the point of being writ up in song and story as Rama the Bird Girl if all you can say is 'cluck'?"

I looked at Rama, who somehow wasn't quite as beautiful as she'd been an hour ago, but was still maybe a shade above average. "I don't see no wings or feathers on her," I said. "What makes her the Bird Girl?"

"Mostly the way she talks," admitted MacNamarra. "Even out here in the middle of nowhere she can attract men, but though most of 'em can go for days without saying a word to her, sooner or later every last one of 'em either asks what's her name or where's the bathroom or what's that roaring off in the distance, and then she answers, and another potential son-in-law has flown the coop." He spat on the ground. "Hell, I even built an extra house, just for her and her husband," he added, gesturing toward the chartreuse mansions.

"Looks like you're expecting lots of grandchildren," I noted.

"If you can find a second thing to do in this hellhole, let me know," he said. He kind of squinted at me. "What are you doing in this jungle, anyway?"

"Mostly looking for a way out," I said. "I'm a preacher by trade."

"What religion?" he asked.

"Something me and the Lord worked out betwixt ourselves of a Sunday afternoon back in Moline, Illinois," I said.

"So what are you doing down here in South America?" he asked.

"Well, the truth of the matter is that I was kind of invited to come here," I answered him.

"South America asked you to come here?" he said, cocking an eyebrow.

"Actually, I was invited to come here by 33 *other* governments due to some minor disagreements over the finer points of the law," I admitted. "Still, I figger as long as I'm here I might as well hunt up the perfect spot to build the Tabernacle of Saint Luke."

"Saint Luke, huh?" he said. "He writ hisself a pretty good gospel. One of the six or seven best, that's for sure."

"This here is a different Saint Luke," I told him.

"I ain't never heard of a second one," he said.

"You're talking to him," I said. "I figger calling it the Tabernacle of Saint Lucifer might put some parishioners off their feed."

"A telling point," he agreed, nodding his head sagely. "You're gonna make a fine addition to the family, Reverend."

"Well, I been mulling on it the last few minutes, Brother Corny," I said, "and I think I may have been a little hasty losing my heart to Rama."

"Nonsense!" he said. "You ain't looking at it the right way. She's mighty easy on the eyes, pleasant as anyone can want, a fine cook, and she ain't never gonna tell the punchline of your joke after you've spent five minutes building up to it."

"I don't know, Brother Corny," I said. "I got to think about it a little more."

"You're right welcome to," said MacNamarra. "Spend the night if you like. Hell, spend the summer."

"Ain't we *in* summer?" I asked.

"Spend Christmas and New Year's and Opening Day," he went on. "Take as long as you want."

"That's right reasonable of you, Brother Corny," I said.

Then he picked up his shotgun and aimed it at me. "Yep," he said. "Take as long as you want, Reverend. Ain't no hurry at all. But you ain't leaving here a bachelor, and that's a fact."

"You'd really kill me?" I asked, kind of startled.

"Naw, wouldn't be Christian," said MacNamarra. "I'd just blow your legs off. Did I mention that my Rama is a hell of a nurse, too?"

"Tell me, Brother Corny," I said, "what was Rama's mother like?"

"Kind of flighty," he said. "Finally run off with a feller from Kentucky what had this idea about building some kind of franchise, whatever that is. Left me stuck down here with two daughters."

"Two?" I said. "What happened to the other one?"

"Nothing," he said. "She's out hunting our dinner."

Suddenly a rifle shot rang out.

"Well, she either caught it, or she ran into one of Rama's former suitors."

"Cluck cluck cluck!" laughed Rama.

Either the gunshot or the clucking got me to thinking, and I turned back to MacNamarra. "What does your other daughter look like?" I asked him.

"She's the prettier of the two," he said. "I'm sorry, Rama, but it's the truth."

Rama nodded her head in agreement.

"Well, there's no sense rushing into marriage," I said. "Maybe I should meet your other daughter before I make up my mind."

"I don't know," he said. "I kind of had my heart set on marrying Rama off first. I love her like only a father can, but truth to tell, she ain't half the shot her sister is, and if one of 'em's got to grow up to be a ugly old maid what does nothing but tend to her father's needs, it makes sense for that to be Bella."

"Bella?" I repeated. "That's her name?"

"Yeah," he said. "It was Anabella or Arabella or something-else-Bella when she was born, but I never could remember which — but I always remembered the Bella part." He looked across the clearing at a vision of feminine loveliness what was just emerging from the jungle with a rifle in one hand and a young tapir slung over her shoulder.

"Oh, we're gonna eat well tonight, Reverend!" he said. "Hey, Bella, come on over here. There's someone I want you to meet!"

Not many women could make Rama look like a boy in comparison, but Bella was one of 'em. I made a mental note to thank my Silent Partner for arranging for me to meet her before I hooked up permanently with her sister.

Bella kind of undulated across the clearing toward me with a big friendly smile on her face. Her hair was kind of sand-colored — that's dry sand, not the way it looks after a monsoon or maybe being trampled by a herd of terrified elephants — and her skin was smoother than any satin I ever seen. And I'd have given odds that there wasn't a straight line anywhere on her.

"Bella," said MacNamarra, "this here is Reverend Lucifer Jones, who's announced his intention of marrying into our family, one way or t'other."

"Howdy, Bella," I said, taking her hand in mine. I was going to kiss it in a courtly manner until I saw it was covered with tapir blood. "I'm mighty pleased to make your acquaintance, and if I can be allowed to say so, you and your sister are the two most beautiful women it's been my pleasure to encounter on this continent."

"Gobble," she said.

"We'll get around to it," I said, "but it ain't dinnertime yet, and besides someone's got to clean and baste the tapir."

"Gobble gobble gobble," said Bella.

"Uh...Brother Corny," I said, "would I be correct in assuming that ain't no verb?"

"What can I tell you?" he said. "I got *two* bird girls. Built a mansion for each of 'em and their husbands." He started fingering his shotgun again. "I'd sure hate for you to disappoint me, Reverend."

I took another look at his gun and decided that if push came to shove, I'd be even more disappointed than him, to say nothing of being more full of holes.

"Brother Corny," I said, "such a thought couldn't be farther from my mind. I'll be mighty glad to stay for dinner and decide which one of your beautiful daughters I plan to pay court to."

"Now that's more like it!" he said enthusiastically. "Hell, I might even break out a bottle of my prime drinkin' stuff!"

I allowed as to how that could ease the pain of kissing my bachelorhood good-bye, and he told the girls to go clean and cook the tapir and got a couple of clucks and a gobble in response, and then he asked me if I'd like to see the insides of the chartreuse mansions.

"Ain't no hurry," I told him. "I figger I'll be moving into one of 'em soon enough."

"I like your attitude, Reverend Jones," he said, slapping me on the back and damned near sending me sprawling.

"How'd you ever get in the middle of this here jungle in the first place, Brother Corny?" I asked.

"We was looking for Buenos Aires," he answered. "Saw a bunch of little naked folk off in the distance, and figured we must have hit the place during carnival season. We followed the parade for a few days, and then one morning they was all gone and we were stuck here in the middle of nowhere, so I got to work building Chicky and me a house, and—"

"Chicky?" I interrupted him.

"I always called her my little chickadee," he explained. "Of course, that was before she done produced two ever littler ones."

Well, we swapped life stories for the next hour, and he spent another hour asking me about the Clubfoot of Notre Dame and the Insidious Oriental Dentist and some of my other adventures and exploits and encounters, but if you're reading this here account you probably already read them books so there's no sense my repeating it all here. Anyway, I'd just brung him up to the present when Rama and Bella came out and clucked and gobbled at us, and he allowed as to how that meant dinner was ready, and we went inside and sat ourselves down at a table he'd made out of some defenseless tree that probably never did him no harm, and then the girls brought out a slab of meat that tasted as good as it smelled and a lot better than it looked, and we fell to feeding our faces.

When it was over MacNamarra lit up a cigar and told me that I'd brung him up to date about me, but I'd kind of left out the rest of the world, and he was sort of curious about it.

"For example," he said, "did Woodrow Wilson keep us out of that little skirmish over in Europe?"

"For a while," I said.

"Good," he said. "Only problem with all them foreigners is that they speak European and probably don't believe in God and maybe eat their young, but other than that I can't see that they're all that much different from Americans except for being dumber and uglier." He paused for a moment. "How about the fat guy with the girl's name?"

"I ain't quite sure who you're talking about, Brother Corny," I said.

"You know," insisted MacNamarra. "He pitches for the Boston Red Sox. Calls himself Dolly or Honey, something like that."

"You mean Babe Ruth?"

"That's the feller!" he exclaimed. "I sure wouldn't want to find myself alone in the men's room with a guy called Babe. Whatever happened to him?"

"Traded to the Yankees, last I heard," I told him.

"Good," he said. "Ain't no way Boston was ever going to win a pennant with a fat guy named Babe on the team."

"Anything else you got a driving desire to know?" I asked.

"Yeah," he said. "You think my Rama and Bella could make it as Floradora girls?"

"Ain't no Floradora girls no more," I told him.

"Oh?" he asked, looking his disappointment. "What happened to 'em?"

"Talking pictures put 'em out of business," I said.

"Talking pictures?" he repeated, kind of frowning.

"Like unto Charlie Chaplin and Mary Pickford, but with talking," I explained.

He threw back his head and laughed. "Talking pictures!" he guffawed. "By God, I'm gonna like having a son-in-law with a sense of humor!"

He began telling me about how he still had a pile of money in some Missouri and Oklahoma banks, except for the part he'd invested in Anaconda Copper, and I decided telling him about 1929 would just depress him, so I never brung it up.

We talked a bit more, and then he led me out to a tiny shed.

"Good night, Reverend," he said. "I can't tell you how happy I am to have you joining our little family."

I heard a kind of snorting sound from the shed.

"Uh…I don't want to sound unduly alarmed, Brother Corny," I said, "but exactly what is residing in there?"

"Just Sadie, our pet pig," he said. "Don't mind her. She's a right friendly sort, unless you get her mad."

"Maybe I should just sleep in one of the houses," I suggested.

"Rama lives in one and Bella lives in the other," he said. "T'wouldn't be moral, you spending the night under the same roof with one of 'em until after you're married."

Sadie grunted and the shed shook.

"Maybe I'll just sleep on your rocking chair," I suggested.

"Suit yourself," he said with a shrug. "If'n you don't mind being et alive by bugs and having snakes crawl all over you, I can't see why it should bother me neither."

"On second thought, Brother Corny," I said hastily, "I can see that Sadie's a beloved member of the family, and I wouldn't want her suffering no pangs of rejection."

"Well, good for you, Reverend!" he said, slapping me on the back, which was starting to get more than a little sore from all these displays of friendship. "I like the way you think. Hell, build your tabernacle on the property here, and I just might join it. Probably get you three or four Indians, too, provided your religion ain't got nothing against nudity or cannibalism or virgin sacrifice or any of them other little local customs."

I thanked him for his concern and his confidence and his pig, and then I went off to spend the night with Sadie, who truth to tell smelled better and hogged the sleeping area less than some women I could name.

Came morning I wandered over for some breakfast, and Rama and Bella were all scrubbed up and looking their prettiest, than which not a lot of things and hardly no women were prettier, and MacNamarra asked me if I'd made my choice yet, and I told him I was still considering which of these lovely damsels I was going to grace with my hand in marriage, and I realized that I was going to have to come up with some kind of answer pretty soon, because while he smiled and allowed that it was a pretty tough decision, I noticed that his shotgun wasn't never out of his reach.

I began reviewing my options. There were probably worse fates than marrying Bella and having an occasional friendly rendezvous with Rama, or vice versa. Hell, MacNamarra was so desperate to marry 'em off I don't think he'd have raised any serious objections to me marrying both of 'em in the same modest little ceremony on his front porch — but I knew that sooner or later I'd get a little tired of bird talk. Probably in something under three minutes.

I could high-tail it for civilization, but I didn't know where civilization *was*, and besides I wasn't quite as young as I'd once been and I figgered it was mighty unlikely that I could outrun MacNamarra's buckshot.

And then it occurred to me that there might very well be an alternative that didn't involve getting hitched *or* getting shot. It wasn't no sure thing, but it made a lot more sense than a long lifetime of chirping or a very short lifetime of no chirping.

"Hey, Brother Corny," I said, "as long as I'm gonna spend the rest of my natural life here, how's about me going out hunting with Rama and Bella and kind of getting the lay of the land?"

"Sure," he said. "Whoever you marry, you figger to get her pregnant right away and keep her pregnant for years and years, so you might as well start acquainting yourself with the landscape."

"Fine," I said, standing up. "Ain't no time like the present."

"Girls," said MacNamarra, "go with him so he don't get hisself so lost that he can't find his way back here. And if he tries to run off, fire two or three warning shots into his bow."

"You mean across my bow," I corrected him.

"I know what I mean," he said. "Okay, girls, get a move on."

Rama and Bella headed off toward the jungle, and I didn't seem to have no choice but fall into step behind them. We wandered far and wide, to say nothing of high and low. Every now and then Bella would start gobbling and pointing, and sure enough there's be a jaguar watching us from an overhanging branch, or Rama would begin clucking a blue streak and I'd see an anteater staring at us from behind some bushes.

But I wasn't after jaguars or anteaters, nor any other fish or fowl. I never did find what I was looking for, and at day's end we went back to the chartreuse mansions, and I reacquainted myself with Sadie, but we were off again the next morning, and the morning after that, going farther afield each time — and on the fifth day we finally ran into a couple of well-muscled good-looking young men, each wearing a little dinky loincloth and carrying a bow and arrows, and it was clear that they were just about the right age for getting hitched.

Thank you, Lord, I said silently. *Now I owe You one.*

"Howdy," I said to them when they became aware of our presence, and I could tell right off that they were smitten by Rama's and Bella's beauty. "I hope we ain't intruding on your hunting grounds, and by the way where's the nearest city?"

"Quack quack quack," said the one on the left.

By God, Lord, I thunk, *You outdone Yourself this time!*

"Does your friend always talk like that?" I asked the one on the right.

"Squawk squawk squawk squawk squawk," he said.

I took a quick look at the girls, and I could tell they'd already lost their hearts and were preparing to lose a couple of other things as well, and there wasn't no doubt that the young men were hopelessly in love too.

The five of us went back to the chartreuse mansions, and when MacNamarra saw what I had in tow, and especially when he *heard* what I was bringing back for his girls, he was so happy he forgot all about shooting me. He broke out his drinkin' stuff again, and before dark I presided at the ceremony what joined the bird boys and the bird girls together for all eternity, and then I stood clear just in case Brother Corny had a tractor and was going to let the girls use it to plight their troughs, and after spending one more night in Sadie's company while each girl honeymooned in a chartreuse mansion, I announced that it was my intention to be on my way, because when you're a man of the cloth whose business is saving sinners, you just naturally got to go to where the sinners congregate, and that meant a city.

"I'll come with you," said MacNamarra.

"I'd of thunk you'd be the happiest man in the world," I said.

"I am."

"Then why are you leaving now that you got both of your girls married off?"

"Truth to tell, Reverend," he answered, "that bird talk was driving me crazy, and now suddenly there's going to be twice as much of it as there was. I got to go where they speak some human language."

"Well, it'd be un-Christian to refuse you a favor," I said, "so pack up your gear and let's be going."

"I promise I won't be no bother to you," he said. "I just got to hear a human voice. Yours ain't much, and it don't make sense very often, but it's better than clucking and gobbling."

He kissed the girls good-bye, slung his shotgun over his shoulder, packed a satchel of ammunition and another of drinkin' stuff, and off we went. He wasn't too bad a traveling companion, except that he'd kick me awake two or three times each night and ask me to talk at him.

I think we'd been on the trail a week when we came to a village smack-dab in the middle of the jungle. It wasn't much of a village, just four or five huts, and sitting in front of one of 'em was an almost-naked lady who was about MacNamarra's age and maybe three or four times his weight.

"Good morrow, Madam," he said, bowing low to her. "Has this here village got a name?"

She answered him in the very same language them guys what wasn't Indians had used on me a couple of weeks earlier, and she guv him a great big smile, and I could see that her teeth were busy rotting away, and even from where I stood I could tell that she hadn't bathed in the last ten or twenty years, but none of that bothered MacNamarra.

"Ain't she got the most beautiful voice you ever heard?" he asked me.

"Did you understand a word she said?" I shot back.

"What difference does that make?" he said. "She didn't chirp, and that's all that matters." He reached out and shook my hand. "It's been nice knowing you, Reverend Jones, and I can never thank you enough for what you done for my daughters, but I'm smitten with this here delicate little frail flower, and I'm going to spend the rest of my natural-born days just listening to her dulcet tones."

"If that's what you want, Brother Corny, I wish you all the luck in the world," I said, though from the way his delicate little three-hundred-pounder was talking a blue streak at him I figured he'd already found all the luck he needed.

I bid him a fond farewell, and headed off toward where I thought civilization was hiding, primed and ready to finally build the Tabernacle of Saint Luke.

THE LOST CONTINENT OF MOO

You know, there's one thing I ain't never figgered out, and man and boy it's been bothering me most of my blameless life, and even now as a old man I haven't come up with an answer, and I've had a lot of time to think about it since it was always happening to me, even back in 1935 which is when the tale I'm telling you took place, and though I've wandered the face of five continents (or maybe seven, if you count them two little ones down south) I still don't know why it takes me such a short time to get lost and such a long time to get found again.

In fact, that was my very thought as I left Cornelius MacNamarra's chartreuse mansions behind me and moseyed alongside the Amazon, waiting for civilization to raise its head so I could get together with it and finally get around to the serious business of building the Tabernacle of Saint Luke. But the closest I came to civilization in the next week was a couple of little fellers who were wearing paint on their faces and not much else. They didn't speak no known language, which is something they had in common with the French, and they kept staring at me as if they were wondering how my head would look in their trophy case, so I finally took my leave of them.

I wish I could have took my leave of everything else, because I kept getting et by mosquitoes and hissed at by snakes and growled at by jaguars and giggled at by monkeys, and after I'd footslogged maybe another hundred miles and still hadn't seen no shining cities filled to overflowing with sinners who were in desperate need of a man of the cloth like myself, I figgered maybe the cities had all migrated to the south when no one was looking, so I took a left turn and put the Amazon River behind me.

Now, I knew South America had a bunch of cities even back then, places like Rio and Buenos Aires and Caracas and Saigon, but it was like they'd seen me coming and had all tiptoed away before I could lay eyes on any of 'em. I picked up a female companion named Petunia along the way. She was a real good listener, but she didn't say nothing and she smelled just terrible, especially after a rainstorm (of which we had an awful lot), and after a few days I finally had to admit that I just didn't have much in common with lady tapirs, and we parted ways.

I kept trudging along, keeping my spirits up by reading my well-worn copy of the Good Book, and finally, after another couple of weeks, the forest started retreating, the mosquitoes found other things to do, the animals took umbrage when I kept reciting the Eighth and Fourteenth Commandments at 'em, and even the rain decided it had urgent business elsewhere. The land flattened out, the sun came out of hiding, and suddenly I was in this pasture that must have been a couple of hundred miles long, give or take a few inches.

And as I looked over my surroundings, I began to realize that this wasn't like no part of South America I had ever seen, and I'd seen an awful lot of it, starting with San Palmero and working my way through the Island of Annoyed Souls and this big wet area everyone called the Amazon Basin though I didn't see nary a single wash basin, with or without no love-starved Amazons, the whole time I was walking through it.

I kept looking around and thinking that maybe I'd fallen asleep and sleepwalked to some new country. I was still mulling on it when I realized I'd been walking forever and a day, and I decided to lay down right on the grass, and if there'd been a desk clerk I'd have told him not to wake me 'til maybe half past Tuesday, and then I was snoring to beat the band.

I woke up when something kind of cold and sort of wet and more than a little bit pushy rubbed against my face.

"I'm sleeping," I said.

It nudged me kind of gently.

"Go away," I said, scrunching up my eyes. "It's a holiday somewhere in the world. I'll get a job tomorrow."

Then whatever it was pressed right up against my ear and said *"Moo!"*

"What in tarnation was *that*?" I bellowed, jumping to my feet.

Suddenly I heard a dozen more *moos*, and I looked around, and damned if I wasn't surrounded by some of the fattest cows I'd ever seen. There were hundreds of 'em, maybe thousands, and they'd all snuck on me my while I was sleeping.

And then I thought, well, maybe they didn't exactly *sneak* up. Maybe they *live* here.

"Moo!" said a few dozen of 'em, staring at me with big brown cows' eyes, as if they were begging me to come on over and choose a steak for dinner.

And then, being a educated man, I remembered my history books, or at least some stories I'd heard in Red Charlie's Waterfront Bar in Macao, which comes to almost the same thing, and I realized that somehow or other I *had* stumbled onto a new land what no one else had ever seen before, and it didn't take but forty or fifty more cows joining the chorus to for me to figger out that I was probably the first white man ever to set foot on the Lost Continent of Moo what had been writ up in fable, song and story.

I looked off into the distance, hoping to see a shining city filled with Moovians or whatever they called themselves, where I could build my tabernacle and set up shop, but there wasn't nothing out there but cows. Now, I knew there had to be people somewhere, because in all my experience I ain't never come across a cow that could sing songs or tell stories about lost continents.

And while we're speaking of lost continents, them of you what's read *Encounters,* the story of my attempt to bring the word of the Lord to the sinful nations of Europe, will know right off the bat that this here wasn't the first lost continent I discovered. In fact, it seems that one of the things I'm really good at, other than helping poor sinners (and especially fallen women) see the light and the glory, is finding lost continents. It ain't generally known—and in fact if you didn't read my book it probably ain't known at all—but not only did I find the lost continent of Atlantis, I actually bought it. Of course, it was buried under a few fathoms of water, but I'd be there still if the Greek government hadn't objected to my placing a bunch of ads in the local paper offering to sell lots with a Mediterranean view. But that's another story, and one what's already been told with grace and elegance.

Anyway, after I'd wandered a couple of miles, stepping in all kinds of things that a gentleman would never discuss with you except to say they were vile and foul-smelling and mostly plentiful, I heard a shout off to my left. I turned and saw a guy riding up on a horse. He was kind of dressed like a cowboy, except for the chaps and the belt and the shirt and the hat, and he galloped up to me, and then just when I was sure he'd escaped from some hospital for the pixilated and thunk I was a polo ball or whatever it is that they hit with them sticks, he pulled his horse to a stop and said something to me in some alien tongue.

"I don't understand a word you're saying, Brother," I replied, "but allow me to introduce myself. I'm the Right Reverend Doctor Lucifer Jones, and I'm pleased to make your acquaintance."

He jabbered something else I couldn't follow.

"Before we resort to sign language, Brother," I said, "perhaps you could tell me if I've indeed stumbled onto the lost continent of ancient legend."

As I said it, I indicated the land with a wave of my hand, and cocked an eyebrow so he'd know I was asking a question.

It worked, because he shot me a friendly smile and said, "Pampas," which I figgered was how they said Moo in Mooish.

"Thanks, Brother," I said. "And now I wonder if you can tell me where I can find the king of Moo?"

He just stared at me, puzzled, and then I realized I'd made a simple mistake.

"Strike that, Brother," I said. "Where can I find the king of Pampas?"

He kind of frowned, and I began thinking that my initial appraisal was right, except maybe for the polo part.

"Well, thanks anyway," I said, "but I can't waste no more time here. I got to scout up the people and start bringing the Word to any godless sinners I find among 'em, so I guess I'll be going now." I gave his horse's neck a friendly pat, and noticed some weird kind of trinket he had with a ball attached to each end.

He saw me staring at it, and said "Bolas."

"Thanks, Brother," I said. Then, remembering my manners, I added "And bolas to you too."

I headed off to my right, but he immediately urged his horse forward and blocked my way. Then he started jabbering at me and pointing to my left. I looked where he was pointing, and all I could see was maybe twenty thousand cows, give or take a couple.

"That's mighty considerate of you, Brother, but I'm looking for sinners of the two-legged kind," I told him. "Besides, mighty few cows contribute to the poor box, and that's a serious consideration when you're figuring out where to build your tabernacle."

I walked around his horse and began heading off again, and again he blocked my way.

"Just what seems to be your problem, Brother?" I said, starting to get a bit riled.

He began talking a blue streak, but I didn't hear no familiar words like "pampas" or "bolas," and finally I held up my hand for silence.

"I appreciate your concern," I said, "and as near as I can figger it, either you think I'm here to convert your cattle, or I look so hungry you want me to take a couple of hundred cows home with me, or—and now that I come to think of it, them first two don't hold a candle to the next reason, which is that you got all your womenfolk stashed in the direction I'm going." I gave him a reassuring smile. "You don't have to worry none, Brother. The way I smell after walking through your pasture, I doubt that any woman of quality would let me get near her—and if she would, that just means she's been stepping in all this stuff too, and I ain't wildly interested in getting much closer than fifty feet to her, or maybe a hundred, depending on which way the wind's blowing."

I began walking yet again, and this time he just sighed and frowned and shook his head, and finally he dug his spurs into his horse and headed off toward all the cattle he'd been trying to introduce me to.

It took me a whole day and a night to get out of that cow pasture, but finally I came to what was either a large rocky hill or a small rocky mountain, and I followed a footpath up it, and pretty soon I became aware that I was being watched by unseen eyes, which in my broad experience are just about the worst kind of eyes to be watched by, and finally the footpath widened a bit, and suddenly I was facing a mighty impressive stone building which sure didn't resemble no other building I'd ever seen. Of course, the 200 naked warriors, each of 'em with a spear and an expression that would have meant their shorts were too tight if any of 'em had been wearing shorts, might have had a little something to do with it.

Finally they stood aside, and a kind of short, pudgy white man moseyed out of the building while they all bowed down as he passed by. He was wearing a loincloth, which meant he was dressed a lot better than any of his friends and neighbors, and he had a half-smoked cigar in his mouth. He was kind of bald, and a little bit cock-eyed, and he had such a thick unkempt beard that it instantly said to all and sundry that he wasn't on speaking terms with his barber, and his bare feet were pretty caked with all the stuff I'd been doing my best to avoid, but outside all that I suppose he was as presentable as most people, and certainly more presentable than some I'd run into lately.

He walked up to me, stopped about four feet away, put his hands on his hips, jutted out his chin, and said, "Who the hell are you?"

"You speak English," I said, surprised.

"I speak English a hell of a lot better than you answer questions," he said. "Now, who are you?"

"The Right Reverend Honorable Doctor Lucifer Jones at your service," I said. "Weddings and baptisms done cheap, with a group rate for funerals. And who do I have the pleasure of addressing?"

"Rakovekin, Lord of the Outer Realm, Messenger of the Almighty, Spokesman for the Elder Deities, and Commander of the Legions of the Dead."

"That's quite a mouthful, Brother," I noted.

"Yeah, it can get tedious," he admitted. "Especially at parties when I have to meet a lot of new people. You can call me Henry."

"Forgive me for pointing it out, but Henry don't sound like no South American name."

"And the other one I gave you did?" he asked.

"Now as I come to think on it, no, I suppose it didn't neither," I answered.

"Henry's what they used to call me before I stumbled onto this place."

"I could tell right off you weren't no native," I said.

"Only place I'm native to is Hackensack, New Jersey," said Henry.

"What's a Hackensack boy doing thousands of miles from home on this here lost continent?" I asked.

"Being a god," he said.

"Pleasant work?" I asked.

"Most of the time," he said.

"Maybe I'll take a stab at it and join you, since I spend so much time consulting with the Lord anyway," I offered. "What's the job pay?"

"We only got room for one god around here, and I'm it," he said. "Now, you're welcome to stick around a day or two until you're rested up, and you can even grab some grub to take with you on your long and arduous journey to anywhere else in the world, but you can't stay here on no permanent basis."

"How did *you* find this here lost continent, Brother Henry?" I asked him.

"Didn't know it was no continent, and it sure as hell ain't as lost as it used to be," he grumbled. "You're the fourth white man to wander in here in less than ten years."

"What happened to the other three?"

"I sent two of 'em packing."

"And the third," I said. "Is he still here?"

"Parts of him are."

Which made me think that there were maybe worse ideas than sticking around just a day or two and then hitting the road.

"But to answer your question, Reverend Jones," he continued, "I came down to this part of the world to hunt elephants."

"I don't want to put no damper on your enthusiasm, Brother Henry," I said, "but there ain't no elephants within a couple of thousand miles of here, except them what's on display at zoos."

"Well, if push had come to shove I'd have settled for 'em," said Henry. "They don't run so fast nor so far when they're in a cage, and they sure can't find much natural cover there."

I could see right off that he was a natural-born sportsman who was put off his feed at the thought of littering the landscape with escaped animals what had been gutshot or worse, and I figgered if I could befriend him over the next couple of days I could maybe send him off to a zoo in Argentina or Brazil and try my hand at the god business myself.

"Anyway," said Henry, "I was wandering the landscape looking for elephants without no success when I stumbled onto this place. I couldn't see no one around, so I just followed the path right up to the temple, and I was so danged tired that I walked into it to get out of the sun and kind of catch my wind, and that stone altar in the middle of the place looked so inviting that I doffed most of my duds and lay down on it to take a little nap." He shook his head in wonderment. "Next thing I knew there were twenty naked men kneeling down in front of me. At first I thought they were shooting craps, which is what's usually going on when a bunch of Hackensack men get down on their knees, but then they saw I was awake and they began bowing and chanting. After awhile I asked one of 'em what it all meant, and he told me that I was clearly the god of prophecy that had been sent down to lead them to their former glory, and he started giving me my name and my titles. I know you thought I'd guv you a tongue twister when I introduced myself, but actually I got 38 more titles to go with the ones you heard. At first I thought reciting 'em all would charm the ladies, but the truth of the matter is that most of 'em fall asleep before I hit Number 20."

"Speaking of the womenfolk, Brother Henry, just where are they all hiding?" I asked him.

"Oh, they're off tilling fields and fetching water and toting firewood and other womanly duties like that," he said. "All except for the priestesses, anyway."

"And what about the men?"

"Mostly they're worshipping me in private, and getting ready to go to war."

"War?" I repeated. "You planning to attack two hundred thousand head of cattle?"

"No, we're after the gauchos that herd the cattle," he said. "Then I figure once we've won that little skirmish, we'll drive the cattle all the way to Buenos Aires so we'll have a little something to nibble on while we're carrying out our war of conquest."

"I like a man who thinks ahead," I said. "I can tell we're going to be great friends, Brother Henry."

"Well, as long as you're here, Reverend," he said, his expression softening a bit, "I might as well show you around my earthly kingdom." He lowered his voice confidentially. "Truth of the matter is that I ain't yet figured out where they're hiding my heavenly kingdom."

He headed off to the interior of the building, leaving all the menfolk behind, and I fell into step behind him.

"This here's the Great Temple of Rakovekin," he said. "I keep trying to get 'em to call it the Great Temple of Henry, but they're a stubborn lot."

I saw a bunch of half-naked women puttering around lighting candles and such, and I shot the closest of 'em a great big smile. "Them's my Heavenly Handmaidens," said Henry. "Each and every one of 'em a virgin."

"Yeah?" I said.

"Well, except for them what ain't," he replied with a shrug.

I kind of winked at another of 'em, and she giggled and blushed, and I pretty much decided then and there that since food grew on trees and bushes and Heavenly Handmaidens only seemed to grow in Moo, I'd take a couple of 'em with me when I left and trust to the Lord that I could find food along the way.

"Over here," said Henry, pointing to a big stone slab, "is the altar I fell asleep on that first day."

I looked closer. It had a lot of bloodstains on it.

"I see you don't believe in sacrificing turnips," I noted, and he threw back his head and laughed.

"Rev," he said, "I had a feeling the second I saw you that we was going to become friends." He patted the stains lovingly. "No, these come from men who thought they could lay hands on the High Priestess."

"You got a High Priest, too?"

"We did," he said. He pointed to one of the stains. "I believe that's what's left of him."

"She's inviolate, huh?" I said.

"No," he answered. "Last time I saw her she was in gold, such minimal duds as she was wearing. Mostly a crown, a couple of armbands, and some sandals, as I recall."

"Sounds like she was dressed for mighty warm weather," I said, "which I must admit we got a lot of in this here neck of the woods."

"Just between you and me, it's more like an armpit of the woods," said Henry confidentially, "which is why I plan to pillage and plunder my way to Bahia."

"I thunk you were making war on Buenos Aires," I said.

"As long as it begins with a B and it's got electricity and running water, makes no difference to me," answered Henry.

"Getting back to your High Priestess, has she got a name?"

"Of course she has a name," he said. "Why?"

"Truth to tell, Brother Henry, I got an affinity for gorgeous half-naked High Priestesses," I said. "Some people like Ford roadsters, some people like fine Waterford crystal, but me, I like—"

"I get the point," he said. "I may introduce you to her, but you have to understand up front that she belongs to me. If you touch her or make a play for her, it'll bring all my heavenly wrath down on your head. That altar's always got room for another bloodstain."

"I don't rightly hold with one human being owning another, Brother Henry," I said severely. Personally, I figured taking out a short-term lease on the High Priestess was a different matter altogether, but I decided not to discuss the finer points of it with him at that particular moment.

"I fully agree, Reverend Jones," he said.

"You do?"

"Absolutely," he said. "No human being should ever own another." Then he smiled and added, "Damned lucky for me that I'm a god and not a human being, ain't it?"

I had to admit that I didn't have no logical answer to that. In fact, I was just about to change the subject and maybe get him talking about the Brooklyn Dodgers or Equipoise or some other subject that was near and dear to folks what grew up near Hackensack, when my attention and my breath was both took by the most beautiful High Priestess anyone ever laid eyes on, and one look was enough to convince any red-blooded man or god that eyes were the very least of all the things he wanted to lay on her.

"Close your mouth, Reverend," said Henry. "You never know what'll fly into it in these here parts."

She kept approaching me until she was just a couple of feet away, than stopped and smiled at me.

"Hello," she said, extending a delicate hand. "My name is Valeria."

"Miss Valeria, ma'am," I said, "I just want to state for the record that in a lifetime of admiring half-naked High Priestesses and other delicate morsels of femininity, I ain't never seen nothing to compare to your beauty, and if you're ever in the need of a little nocturnal spiritual comfort, all you got to do is say the word and I'll be there with bells on."

She giggled. "Why would you wear bells?"

"You prefer feathers, just say the word," I told her.

"That's enough, Reverend," said Henry. "Let's not forget who's the god and who's the mortal here."

"So you ain't told her?" I said.

"Told her what?" he demanded.

"That any mortal what sleeps with a god will die of a hideously disfiguring disease," I said as Valeria kind of gasped and took a couple of quick steps backward. "I thunk everyone knew that."

"Valeria, honey, he's just making that up!" said Henry.

I pulled my bible out of my pocket. "It's all right here in the Book of Salome, Chapter 7, Verse 3." (Actually, the Book of Salome ain't got no Chapter 7 or Verse 3, but I had a soft spot for them because those were the numbers of the last Daily Double I hit at Saratoga just before I was gently requested to leave the country by a handful of gendarmes and politicians and other select authorities that didn't have no sense of humor or proportion.)

"Let me see that!" said Henry, reaching for my bible.

I pulled it back, and shot Valeria a triumphant smile. "Think about it," I said. "Would a *real* god have to look at the bible to remind himself of what it said?"

"But it didn't say that at all!" shouted Henry.

"And now I suppose you're gonna deny that you ever touched the last 200 women what died in these here parts," I said.

"Valeria, baby, you ain't going to listen to this intruder, are you?" said Henry, reaching out to her.

She jumped back out of reach. "Don't touch me!" she cried.

"But Valeria, sweetie!" he said. Probably he was going to say more, but she turned and ran away before he could get the words out.

"You're going to feel the brunt of my godly wrath for that, Lucifer Jones!" he vowed.

"Come on, Brother Henry," I said. "I got you by two or three inches, maybe 20 pounds, and at least ten years. Let's bury the hatchet, admit we both stumbled onto a happy situation here, and split the spoils. You can have everything to the left of the path that led up here, I'll take everything to the right, you can have Valeria on Mondays, Wednesdays and Fridays (if you can convince her that she'll survive being touched by you), I'll take her to my side of the path on Tuesdays, Thursdays, and Saturdays, and we'll toss a coin for Sundays, provided you got any coins hidden in your loincloth."

"I got a better idea," he said.

"Yeah," I replied. "What is it?"

"I think I'll kill you and keep everything just the way it was."

"You don't scare me one bit," I said. "You're taking this god business a little too seriously, Brother Henry. You're all alone in a strange land, wearing naught but a loincloth. Even Jesus had twelve disciples to do his bidding."

"Conspicuous consumption," he said. "I only need six disciples, and I got 'em all right here." He reached into his loincloth and pulled out a snub-nosed revolver.

"You know, Brother Henry," I said, "now that I come to mull on it, Valeria ain't close to the most beautiful woman I ever seen. Her nose is too big, and her eyes are kind of crossed, and when she smiles I can see she's missing a molar or two, and—"

"Shut up!" he screamed. "You're talking about the woman I love!"

"Well, upon reconsideration, missing that molar makes her an exotic creature of mystery, and anyone who can look in two directions at once has got to be a definite value when you're out hunting or maybe running for your lives from a bunch of outraged infidels, and—"

"Enough!" he said. He aimed the gun at me. "You got any last words?"

"Like I was saying, from the neck down, she's just about perfect."

"Stop talking about her!" he snapped. "You got any *other* last words?"

"Well, now that I come to think of it, I do have a question," I said.

"Just one."

"You got any dangerous snakes in these here parts?"

"All right," he said, shaking his head in disgust. "I done my best, but you're just not taking this seriously. Prepare to meet the Lord."

"Not to be argumentative," I said as he cocked the pistol, "but weren't you claiming that *you* was God?"

"He's my brother," said Henry. "He's minding the store while I'm busy here."

His finger tightened on the trigger.

I kind of scrunched my eyes up so I wouldn't see the bullet coming. The strange thing was that I didn't hear it nor feel it neither.

"*Shit!*" screamed Henry. "Get this thing off'n me!"

I opened my eyes and saw that Henry, who'd been wearing naught but a loincloth a few seconds earlier, was now wearing a wraparound anaconda what was maybe 25 feet long.

"Don't just stare at me!" he yelled. "*Help* me!"

"I don't mean no impertinence, Brother Henry," I said, "but wasn't you just preparing to shoot me before this here snake came to my rescue?"

"That was *then*!" he said kind of desperately. "This is *now*!"

"You're still holding the gun," I noted.

"He done paralyzed me with his fiendish venom! I can't move my fingers!"

"Anacondas ain't got no venom," I said. "You're thinking of rattlesnakes."

"I'm thinking of being crushed to death!" cried Henry. "Help me!"

"Or maybe cobras," I said. "I seem to remember that King Cobras are loaded with venom." I stopped and scratched my head. "You know, now as I come to think on it, I don't recollect that I ever saw a Queen Cobra. I wouldn't know how to tell 'em apart anyway; I don't imagine they can be much curvier."

"I'm dying and you're lecturing me on herpetology!"

"I ain't so much lecturing as discussing," I pointed out.

Suddenly the gun fell from his hand.

"Okay, I'm unarmed!" he said. "*Now* will you get this blasted critter off me?"

"Well," I said, "it'd be an act of Christian charity, there ain't no denying that."

"Then do it!"

"On the other hand, it might well be an act of Christian suicide," I said. "I got to think this over."

"Don't take more than about 20 seconds," he groaned, "because I'm gonna be all out of air in less than half a minute!"

"What's going on here?" said a feminine voice. For a moment I thunk maybe the snake's wife was getting jealous, but then I saw it was Valeria, who'd come back when she heard Henry screaming.

"Get your damned pet off me!" wheezed Henry.

"I've warned you not to tease him!" she said harshly. Then she turned to me. "Was he abusing my snake?"

"Just the opposite, as near as I can tell," I said.

Henry tried to agree with me, but though he moved his lips nothing came out.

"I certainly don't want to take sides in this little dispute, ma'am," I said, "especially since he was about to shoot me for saying how much I admired your rare and ethereal beauty, but he's turning purple."

"Oh, all right," she said. "Bubbles, sit!"

The snake released Henry and coiled itself on the ground.

"Down!" she said, and suddenly he lay down belly to the ground, which was an awful lot of belly to hit the ground all at once.

"That dagnabbed snake is always sneaking up on me!" muttered Henry, trying to catch his breath.

I stepped over and picked up the gun before he got back enough strength to reach for it.

"That's a mighty well-trained snake, Miss Valeria, ma'am," I said.

"I've had him since he was a puppy," she said.

"Well, you learn something new every day," I said. "I didn't know snakes was ever puppies."

"They aren't," she answered. "But I don't know what to call a baby snake."

"How about Godless Spawn of Satan?" wheezed Henry, finally dragging himself to his feet.

"Shut up!" snapped Valeria.

"Can Priestesses say 'Shut up' to a god?" I asked.

"When they look like *him*, they can say a lot worse," she said. "Why was he trying to kill you?"

"He was afraid I was going to horn in on the god business, and also he didn't want me declaring my undying love for you."

"What is it with you gods?" she said wearily. "Can't you keep your passions, or at least your hands, to yourselves?"

"Now, Valeria, honey…" began Henry, but Bubbles starting hissing and he decided that silence was the better part of valor.

"I don't want to put no damper on your religious beliefs, Miss Valeria, ma'am," I said, "but someone's got to be the one to let you know that Henry here ain't no god."

"That's a fine time to tell us," she said angrily, "after we've been worshipping him for fifteen years and giving him a steady supply of virgins."

"You got *that* many young women around here?" I said. "I sure didn't see 'em on the way in."

"When we ran out of girls we gave him cows," she answered. "He was usually so drunk he didn't know the difference."

"I know they didn't jabber all night," said Henry sullenly.

"Before I let Bubbles keep him, how do you know he's not a god?" she asked.

"Can he bring rain?" I said. "Can he make seven passes in a row at the craps table? Can he turn water into Napoleon brandy? How many winners can he pick if the track comes up muddy?"

"Those are all godly qualifications?" she asked.

"The bringing rain one's just a trick, but the others are all legitimate," I said. "Hell, even minor league gods like Zeus and Jupiter can do most of them things."

"I see," she said, glaring at Henry. "My people have been a victim of false doctrine."

"Well, then it's only just and fitting that I was guided to this here lost continent to bring you the Word," I said, "me being the Lord's business agent, so to speak."

"What will we do with *him*?" she asked, indicating Henry, who was starting to shiver even though it was shorts and sandals weather.

"You're not going to listen to this charlatan, are you?" demanded Henry. "I *am* a god, goddamn it! I'm Rakovekin, Lord of the Outer Realm, Messenger of the Almighty, Spokesman for the Elder Deities, Commander of the Legions of the Dead, Defender of..."

"You're not going to list all 38 titles, are you?" she asked in bored tones.

"I got an idea, ma'am," I said. "Let him rassle Bubbles two out of three falls. If he's a god he shouldn't have no trouble winning."

She looked like she was considering it, and finally nodded her approval. "I see no reason why not."

"Well I see one," complained Henry. "How can I pin something what ain't got no shoulders? I can't give him no full nelson or stepover toe-hold, because he ain't got no arms nor legs neither."

She turned to me. "Lucifer, have you an answer?"

"Since Bubbles ain't got no arms, he can't put no Mongolian death grip on you," I said to Henry. "And he ain't likely to trip you or kick you when you're down. As I see it, that makes it a fair fight."

"If it's a fair fight, you can book my bet," said Henry. "I want to put fifty dollars on the snake."

"I'm happy to book it," I said, "long as you understand that I'm giving seven thousand to one on Bubbles. If you win, I'll owe you a little less than a penny."

"See?" he said to Valeria. "That *proves* it ain't a fair fight!"

"Miss Valeria," I said, "I put it to you: couldn't a real god beat them odds?"

"I think you have a point, Lucifer," she replied.

"And if he combs his hair just right maybe no one'll notice it," said Henry bitterly.

"Come on now, Henry," I said, "there ain't no cause to get riled just because you lost fair and square."

"I ain't lost nothing yet!" he yelled.

"That's because you ain't rassled Bubbles yet," I said. "But you already lost the love and respect of the delicate frail flower what won my heart the second I seen her."

"She's *mine*!" he roared.

"She's already guv you everything she's got except her crown and a couple of armbands," I said. "Ain't that enough?"

"To hell with the snake!" he said. "I'll rassle *you* for her!"

I turned to Valeria. "You gonna let him insult your snake like that, ma'am?"

She frowned. "He *did* insult Bubbles, didn't he?"

"It was a slip of the tongue!" said Henry, backing away. "I didn't mean nothing by it. I think Bubbles is the nicest, pleasantest, friendliest, most beautiful representative of all the hellborn man-eating critters I ever met!"

"That's it!" snapped Valeria. "Bubbles?"

Bubbles kind of snapped to attention, as much as a 25-foot-long killer snake can anyway, and waited for her orders.

"He's all yours."

Henry didn't waste no breath screaming or cursing. He just turned and lit out like Jesse Owens, and Bubbles took off after him like Man o' War but without the legs and the jockey. Henry was still leading by a couple of lengths as they swung around a stand of trees and was lost to sight.

"I thank you for all your help, Lucifer," said Valeria, "but now we are without a god."

"I think we can fix that without no undue effort, Miss Valeria, ma'am," I said.

"How?" she asked with a eager little tremor of excitement.

Well, let me tell you, when you're built like Valeria and you ain't wearing naught but a crown and some gold armbands, and a tremor sweeps over you, even a eager little one, it just naturally is going to have a positive effect on any nearby menfolk. It's positive effect on me was that I was positive I wanted to spend the rest of my life within arm's reach of that gorgeous body, except when answering calls of nature or playing cards with the boys once I taught 'em the intricacies of poker and figured out what a bunch of naked savages had to bet.

"Easy," I answered. "I ran old Henry out of here, with a little help from your snake, so I figger that makes me an even greater god than he was."

"But he wasn't a god at all," she said. "You proved it."

"Then no matter what kind of god I am, I'm a greater one than he was," I said with impeccable logic. "Now, I figger if you and me get hitched, that'll elevate you to the status of apprentice goddess, so the people'll be twice as happy with twice as many gods to worship, and it'll give 'em a purpose in life, which'll be to gather food and drink and firewood for us while we're getting to know each other better."

"It's tempting," she said with a little flutter of emotion, and let me tell you her flutters put her tremors in the shade. "But we have been fooled once already. We must be sure you are truly a god before I agree to become your consort."

I was about to tell her that I didn't want her to become my consort and would settle for her becoming my ladyfriend, but she looked like she had her mind made up, so I asked her what kind of godly test she had in mind for me, adding that I didn't do no heavy lifting because I'd pulled a muscle or two tossing the moon into orbit, and also that I didn't speak Sumarian, Aramaic, French, or no other nonsense languages.

"We must devise a proper test for your divinity," said Valeria. She lowered her head in thought for a moment, then looked up. "I suppose if you can swim across a piranha-filled river and live through it, that would prove you were an immortal."

"I'm allergic to water," I said. "How about a spelling bee?"

"Or perhaps if each man were to hurl his spear at you, point-blank, and they all bounced off..."

"Ping-pong," I suggested. "I'll take on all comers at ping-pong."

"Or we could cover you with *marabunta*."

"What's *marabunta*, ma'am?" I asked. "Something like peanut butter?"

"Army ants."

I never knew that a beautiful naked High Priestess could be so bloodthirsty and single-minded all at the same time.

"I wish I could accommodate you, Miss Valeria, ma'am," I said, "but you got to understand that no two gods are alike. We're as different as baseball players and pole vaulters and shoe salesmen."

"And what makes you a god?" she asked.

"Well," I said after some thought, "I play a mighty mean game of tiddly winks."

"Tiddly winks?" she repeated. "I have never heard of it."

"Darn," I said. "I guess that means I can't prove my godliness to you. I suppose you'll just have to take my word for it and move in with me. If you want to bring a couple of them lesser priestesses to act as cooks and housemaids, that'll be okay too."

"I really feel we must end all controversy before it begins, Lucifer," she said.

"You're looking at this all wrong," I explained. "Let 'em controverse for a few years and get it out of their systems. In the long run it'll do 'em a world of good."

"It will?"

"Sure," I said. "Now instead of falling asleep right after a few hours of connubial bliss, we'll make it a law that they have to spend an hour a night discussing whether or not I'm a god. That's probably a lot more than most husbands and wives ever spend talking to each other after they tie the knot."

She stared at me kind of funny-like. "I can believe all gods are different. You sound nothing like Henry."

"Well," I said condescendingly, "you know them New Jersey gods."

"I shall have to think about this," she said.

"Fine," I said. "We can talk about it right after you and me consummate our godly relationship. In fact, now that I think about it, I just remembered that I ain't got no apartment here, so I reckon I'll move into yours."

She shook her head. "No, I think it best that you keep your distance until this matter is resolved."

"But Miss Valeria, ma'am, this is one of the best ways I know to prove my godhood."

"What are you talking about?" she demanded.

I leaned over and whispered what I was talking about into her ear, then stood back with a triumphant smile. "Now be honest," I said as her face turned a bright red, "could any mortal man do *that*?"

I saw the slap coming, but I couldn't duck it.

"In answer to your question," she said with as much dignity as a naked High Priestess could muster on the spur of the moment, "no mortal man would ever be allowed to do *that* or even suggest it."

"So that solves it and now I don't have to prove I ain't a mortal man?" I asked, rubbing my jaw where she'd loosened a tooth or two.

"Now you have to prove that you're not a demon from the pits of hell," she answered.

She put two fingers in her mouth and whistled, and suddenly the temple was filled with all them men what had been busy worshipping Henry when I arrived, and I found myself facing the business ends of a bunch of spears.

"You're going about this all wrong, Miss Valeria," I said. "If I'm a demon I'm gonna kill all your spear-toting friends and relations here, and if I'm not they're going to kill me and you're going to feel just awful about having made such a mistake."

She stared at me. "If I'm wrong I don't believe I'll lose a minute of sleep over it."

"Being a compassionate god or demon, I just can't countenance such bloodshed," I said. "I'll tell you what: I'll rassle one of 'em. If I win, everyone admits I'm a god, or at least a demon what's a hell of a good rassler, you move in with me, and they all agree to worship me."

"And if you lose?"

"Then I'll take your solid gold armbands as a romantic remembrance and be on my lonely and heartbroken way."

Whilst we'd been talking, the whole population of Moo had shown up and kind of gathered around us in a big circle, and a guy who must have been seven feet tall and almost as wide stepped forward. "Let me be the one to fight him, High Priestess!" he shouted.

Pretty soon half a dozen other guys, who all looked like the first one's bigger, stronger, nastier older brothers were begging for the chance to face me in hand-to-hand combat.

"You are all splendid examples of our race," said Valeria. "I find it difficult to make a choice." She turned to me. "Lucifer, I will allow you to choose your opponent."

"You're sure?" I said. "I mean, once I choose, you promise you won't go back on your word?"

"The word of the High Priestess is absolute law," she said.

"Okay," I said. "I choose you."

"I beg your pardon?"

"You heard me," I said. "You told me I could choose my opponent in this here rasslin' match. I choose you."

"But I meant…"

"And you told me in front of everyone that the word of the High Priestess was in purple."

"Inviolate," she corrected me. Then she turned to the assembled warriors and priestesses and lesser beings. "I gave my word." She took her crown off and handed it to another gorgeous naked lady who I guessed was her Vice High Priestess.

The crowd formed kind of a circle around us. I'd have took off my shirt, but I'd been wearing it so long it was kind of stuck to me, so I just spit on my hands, rubbed 'em together, and got ready for the referee to ring the bell.

It was when Valeria punched me in the stomach that I realized that we didn't have no referee nor no bell, and when she sunk her teeth into my ear I figgered out that we didn't have no rules neither.

I pulled back, leaving some ear in her mouth, and we started circling around each other. Then she reached out to grab me, and I reached out to grab her, and a second later she slapped my face again.

"Don't do that!" she snapped.

I didn't know whether to apologize or tell her to protect herself in the clinches, so I settled for circling around her again and grabbing a little lower this time, which just got me another slap in the face.

"Damn it, Lucifer, are you wrestling me or molesting me?"

Before I could answer she launched herself through the air at me, and I fell over backward with her on top of me. After that things happened real fast for the next few seconds, and then she slapped me yet again.

"No kissing!" she yelled.

I grabbed a hold of her left wrist with my right hand and her right wrist with my left hand. She wrapped her legs around my waist and started squeezing the air out of me, and while she was doing that she wrapped her other legs around my ankles so's I couldn't move, which surprised me because up until that very moment I'd thunk she only had two legs.

Then she wrapped some more legs around my thighs, and then I heard her legs starting to hiss, and I realized that Bubbles had decided his mistress was in trouble and had come on over to protect her.

"Foul!" I yelled.

"What are you talking about?" she grated. "I haven't done anything to you yet."

"You get that snake off'n me or I'm gonna bring my godly wrath down on both your heads!" I said.

She twisted around to see what I was talking about.

"Bubbles!" she cried. "Go back to your dog house!"

Bubbles looked plaintively at her.

"Now!"

Bubbles gave my legs one final squeeze for good measure and crawled off.

Valeria watched him slither off, and since her attention was took elsewhere, I gave her a delicate little pinch in a delicate little place to see if I could encourage her to get off me, and all I can tell you is that if basketball players could jump like that they'd have to give serious consideration to raising the hoop to maybe twelve or fifteen feet high.

As for me, I figgered if I got up she'd just knock me down again, and if I actually put any hold on her, she'd either slap my face (depending on where the hold was) or Bubbles would come hissing and sliding to her rescue again, so I reasoned that the best thing was to stay right on the ground where I was.

"Get up, Lucifer!" she snarled. "I'm going to tear you to pieces!"

"I can't," I said. "Your snake done busted up my legs."

"I didn't hear anything break," she said.

"Muscles don't make as loud a snapping sound as bones do," I said. "But if you want this to be a fair fight in front of your people, we're gonna have to postpone it until I got my legs back under me."

"All right," she said reluctantly. "But if you're lying..."

"Gods ain't capable of lying," I said, crossing my heart.

"I'd have sworn there were a lot of things gods weren't capable of before I got in the ring with you," she said bitterly.

"I suppose that means you don't want to kiss and make up?"

She just glared at me and then ordered a couple of the bigger guys who had wanted to rassle me to carry me over to the altar, where I'd have room to lie down and stretch my feet out. One of them pulled his knife out and turned to her.

"As long as he's here anyway, Priestess," he said, "it seems a shame to waste the opportunity."

"No, I must keep my word," said Valeria. "We will continue our battle when his legs have healed."

"You know," I said, "as long as we're postponing it, we could pass the word to neighboring continents and sell tickets."

"What's a ticket?" asked Valeria.

"What's a neighboring continent?" asked the guy with the knife.

Well, I could see that they were just a bunch of ignorant peasants, half of 'em beautiful and half of 'em ugly, and all of them badly in need of a god what could teach 'em the ways of civilized societies. But before I could tell them why they were in serious need of me, Valeria ordered them all out, except for two nubile lesser priestesses what wasn't wearing no more clothes than she herself was.

"On the off chance that you really are a god, you will stay here in the temple until you can walk again," said Valeria. "I am leaving these two handmaidens to bring you food and tend to your wounds."

"You ain't staying your own self?" I asked.

I thunk she was gonna slap me again, but instead she just glared at me for a moment, then turned to the two girls.

"You know your duties," she said. "But be very careful whenever you get within arm's reach of him."

"But isn't he a god, High Priestess?" asked one of them.

"Possibly," said Valeria. "But if so, then he is a dirty old god. You have been warned."

Then she was gone.

I sat up and slung my feet over the side of the altar. "Well, ladies," I said, "what's for dinner?"

"Henry, if they catch him before sundown," said the one on the left.

"Are you really a god?" asked the other one.

"Cross my heart and swear to myself I am," I answered.

"What's heaven like?"

"Funny you should ask," I said. "I thunk we might just experience a little bit of it before we eat."

"You can actually transport us to heaven?" she asked, all kind of wide-eyed and trusting.

"Sure can."

"How?"

"Come on over here and I'll show you," I said.

About three seconds later she slapped my face.

"Don't they teach you anything in priestess school besides sunbathing and face-slapping?" I asked, rubbing my cheek.

"Don't they teach you gods anything besides pinching and grabbing?" she shot back.

"I was just practicing my rasslin' holds," I said.

"I *know* what you were practicing," she said.

"Actually, it looked like fun," said the other one. "And, well, if he really *is* a god, it'd be a shame to miss an opportunity to learn what lies ahead of us in heaven."

"You know," said the first one, "I never looked at it that way."

"Sure," said the other one. "And if he's as clumsy as Henry, then we'll know he's a mortal and we'll feed him to Bubbles."

"No," said the first. "The High Priestess says Bubbles is gaining too much weight. We'll just chop him up into little pieces and feed him to the piranhas."

"I don't know," said the other one. "Then they'll want to be fed every day, and it won't be safe to go swimming." She paused for a moment, considering their options. "We could tie him up and put a bunch of hungry scorpions on his belly."

The first one made a face. "I don't like scorpions."

"Rats, then," suggested the other. Then she shook her head. "No, that won't work. Bubbles has eaten most of the rats. I suppose we could make him swallow a bunch of *marabunta* and let them eat their way out."

"Remember that Chinaman who wandered in here, delirious from fever, and kept raving about the Death of a Thousand Cuts?" said the first.

Well, the two of 'em kept discussing the penalties for my potential failure in their delicate ladylike way for the next ten minutes, and got so wrapped up in it that they didn't even notice that I'd climbed down off the altar and had made my way to a side door.

"All right," announced one of 'em at last. "We're ready to be transported to heaven on a sea of sexual bliss."

"Or else," said the other ominously.

They may have said some more things, but by then I was running back down the hill I'd climbed when I first found the lost continent of Moo, and I didn't slow down nor miss a step until I'd put quite a distance betwixt me and it.

I was mentally patting myself on the back for making good my escape when I felt a thumping somewhere between my shoulder blades. This struck me as kind of unusual. I knew I had a right powerful brain, but I didn't know it was strong enough to translate mental pats into real ones, so I turned around and who should I find myself facing but Henry, who was covered by dirt and a bunch of cuts where he'd brushed by thorny bushes on his way out of Moo.

"I hate you!" he said. "You ruined the god business for both of us!"

"Maybe not," I said. "There's a couple of heavenly hand-maidens in the temple that are just waiting to be transported on a wave of bliss, or maybe it was a sea of passion. Anyway, it was something wet, I'm pretty sure of that. Just go back up there after dark and they'll think it's me."

"What the hell good will *that* do?" demanded Henry. "I see they ran you off too."

"No, I run off on my own," I said. "Believe me, there's two beautiful naked priestess just dying for a little male companionship."

"Really?" he said, his face brightening under the dirt and the beard.

"I give you my godly word on it," I said. "Just make sure it's dark when you get there, and it probably wouldn't hurt none to lose your beard first, or at least convince 'em it's fast-growing since I didn't have none when I took my leave of them a few hours ago."

He stuck out his hand. As first I thunk he was looking for money, but then I realized it wasn't palm up so I took it and we shook in friendship.

"I guess you ain't all that bad a guy, as lying, backstabbing, claim-jumping bastards go," said Henry.

"And you're certainly better than the average greedy, uncouth, foul-smelling fiend from New Jersey," I said.

So we parted friends after all, and I figured it was time to continue my quest for the perfect spot to build my tabernacle. I wandered across that huge cow pasture for almost a week, and finally I came to a little outpost made all of logs except for the parts that weren't, and I walked in and made a beeline for the bar.

"What'll it be, stranger?" said the bartender.

"Gimme a shot of your best whiskey and a chaser," I told him.

"What kind of chaser?"

"Another whiskey," I said.

"You're new around here, ain't you?" he said. "Where do you hail from?"

"I just arrived from the lost continent of Moo."

He stared at me for a moment. "Funny," he said. "You don't *look* Mooish."

"Tell me something, Brother," I said. "Where's the nearest civilized city what's got an abundance of sinners, especially of the female persuasion, that's in serious need of saving?"

"Well, you've got a lot of choices," he answered. "It's getting close to carnival time in Rio off to the east, they say they just discovered emeralds up north in Equador, I hear tell they found some lost Inca city filled with gold and other trinkets off to the west in Peru, and the gauchos are having their annual round-up just south of here and there figures to be a lot of money at the other end of it, ready to buy a few million tons of beef, and where there's money there's almost always sinners."

"True, true," I agreed. "Thanks for your help, Brother." I downed my drinks, had a few more, got my face slapped yet again when I thunk one of the ladies at the bar was looking lonely and lovelorn, and finally I wandered outside to watch the sunset.

I'd been guv a lot information about where to go next. Too much, you might say. So I did the only reasonable thing. I waited until the breeze died down, turned my left hand palms up, spat in it, then slapped my right hand down right hard, and decided that whichever the way the spit flew was the direction in which a passel of sinners would soon find themselves saved.

As my next narrative will show, it wasn't near as easy as it figgered to be.

CARNIVAL KNOWLEDGE

wandered north and east until I finally came to Los Blancos, which had two hotels, three restaurants, a whorehouse, and five bars, none of which felt inclined to extend credit to a man of the cloth. I finally got a grubstake together when I taught some of the locals a little game what had to do with statistical probabilities and the number 21. It was when they became more interested in the number 54, which was how many cards there were in the deck once you counted the two aces that slipped out of my shirtsleeve at a most inopportune time that I felt a need to take my leave of that fair metropolis, and the sooner the better.

I'd won just enough money to buy passage with an itinerant bush pilot, whose profession was sadly misnamed as there wasn't a single bush aboard his little three-seater. I figgered I might as well go to Buenos Aires, since I was in Argentina anyway, but he explained that this was carnival week in Rio, and that's where people from all over South America was headed, and I figured if *they* were going to Rio probably their money was going along with them, and I just might get my hands on enough contributions, freely given and otherwise, to finally get around to building the Tabernacle of Saint Luke—and even if not, there had to be a passel of fallen women in serious need of salvation, and taking the sins of fallen women unto myself was one of the things I did best, me being one of God's personal representatives.

"Tell me about this here carnival," I said after I agreed to let him take me there. "Got a lot of sideshow games of chance in it?"

"No, Señor," he replied.

"Elephants and lions and other trained critters like that?"

"Certainly not, Señor."

"Well," I said, "we can play guessing games all the way to Rio, or you can tell me what makes carnival week different from any other time of year."

"Everyone dresses up in costumes, and they march through the streets, and everywhere there are bands and dancing. The whole city is filled with revelers."

It sounded a lot more like a costume party than a carnival, but I didn't want to disagree with him, especially not at 7,000 feet of altitude and no parachute, so I just sat back and started making plans. I figured I'd go dressed as a preacher what had been stuck in the South American outback for a couple of months, which would at least save me the cost of a costume, and with people coming from all over the continent, there figured to be enough sinners for me to get right down to the business of saving souls, since if you're going to save sinners you just naturally got to go to where they all congregate, and when the pilot started describing some of the ladies' costumes, which sure as shooting sounded a lot more like the ladies' lack of costumes, I knew that I'd somehow lucked out and was going to the very best place to find a bunch of blackened souls what was in serious need of some spiritual soap and water.

"Not only is it Carnival," he continued as this great big city came into view, "but if you are lucky you will have the opportunity to see the Pebbles of God."

"I speak to God every day," I said, "and He ain't never mentioned no pebbles to me. You make 'em sound like they're mighty special, at least as pebbles go."

"That is merely the name for them, Señor," said the pilot. "They are actually a matched set of perfect blue-white diamonds."

"You don't say? Worth a lot, are they?"

"A king's ransom," he answered. "Maybe an emperor's."

"And they're going to be on display during this here costume party?" I asked.

"They won't be out on the street with the revelers, of course," he explained. "But they have been moved to the Presidential Palace under heavy guard where certain select dignitaries will be allowed to view them."

"How do these here dignitaries get themselves selected?" I said.

He shrugged, which damned near sent the plane into a tailspin. "Who knows, Señor?" And then he added, kind of suspiciously, "Why do you ask?"

"Well, Brother," I said, "as a man of the cloth, I figger I might be offended by all the drinking and scanty costumes and the like. I kind of yearn for something more sedate, like admiring works of art."

"There is an excellent art museum on San Paulo Street," he offered.

I shook my head. "Probably filled to overflowing with paintings of shameless naked women," I said. "No, I think I'd better stick to admiring God's marbles."

"The Pebbles of God," he corrected me.

"Whatever," I said with a shrug.

Then he got busy landing the plane, and the conversation kind of lay there like a dead groundhog, and finally we bumped down—I was going to say that we touched down, but I wouldn't want my Silent Partner to strike me dead for lying to you—and I got out of the plane and wandered over to the Customs and Immigration shed, which was composed of rotting wood and a leaky roof, and lit by a gas lantern.

"Welcome to Rio," said a uniformed man with a bushy mustache and a toothy smile.

"Glad to be here, Brother," I said. "Which way to the diamonds?"

"It is the wrong time of year," he said apologetically. "We do not play baseball during Carnival."

"Okay, then," I said. "Just point out the Presidential Palace and I'll be on my way."

"I am afraid no one is allowed in or out of the palace since the robbery, Señor," he told me.

"What robbery are you referring to?" I asked, hoping that it was something trivial, like maybe someone stealing Mrs. President.

"The Pebbles of God, Señor," he said. "You have heard of them?"

"Once or twice," I said. "What happened?"

"I do not know, Señor," he replied. "I have been at my station all day. But we received word about an hour ago that an incredibly brazen thief somehow got past all our security and stole the Pebbles. They are searching the city for him even as we speak, but with Carnival going on...." He shrugged. "Ah, well. We have the finest police force in the world. I'm sure that eventually they will apprehend the thief and recover the diamonds. Now then, Señor, have you anything to declare?"

"Just that I'm as outraged as you are, and that Satan's probably warming up a seat in hell for him even as you and I shoot the breeze," I said.

"I mean, have you anything to declare for Customs?"

"No," I answered. "Us men of the cloth travel light." I showed him my wallet, which was empty, since I'd put what little money I had left inside my shoe.

"Thank you, Señor," he said, looking at it and handing it back to me. "By the way, your driver's license expired nineteen years ago."

"Yeah?" I said, taking a look. "You know, I could have sworn it was only seventeen years out of date. Thanks for pointing it out to me."

Before he could answer I was heading through the airport and out into the street, where I caught a double-decker bus and headed off toward the center of town. I figured since the Pebbles of God were no longer available, the least I could do was join the party that seemed to be going on all around me, and maybe share a little carnival knowledge with an obliging lady of quality.

Everywhere I looked people were wearing costumes (or in the case of some of the young ladies, not quite wearing them), and they all were smiling and laughing and dancing the samba, which for them of you what ain't never seen it is a kind of rhythmic form of palsy where you take a ton of steps but don't get nowhere.

The bus was slowing down for a corner when my eyes fell on the prettiest morsel of femininity I ever did see. She had long black hair flowing down to her waist, and the kind of figure that made you think she had room for an extra set of lungs, and her hips were vibrating like unto a rattlesnake about to strike. I couldn't quite figure out her costume, but mostly it looked like a naked lady covered with gold and silver glitter and maybe a set of false eyelashes and not a hell of a lot more.

I hopped off the bus and made my way through the dancers right up to her side.

"Howdy, ma'am," I said. "I hope you don't mind this intrusion, but I got to tell you that your beauty done dazzled me from afar, so I thunk I'd come on over and let it dazzle me from close up."

She flashed me a smile that would have made me bay at the moon if I could have spotted it amidst all the balloons and confetti.

"You are rich Americano, no?" she said in the most beautiful feminine voice.

"Yeah, that's me," I said, because I figured hitting .500 already put me ahead of Babe Ruth and Ty Cobb.

"I am Conchita," she said. "You put me in movies, maybe?"

"Sure, I'll be happy to," I said, making a mental note to buy a little eight-millimeter camera the next morning, and maybe purchase some film in a month or two, after all the tourists went back home and the prices began dropping.

Well, we got to talking, and one thing led to another, and before long Conchita had samba'd her way to a little hotel on a side street, and then she samba'd up the stairs, and then she samba'd into the big double bed, and sometime during the night while I was snoring peacefully she samba'd back out and about an hour before sunrise she samba'd in back and brung her six brothers with her. One of 'em looked like Primo Carnera, only meaner, and he was the runt of the litter. She introduced us and asked me to name the date, and I told her I couldn't rightly remember but I thunk we were in June, or maybe April, or possibly October, and she laughed musically and said that she didn't mean today's date, she meant the date for our nuptials.

The whole family seemed mildly upset when I explained that offering to buy a cheap camera didn't constitute a bonafide proposal of marriage back where I came from. Then she started crying, and her brothers began ripping the room apart and looking like they was about to leave the room alone and start in on me, so I kind of rushed out the doorway and down the stairs. By the time I hit the main floor I realized I didn't know how to get in touch with Conchita in case she wanted to go out on another date at some point in the future when everyone had calmed down, but them brothers were thundering down the stairs so fast that I figured that it was better to have loved and lost than to have loved and been dismembered, so I took off down the street and tried to lose myself in the crowd, which was still there and still dancing, even though the sun was thinking of coming up.

"There he is!" yelled a voice, and I saw that one of Conchita's brothers—the one with steel teeth and hobnailed boots—had spotted me. I raced down an alley, turned onto the next street, damned near bumped into the brother who carried a hand axe for comfort, spun around, and headed off in a new direction. Before long all six of 'em was hot on my tail, and the only thing that saved me was that the crowd was getting thicker and thicker, and none of us could make much headway.

Finally I spotted a big building where a bunch of gents in sparkling white suits and ladies in sparkling pink skins were gathering, and I made a bee-line for the door. I don't think Conchita's brothers saw me, because they were no more than fifteen seconds behind me, and no one entered the place for the next half minute. I looked around, and saw that I was in a warehouse, and that this was where a bunch of men were getting into their costumes and a bunch of ladies were getting out of them, so to speak. I figgered the best way to become incognizant was to put on some of the duds the men were wearing, but they seem to have brung their own, because big as the place was I couldn't find no spare costumes hanging on the walls.

Finally I walked up to one of the men and offered him five dollars for his sequined tuxedo.

"Ten," he said.

"Okay, ten."

"And a date with Jean Harlow," he added.

"I don't know Jean Harlow," I admitted.

"Then the deal's off," he said.

"Hang on a minute," I said. "I know a right friendly local girl named Conchita."

"Conchita with all the brothers?" he said. "You and 500 others." He crossed himself. "Those brothers made short work of at least 490 of them."

"That's why I need a disguise."

"You need a priest."

"I *am* a priest," I said desperately. I held up my well-worn copy of the good book.

"Really?"

"Well, a minister," I said. "The Right Reverend Doctor Lucifer Jones. Same position, different league."

"If you're a minister, what were you doing with Conchita?" he asked me.

"Showing her what sins to avoid if she wants to move to the head of the line at the Pearly Gates."

"I think I may convert," he said with a great big grin. "Will you bless me, Father?"

He still had the wrong religion, but I didn't have no time to argue.

"Domino nabisco, my son," I said. "Now help me find some duds before them brothers of hers bust the building down."

Suddenly a trumpet blared and everyone began rushing to the door.

"I am sorry," he said apologetically. "My group is beginning our march through the city now. We must continue our discussion later." As he reached the door he turned and yelled back, "If I see Conchita, I'll give her your regards."

Then he was gone, and I was all alone in the building. At least I thought I was when I heard a very cultured, very familiar voice say, "I see Fate has brought us together once again, Doctor Jones."

I kept my eyes on the door, because I didn't want to turn around and find out for sure that the voice belonged to who I thunk it belonged to.

"Have you no word of greeting for an old friend?" it said.

"Show me an old friend and I'll let you know," I said.

"But it's me, Erich von Horst," he said, walking into my line of vision, looking as trim and elegant as ever, kind of like a head-waiter without a hair out of place.

"So it is," I said, walking around him and heading to the door. "And it's sure been nice seeing you again, but I got urgent business elsewhere."

"I overheard what you were saying," he replied. "If you go outside, you'll run into the girl's brothers."

"The worst they can do is bust my arms and legs and maybe break my back and gouge out my eyeballs," I said, still walking away from him. "That makes it an easy choice."

He grabbed my arm. "I believe the heat has gotten to you," he said. "You really should start wearing a hat. You know what the vertical rays of the sun do to Englishmen."

"I'm from Moline, Illinois."

"Same thing," he said, kind of pulling me over to a chair and sitting me down. "You look well, Doctor Jones. How has life been treating you?"

"Just fine until about two minutes ago," I muttered.

He threw back his head and laughed. "Good old Doctor Jones!" he said. "Always Johnny on the spot with a witty remark."

"I hope you didn't come here all the way from England just to bamboozle me again," I said. "Because if you did, I got to tell you on the front end that I ain't go no money."

"When did I ever try to relieve you of your money, my good friend?" he asked innocently.

"Tanganyika," I said. "Morocco. Mozambique. Greece. England."

"You may have emerged the poorer party, but you were not the innocent one."

"We ain't neither of us innocent of much," I said bitterly, "but every time we hook up I wind up un-innocent and broke and you wind up un-innocent and rich."

"Then perhaps you'll let me make it up to you," said von Horst.

"I don't want to hear this," I said.

"There are millions involved."

I got up. "I'm going out into the street and challenge Conchita's brothers. I'll be safer."

"The Pebbles of God," he said softly.

I sat back down.

He grinned. "I thought that would interest you."

"Only because I'm a religious man, and I won't have you robbing my Silent Partner."

"Oh?"

"Well, not alone, anyway."

"What if I told you that I know who stole them?"

"If I'd known you were in the country, I could have given 500-to-1 odds that I knew too."

"So...are we partners?" said von Horst.

"You already got 'em," I said suspiciously. "What do you need a partner for?"

"The police are watching my every move," he explained. "If I try to leave the city, they'll stop me and search me."

"No," I said.

"No, what?" he asked.

"No, I ain't gonna try to smuggle them out of the city for you," I said. "I'm a foreigner too. They'll search me, find the diamonds, and I'll rot in some Brazilian jail while you go free as a bird."

He shook his head. "Oh, ye of little faith."

"I got faith, and to spare," I shot back. "What I ain't got is a death wish."

"Everything has been arranged," he said. "You will be able to leave the city right under the nose of the police."

"And they'll ignore me, huh?" I said sarcastically.

"No, my dear friend," he replied. "They'll *applaud* you."

"What in tarnation are you talking about?" I demanded.

"It is *Carnival!*" he said. "And you are in a costume warehouse!"

"The most valuable diamonds in the country have been stolen, and you think that anyone wearing a costume can dance right out of town?" I said. "That's the stupidest thing I've ever heard."

He shook his head. "No, they'll search you top to bottom," he said. "But they'll never find the Pebbles of God."

"If they're that well hid," I said, "why don't you take 'em out yourself? What do you need *me* for?"

"While you're taking them to our appointed meeting place, I'm going to be convincing the police that I still have them," he explained. "I have been hiding since I stole them, but once you're on your way, I plan to show myself and lead them a merry chase in the opposite direction, which will take most of their attention away from you, and result in at best a cursory examination. Possibly the police will catch me, possibly they won't—but even if they do, they will eventually have to let me go since I won't have the diamonds." He looked sharply at me. "Your fee will be one-third of the take."

"Seems to me that the guy what's carrying the diamonds is taking most of the risks," I said, "and ought to be making most of the money."

"All right," he said. "Fifty-fifty."

"Sixty-thirty," I said.

He frowned. "That's only ninety."

"God gets ten percent. As His spokesman on Earth, I'll hold it in escrow for Him."

He considered it for a moment, then shook his head. "Fifty-fifty or it's no deal."

"What about God?" I demanded.

"You can split your half with Him any way you want," he said. "Now, are you in or out?"

"First show me how you think I'm gonna waltz right by the police and then I'll tell you."

"Here," he said, pulling a glittery toga and a pair of gold sandals out of a pocket. "Put these on."

He began walking off.

"Where are you going?" I said.

"Just get dressed," he answered, opening a side door I didn't even know was there. "I'll be right back."

I doffed my duds and clambered into the toga, which truth to tell felt a little drafty down at the south end of it, and then strapped on the sandals. I'd just finished when I heard a snort that sure didn't sound like von Horst. I looked up, and there he was, leading in a smart-looking chestnut horse what was attached to a gold chariot.

I took a deep breath and wrinkled my nose.

"What's the matter?" he said.

"Your horse smells of fish," I told him.

He smiled. "That's not the horse. It's part of your costume." He reached into the chariot and pulled out a trident with a pair of fish on it. "You're Neptune, King of the Ocean."

"Couldn't I lose the fish and be King of the Desert?" I said.

He shook his head. "Look at all the fish designs on your chariot. You've got to be Neptune. We don't want to draw any unnecessary attention to you."

"I'm a gringo riding a chariot, wearing a skirt, and carrying a bunch of dead fish," I said. "Don't you that *that* will draw attention?"

"Not in the middle of Carnival," he said, pulling a phony beard out of his pocket. "Put this on."

"No one's ever seen the King of the Ocean," I said. "How do you know he wears a beard?"

"Maybe he doesn't," agreed von Horst. "I suppose it all depends on whether you want every policeman in town to know exactly what you look like."

Which is how I wound up wearing a beard.

"You seem awfully well-prepared for this," I said suspiciously. "Why do I get the feeling that you were waiting for me to come along?"

"Because you have a suspicious nature," he replied easily. "I was waiting for *someone* to come along that I could trust. It was just serendipity that it was you."

"Okay," I said. "I look like an idiot and smell like a fish. What has all this got to do with God's Testicles?"

"The Pebbles of God," he corrected me. He reached into the chariot one more time and withdraw a glittering gold crown encrusted with diamonds. "Here they are," he said triumphantly.

"You'll wear them right out of town under the noses of the police. There must be five thousand crowns in the parade, all covered with cut glass. There will be no reason for anyone to suspect that this is what the entire city is searching for."

I took the crown from him and studied it. "What do you think they're worth?" I said.

He shrugged. "Three million, four million, who can say?"

"The fence you're going to sell them to can say."

"Why guess?" he said. "You'll be standing right beside me when we make the deal."

"Where are we gonna meet?" I asked.

"There's a tavern named Carlita's two miles south of the city limits," he said. "Meet me there two hours after sunset."

"Carlita's," I said. "Got it."

"And don't forget to feed and water the horse," added von Horst. "If he dies on you, they'll probably arrest you for animal abuse, and if you're in jail for a few days, even these unimaginative minions of the law will figure out that your crown is more than it appears to be."

"Right. Feed and water the horse, follow the parade south out of town, and meet you at Carlita's after dark."

"Two hours after dark," he said. "If you are late I will assume you have betrayed my trust, and I will report you to the police and claim ten percent of the Pebbles as my finder's fee. We will both be a lot wealthier if you simply do as we have planned."

"I am shocked that you could think such un-Christian thoughts about me, Brother von Horst," I said. "Just see to it that you get to Carlita's on schedule. If you're more than a few minutes late, I'm going to assume that the police have picked you up and I'm on my own."

"Fair enough," he agreed.

I climbed into the chariot and grabbed the reins. "Has this nag got a name?" I asked.

"Dobbin," said von Horst.

"How about that?" I said. "We used to have a horse called Dobbin back on the farm in Moline, Illinois."

"A family pet?"

"Until my father got drunk and mistook him for a moose, or maybe a tax collector."

I clucked to Dobbin, and he trotted out of the building, and a minute later we were in the thick of things, surrounded by dancers and singers and drummers and a lot of ladies what was dressed for extremely warm weather. I stayed with them for almost a mile, until I was sure von Horst wasn't following me, and then I turned Dobbin into a side street, pulled him to a stop, and clambered out of the chariot.

If there was one thing I knew, it was that Erich von Horst didn't have an honest bone in his body. This was the guy who salted the Elephant's Graveyard in Tanganyika, stole the Crown jewels in London, and otherwise flim-flammed his way around the world, usually taking unfair advantage of innocent trusting souls like myself. But I was onto him this time. I knew if he told me the diamonds were in the crown, that was the one place they weren't. They looked like cut glass because they were cut glass.

Still, he wouldn't have gone to all this trouble if he had the diamonds on his person, so they had to be here somewhere. I knelt down and pulled the hubcaps off each wheel, but there wasn't nothing to be found. I went over the chariot with a fine-toothed comb, but I couldn't find no diamonds. Then I thunk of checking Dobbin. I went over every inch of his bridle and harness, checked his teeth for shiny fillings, even pried off his shoes in case von Horst had hid the diamonds there, but I kept coming up empty.

I'd wasted an hour and still hadn't found the diamonds. The sun was getting a little higher in the sky, the day was warming up, and the smell of the fish was making me sick. I figured as long as Neptune had a trident he didn't need no fish on it, and I was about to pull 'em off and toss 'em to a couple of stray cats that had moseyed over to admire 'em close up...

...and then it hit me. What was the one place von Horst was sure I wouldn't look for the diamonds? Inside the fish, which were getting so high and off-putting that he figgered I wouldn't want to have nothing to do with them, but I was just a little too smart for him.

I pulled one of the fish off the trident. The cats started meowing up a storm, figgering I was about to toss it to them, but instead I manipulated the trident and cut the fish's belly open with one of the tines, and sure enough, out fell half a dozen perfect blue-white diamonds. I tossed the empty fish to the cats, cut open the other one, picked up another six diamonds, and gave what was left over to the cats.

I knew I couldn't bring the diamonds out of town with me, because von Horst would be waiting at Carlita's. I looked around and realized I was standing next to a lamppost. I moved Dobbin right up against to it, climbed up onto his back, removed the top of the lamp, and put the diamonds there, where they couldn't be seen from the street. The guys who lit the lamps at night did it with these long-handled candles, so none of them ever climbed up there or got a close look, and I knew the diamonds would be safe until I got the opportunity to come back and collect them.

I got back down on the ground, hopped into the chariot, and turned Dobbin back in the direction of the parade. When we passed a fish market a little farther down the street, I stopped, bought a pair of fish that smelled almost as bad as the two I'd left behind, and stuck 'em on the trident.

Then it was just a matter of joining the revelers, who never seemed to run out of energy, as they danced their way through the streets of Rio. I even saw a couple of Conchita's brothers, but of course they never thought to look at Neptune, so we didn't have no unpleasant or deadly encounters. In midafternoon I struck up a conversation with a mildly naked young lady what was dressed as a harlequin from the neck up and the ankles down. I invited her to join me in my chariot so's we could get to know each other a little better, and for a minute there I thunk she was going to oblige, but then she wrinkled her nose and said that she was happy to share the chariot and other things with me, but not with the fish. It was a tough decision, but I couldn't be sure I'd pass another fishmonger before we left the city, so I reluctantly bid her farewell. I never saw a gorgeous underdressed lady look so surprised in all my born days, and I've had some pretty surprising encounters with a passel of 'em.

In late afternoon I let Dobbin graze on a pair of fruit stands what's owners were off dancing. Pretty soon it started getting dark, and I realized that first, I was about three miles from Carlita's, and second, I was getting powerful sick of samba music, so I turned Dobbin south onto the exit road. I let him stop and munch on some grass and flowers and the like, and we pulled up to Carlita's almost exactly two hours after sunset. I didn't want von Horst examining the fish too closely while I was still around, so I laid 'em down on the floor of the chariot, hopped out, tied Dobbin to a hitching post, and walked into the tavern.

There was so much cigar smoke that I almost didn't see the sultry girl doing kind of a slow dance in the corner. She was barefoot, she had a cigarette dangling from her mouth, and she was kind of doing a solo rhumba in slow motion. The bartender was maybe 400 pounds and drenched in sweat, but just the same he never rolled up his sleeves, unbuttoned his shirt, or loosened his bowtie. There were half a dozen tables, most of 'em filled by people who looked like they either didn't know it was carnival week or didn't much care.

I sat down at an empty table. A couple of friendly young ladies wandered over from the bar, but before they could reach me von Horst entered the place, carrying a brown paper bag, and walked right over to me, waving them away kind of disdainful-like.

"Any trouble?" he asked.

"Only with the fish," I said, just to see his reaction.

His face got all tense. "What *about* the fish?"

"They smelled so bad that I couldn't get any young ladies of quality to ride with me," I said.

"But you still have them?" he said kind of urgently.

"Yeah, they're out there in the chariot."

He suddenly relaxed. "I'm glad to see everything went off without a hitch."

"I don't suppose you brung my clothes with you?" I said. "I don't like the way a couple of these guys are staring at my legs."

"As a matter of fact I did," said von Horst. He handed me the bag. "Maybe you should go change in the men's room."

And that was when I saw how I'd make my getaway.

"Thanks, von Horst," I said. I put a hand to my stomach. "I was about to head off there anyway. I been feeling a mite queasy all day. I think it was the smell of them damned fish."

"Take your time," he said. "My fence isn't due here for another half hour."

And then, because I didn't want him coming looking for me, I had another stroke of brilliance. I took the crown off and guv it to him.

"Here," I said. "You hang onto this."

He just looked kind of surprised, and a bit curious.

"What's past is past," I said, "and I just want you to know that there ain't no hard feelings. I trust you not to run off with the Pebbles while I'm in the john."

"I appreciate that, Doctor Jones," he said.

I picked up the bag and walked to the bathroom. I'd call it the men's room, but from the looks of it it served men, women, children, and the occasional mule what wandered in to get out of the weather. I took off the toga and sandals, got into my clothes, and then climbed out through the narrow window.

When I was about a block away I took a peek back. Dobbin was still tied to the post, and von Horst either hadn't come out to check on the fish, or had maybe got as far as the front door, took a deep breath, and satisfied himself that they were still there.

I hitched a ride into Rio in the back of a truck what was delivering a few hundred live chickens to market, which certainly got the smell of fish out of my nose. I hopped off when we were a block away from the lamppost where I'd left the Pebbles of God, then waited a few minutes until I was sure no one was out on the street where they might see me.

I climbed up the lamppost, reached in, and found to my relief that the Pebbles were still there. I pulled 'em out, stuffed 'em into my pocket, clambered down to the ground, and headed off in search of a place to spend the night, preferably one what wasn't frequented by none of Conchita's friends and relations.

I passed a bunch of Brazilian hotels, and finally came to an American one, and the reason I knew that was that it had a small tasteful sign, written all in American, what said: *Bed and Broad, $7.*

"Howdy," I said, walking into the lobby, which was about the size of a closet, only maybe a little better-lit. "You got any rooms for rent?"

"Nah, we just rent airplanes and gorillas here," said the clerk, which was the kind of answer what convinced me beyond any doubt that he was American.

"You need a better sign painter," I said.

"That's as big a sign as we could afford," he said.

"I wasn't talking about the size of it," I replied. "But it says *Bed and Broad.*"

"I know what it says," he told me.

"And you got no problem with it?" I asked.

"None," he said.

"In that case I just may stay here a month," I said, pulling off my shoe and reaching for my folded-up bill, which I shoved across the counter to him.

"What's this?" he said, frowning.

"My last ten dollars," I said. "But don't worry; I'll have more tomorrow."

"If it's like this, I won't take it tomorrow neither," he said, shoving it back to me.

I picked it up and realized that it wasn't no bill at all, but instead a folded-up letter. It was too dark to read in there, so I took it out and stood under a street light.

My dear Doctor Jones:

If there are three certainties in the world, they are death, taxes, and the nature of Lucifer Jones. If my reading of your character is correct, and thus far it always has been, you instantly assumed that the crown contained nothing but cut glass. It would have taken you less than an hour to examine your costume, your chariot, and Dobbin's harness, come up empty, and finally realized that I must have had an ulterior motive for insisting that the fish be part of your costume. You of course would have cut them open, found the faux "diamonds," and secreted them away before meeting me at Carlita's. (You are welcome to keep them as a memento of our partnership.) I knew you would want to take your leave of the place before I could examine the fish, so I brought your clothes along, giving you the perfect opportunity to escape, which of course you took.

It may interest you to know that you were indeed in possession of the Pebbles of God all day long. They were precisely where I told you they were—embedded in Neptune's crown— but I knew that a man of your deceitful nature would never trust a man of honor and integrity like myself to tell you the truth. I feel your behavior in this endeavor clearly disqualifies you from your share of the profits.

And profits there will be. The diamonds are only part of this little enterprise. The creature you know as Dobbin is actually the champion racehorse Phar Cry, whom I borrowed for a few days and am now returning for almost as much money as I will realize from the Pebbles of God. All in all, a good day's work, thanks in no small part to you.

Your obedient servant,

Erich von Horst

A trio of amiable young men wandered up and asked me if I'd like to join them in a samba.

I kicked each of them in the shins.

.

MERRY BUNTA!

The first time I heard her name, I thunk it was some Brazilian holiday and someone was wishing me a merry one of 'em. I was in Rio, having just experienced some of the side effects of Carnival, which they kept spelling Carnaval, proving once and for all that Brazil ain't never gonna present no threat of worldwide domination, and I figgered I might as well see if this was the place where I wanted to finally build my tabernacle.

Truth to tell, it had a lot going for it. For one thing, it abounded in evil men and scarlet women, and you can't hardly run a religion without an abundance of sinners to save. For another, it had a real pleasant climate, and a lovely beach where most swimmers of the female persuasion left enough clothes at home that it'd get 'em arrested back in the States or applauded in most other places. And, third, there was a bar with a radio that brought in American baseball games, so I could see how Babe Ruth and Dizzy Dean were faring.

Of course, there were some disadvantages too. For one thing, hardly none of 'em spoke American. For another, the local padres weren't real thrilled with competition, especially the vigorous kind of Christianity I preached. And for a third, I didn't have no money, having been flim-flammed by the villainous Erich von

Horst, the details of which I've already writ up and are too painful to go into again.

I still hadn't made up my mind what to do when it was made up for me of a pleasant summer evening, which for reasons I ain't figgered out yet came about in mid-November. I was walking down the street to Madame Sarcosa's House of Exceptionally High Repute, just minding my own business and reciting some of the spicier psalms to myself, when I saw the most beautiful blonde lady I ever did see. I knew right off that she wasn't no native to Rio, since blondes were somewhat rarer down there than mosquitoes, spiders, land crabs, rats and killer snakes—and blondes like this one was rarer than just about anything.

I must have been standing there staring at her slack-jawed, and the way I know this is a few seconds later I started choking on a pair of flies what had flown into my mouth. I must have made some strangling noises, because she suddenly turned and looked at me. I knew a delicate creature like her would disapprove of my spitting on the sidewalk, so I just chomped down on the flies and swallowed 'em, then guv her my biggest, friendliest smile. She smiled back, and I knew beyond any shadow of a doubt that I had fallen eternally and everlastingly in love again.

Then she giggled, and I looked down to make sure my pants wasn't unzipped, and they wasn't, and I couldn't figger out what was amusing her so much, and then I remembered that I was standing right in front of Madame Sarcosa's. I didn't want her thinking poorly of me, so as Ezra Willoughby and Slippery Jim Stevens came out the front door I whipped my copy of the good book out of my coat pocket and began preaching at them to mend their sinful ways.

"Aw, come on, Lucifer," said Ezra. "You're embarrassing us out here in public, and besides it ain't as if you ain't been in there with us the last four nights."

"He just wants us to give the place up so he can have 'em all to himself," added Slippery Jim.

"Shut up, you guys," I said softly. "I'm trying to impress that fair damsel on the other side of the street."

Slippery Jim looked over my shoulder. "I don't see no damsel there."

"What's a damsel?" added Ezra.

I turned, and sure enough the love of my life had vanished.

"What did she look like?" asked Slippery Jim.

"Like unto an angel with blonde hair, a tiny delicate waist, and a extra pair of lungs," I replied.

"Blonde, you say?"

"Like spun gold," I said.

"Sounds metallic and shiny," offered Ezra.

"Like spun hay," I amended.

"Now you've got her smelling like a barnyard," complained Ezra.

"Like spun silk," I said angrily. "And don't make no more comments, because I've run out of spuns."

"She carry a parasol?" asked Slippery Jim.

"No, just a little delicate umbrella," I said.

"I think I know who she is," said Jim. "Merry Bunta."

"Merry Bunta to you," I said. "Now don't just stand there while my entire future is on hold. Tell me who she is."

"You know grizzled old Harvey Bunta?"

"I'm in love and you're telling me about grizzled old guys!" I complained.

"He's a trader. Lives a few hundred miles inland. He comes to town once every eight or nine months to sell whatever he's conned the natives out of."

"What about him?" I asked.

"Sounds to me like you just described his daughter," said Slippery Jim.

"You sure?" I said.

"Pretty blondes and wild elephants in *musth* are equally rare in Rio," he replied. "That's his daughter, all right. I think her name's Merilee, but Old Man Bunta calls her Merry."

"How do you know all this?" I asked suddenly. "You ain't despoiled the fairest flower in all Brazil, have you?"

"No," he said before Ezra could ask what "despoiled" meant. "I just heard him talking to her."

"That's a relief," I said.

He stared at me curiously. "Does she really have to be a virgin for you, Lucifer?"

"No," I said. "I don't put no special stock in virgins."

"Then why did you ask?" he said.

"Because I put even less stock in comparisons," I told him. "One thing I don't need to hear from the woman I'm going to spend the rest of my life with is 'Slippery Jim did it this way' or 'Ezra did it that way'."

"I did no such thing," said Ezra. "But if she's half as purty as you say she is, I *wish* I had."

Just then a horse pulling a cart down the street broke into a trot, and ran right through a puddle in front of Madame Sarcosa's place, and I got all splattered with mud, and I knew I didn't want to introduce myself to Merry Bunta looking like this, so I went into Madame Sarcosa's and asked if anyone there did laundry, and she said that yes, I could toss my duds in with the next load of towels and sheets, and while I was wandering around in my skivvies perhaps I'd like to relax in a room down the hall with a young lady of quality, and since I hadn't sworn my eternal fealty to Merry Bunta yet I couldn't see nothing wrong with it, so that was what I did. Matter of fact, it was so relaxing that I did it all over again, and then once more, and when I finally climbed back into my clothes it was the next afternoon.

I left Madame Sarcosa's and headed across the street to where I'd seen Merry Bunta standing the day before, and tried to figure out where she could have vanished to so quick, and then I saw that she'd been standing in front of a hotel, so I walked in and asked the desk clerk where the Buntas were.

"Beats me, Señor," he said with a shrug.

"Well, why don't you look in your guest book and give me their room number?" I said. "And make it snappy, this being the first day of the rest of my life."

"They checked out early this morning, Señor," he said.

"Did they say where they was headed?"

"Inland, Señor, to Señor Bunta's vast estate."

"I don't want to seem picky," I said, "but the whole of South America is inland from here. You got any more specific address?"

"You don't like inland?" he said. "How about dense, impenetrable jungle?"

"How does he get his mail?" I asked.

"He comes into town twice a year for it." The clerk stared at me. "What business do you have with Señor Bunta?"

"None," I said. "It's his daughter I'm after."

He nodded his head knowingly. "A lovely young girl," he said. "And of course she's in line to inherit the Bunta fortune."

"Yeah?" I said. "How much is Old Man Bunta worth?"

"I do not know, Señor. But I know he doesn't trust banks. He keeps it all in a strongbox on his estate."

"You don't say," I said.

"I just did say."

"And you ain't got no idea how I can find him?"

He shrugged. "Just go inland and ask the natives."

I thanked him for his time and walked back out into the street. I decided not to bother the desk clerk by checking out of my hotel, so I stopped by the local store, bought a toothbrush and a canteen, filled the canteen with beer, and I was ready to find the woman of my dreams, to say nothing of the family fortune.

I faced the west, so the Atlantic Ocean was behind me, and I figured I might as well start marching toward the setting sun, and keep doing it day in and day out until I finally ran into someone who could tell me where Merry Bunta lived.

The first full day was uneventful, and the next ten weren't much different. I never saw a living soul, and truth to tell tapirs ain't much for conversation. I crossed a couple of rivers, which were filled to overflowing with crocodiles or alligators—I couldn't tell one from the other, but I ain't never encountered one of either persuasion what didn't have a lean and hungry look to him, with an emphasis on the *hungry*. Anyway, they'd chased all the snakes up onto solid ground, and some of 'em were more than a little bit reluctant to share it with me, so I started zigging and zagging, still heading west, but in a route that more resembled Merry Bunta's outline than a straight course.

After another six days I came upon a village with a bunch of half-dressed little guys and their women. They must have been hunting monkeys, because they had a collection of little monkey heads that they seemed mighty proud of. They kept jabbering at me about them, but since none of 'em spoke American and I didn't speak no Jabber, I never did find out what it was about these here monkey heads that got 'em so excited. Finally, after an hour or two, as we was sitting around a fire and watching the womenfolk cooking up a big pot of something, I figured I might as well see if any of 'em could help me on my romantic quest.

"Excuse me, Brother," I said as one of 'em was jabbering about the weather, or maybe the snakes that had all kind of gathered around to listen and beg for scraps, "but I happen to be embarked on a search for the woman of my dreams, and I was wondering if any of you could point me in the right direction?"

They just kind of stared at me, so I kept on speaking.

"I know it ain't too likely, you being a bunch of godless heathens what don't speak no civilized language and probably eat your babies, but if anyone can just kind of point me in the direction of my lady love, whose name happens to be Merry Bunta, I'd be much obliged."

Well, actually, I had planned to say "I'd be much obliged", but before I could get the words out they'd all jumped to their feet and pointed off to the west.

"Merry Bunta! Merry Bunta!" they kept shouting.

I couldn't believe my luck, that the first village I'd stumbled upon knew the woman what had captured my heart.

"Now, you're sure?" I said.

They seemed pretty sure. They all kept pointing to the same spot and yelling "Merry Bunta!"

"Well, she sure seems to have established a fan following," I said. "I want to thank you for your help, and now I think I'll head off to find the rarest treasure all Brazil has to offer."

And I took maybe three steps when two of the bigger ones grabbed my arms.

"Merry Bunta!" they yelled.

"Ain't I going in the right direction?" I asked.

They pointed to the west. "Merry Bunta!"

"Then why are you holding me back?" I said. "I know these ain't my Sunday-go-to-meeting duds, but I lost them in a game of chance back in Rio. Besides, once I declare my love, it shouldn't make much difference to her, and anyway I figure neither of us are gonna stay dressed for long."

I headed off again, and this time they just looked at me as if I committed some social error, like maybe I hadn't brung no flowers to their womenfolk, but no one tried to stop me and I soon left the village far behind me.

I traveled west for a few more days. I couldn't remember what berries was safe to eat, so I settled for cooking up some eggs I had found, and you wouldn't believe how mad that made the anaconda what laid 'em, even though I'd left her a few hundred. So I figured I'd only eat fish eggs after that, which I seemed to remember was a pretty ritzy food back in the glittering capitols of Europe, but I guessed wrong again, and I found out that an enraged mama alligator can hold a grudge even longer than an angry mama anaconda. I found me a clutch of condor eggs, but as quick as I'd tap on the shell to bust 'em open, a baby condor would tap on his side of the shell, and before I could figure out what code we were conversing in, out he'd pop, and there went my breakfast. Not only that, but three of 'em decided I was their mama, and I had to keep feeding 'em all the insects I kept plucking out of my hair until they found a lady condor that seemed to be in the adoption business and went off with her.

I'd been getting myself pretty thoroughly lost, though I kept walking toward the setting sun, and just when I was sure I wasn't never going to see another human being again, a passel of 'em burst out of the forest up ahead and started racing toward me, yelling, "Merry Bunta!"

"Well, I'll be hornswoggled!" I said. "How did Merry know to send a greeting party for me?"

Strangely enough, not a one of 'em stopped to answer me. Instead, they just ran by me like I wasn't there.

It was puzzling, but I finally decided I'd run into a tribe what was all near-sighted to a fault, and I kept on heading in my true love's direction.

This here near-sightedness must have been catching, because before night fell I'd come across two more tribes what kept yelling Merry Bunta's name and running right past me, and I figgered that once I'd found Merry and built my tabernacle, I'd import the best optometrist in Brazil once me and God reimbursed ourselves for expenses.

The next morning I came to one lone little guy, wearing a loincloth and not much else. He ran right up to me like Satan was hot on his heels and began repeating Merry's name over and over.

"Hold on, Brother," I said, grabbing his wrist before he could break into a run again. "Can you tell me where I can find Merry Bunta and her father?"

He pointed back the way he'd come. "Merry Bunta! Merry Bunta!" he hollered.

"Fine," I said. "Lead the way."

He got kind of panicky and began trying to pull me in the other direction.

"You're confusing the issue," I said. "I thunk Merry Bunta was *this* way," I added, pointing to where he'd come from.

He nodded his head vigorously. "Merry Bunta!" he said.

"Well, fine, then," I said. "Let's go."

He tried to break loose again, and finally it dawned on me. There wasn't nothing wrong with anyone's eyesight. They just all figured that none of 'em had a chance with Merry when matched up against a handsome young buck like myself, and they were just clearing out because they knew after one look that the race to Merry's heart was already won.

"Okay, Brother," I said. "I understand your motives, and I approve of them. But I ain't met no one what's stuck around more than ten or twelve seconds, and I'm gonna be needing a best man, and failing that a best little feller in a loincloth, so why don't you come along with me, and I promise if you stick around we'll invite you over to dinner of a Sunday at least twice a year."

He pulled all the harder to get free of me.

"All right," I said. "It'd fair break your heart to be in the vicinity of such blonde beauty and know it's been spoken for. I can sympathize with that. Only one of us can win her delicate ladylike hand and all the good stuff that it's attached to. Go on your way, little friend, and no hard feelings."

I let him go. He looked at me like I was crazy, and headed off in the general direction of Madrid and Paris, though of course Rio was in the way.

As I walked I realized that Old Man Bunta must be a pretty good hand with a rifle, because suddenly I couldn't hear a single bird singing. In another couple of hours I figgered that he had about as big an appetite as I'd ever encountered, because not only wasn't there nothing with wings left in the area, but there wasn't nothing with legs neither, not tapirs, not deer, not sloths, not even monkeys. I decided that I approved, because the sooner he et himself to death the sooner I could share his strongbox with Merry. Then I figgered that I didn't want her worrying her pretty blonde head about such weighty matters, and it made more sense for me to just handle whatever was in the box myself.

After another five miles I began to realize that most of the money from the strongbox was gonna have to be spent on seed and fertilizer, because there wasn't nothing growing—not even a blade of grass. The trees was dead, the bushes didn't have no leaves left on them, and I couldn't see nary a flower.

I was still puzzling on why Merry and her father would want to live in a place like this when I finally saw a house off in the distance, and I knew I'd reached my destination at last.

There was a little stream betwixt me and the house, and I knelt down next to it and doused my head in the water. Then I plucked a fish from where it had latched onto my nose and slicked my hair back with my hands, which was the best I could do since I'd left my comb back at the hotel in Rio. For a minute I thunk of taking a quick dip, since I'd been wearing the same duds for months and hadn't had 'em washed since my last friendly visit to Madame Sarcosa's, but I figgered if I did that I'd have to wait a couple of hours for 'em to dry, and I was too anxious to take Merry Bunta in my arms, so I just kept running my hands through my hair til it didn't run into no more six-legged intruders, and then I set off to meet the love of my life.

I'd just about reached the house when an old guy with a shotgun opened the door and stared at me.

"What the hell are you doing here?" he demanded, stepping out onto the porch.

"I'm here to pay court to your daughter, the most beautiful flower in all of God's South American garden," I said, and then added: "That is, if you're Harvey Bunta, and if you ain't, you might as well start packing your things right now, because nothing's gonna stop me from hooking up with the delectable Merry."

"Are you mad?" he said, kind of wide-eyed and surprised that a rival would footslog this far into the wilderness just to beat his time with Merry.

"Mad with passion," I said. And then, since there was still a possibility that he was her father and not a suitor, I clarified it by saying, "With an all-encompassing and almost-Platonic passion."

"You are a fool!" he snapped. "Didn't you see all those men heading toward Rio on your way here?"

"You mean all them little guys in their South American skivvies?" I said. "Yeah, I kept running into them."

"Didn't you pay any attention to them?"

"Sure did," I answered. "I kept asking where I could find Merry Bunta, and they kept pointing me in this direction."

"Idiot!"

"That ain't no way to talk to your future son-in-law, or maybe your rival, depending on who you are, which you ain't told me yet."

"I'm Harvey Bunta, and you are either the dumbest man I've ever met or else you've got yourself a real sweet tooth for punishment."

"Aw, come on, Harvey—or should I call you Dad?—this ain't no way for us to begin our relationship."

"Not to worry," he said grimly. "It'll end in a day or two."

I looked at his shotgun. "You ain't thinking of trying to run me off, are you?"

"Idiot!" he said again. "You're stuck here. We're all stuck here!"

"I can't imagine what you find so attractive about this here place, Harvey," I said. "Ain't nothing growing for miles around."

"This place was greener than you can imagine just two days ago," he said. "Why the hell didn't you listen to those natives?"

"I did," I told him, getting a little hot under the collar that he wasn't taking my word for it. "I kept asking 'em where I could find Merry Bunta, and they kept pointing me in this direction."

"Didn't you wonder why they were all racing hell for leather in the opposite direction?"

I didn't want to give him the real reason, because I didn't want no prospective father-in-law to think I was stuck on myself when nothing could be farther from the truth, so I just said that I figgered it was payday and they were all racing off to Rio to spend their money.

"They were running away," he said.

"From sweet little Merry Bunta?" I scoffed.

"From *marabunta*."

"That's what I said," I told him.

"*Marabunta*," he repeated, and spelled it for me. "*Not* Merry Bunta."

"There's a difference?" I asked.

"Merry Bunta is my daughter," he said. "*Marabunta* are army ants. We're surrounded by about six billion of 'em."

"Six billion?" I repeated. "I guess that's too many for you to stomp on 'em, huh?"

He just glared at me.

"So where are they now?" I asked.

"Their main force is about a mile to the south of us," he said, "and it's headed this way. There's another bunch that's been approaching from the west. They eat everything in their path."

I figgered it was too bad Rosie Sanchez wasn't here, because I had long since come to the conclusion that nothing could eat her beans and tortillas and survive.

"Well, Dad Harvey," I said, "if it's a war they want, it's a war they'll get."

"You call me Dad Harvey again, and the first thing they'll get is your buckshot-riddled corpse."

"These here ants are making you kind of tense," I said. "That ain't no way to talk to your future son-in-law."

"I take great comfort in the fact that you and I will both be dead by sunset tomorrow," said Harvey. "I'm only sorry that Merry will also die beneath the *marabuntas'* onslaught."

That got my fighting blood up, because I was bound and determined that nothing was gonna crawl all over Merry's ripe young body before I did, and I decided it was time to start coming up with a plan of action.

"You got any gasoline, Harvey?" I asked.

"Why?"

"I figger we'll pour it on the *marabunta* and set fire to it."

"I got six gallons of gas. There's seven billion ants out there."

"I thunk you said six billion," I said.

"They multiply fast," he answered.

"Can they swim?" I asked.

"I don't know," said Harvey. "I'm usually so busy watching out for alligators and anacondas and the like when I'm in my boat that I don't pay much attention to what kind of insects are frolicking in the water."

"Well, even if we can't kill 'em all," I said, "at least we can discourage 'em."

"Yeah? How?" he asked.

"You say the main body of the enemy is coming from the south, right?" I said. "I'll just set a fire betwixt us and them, and that ought to discourage them."

"Just how long do you think three gallons of gasoline will burn?" he said.

"I don't know," I said. "But even after it goes out, the ground figgers to be mighty hot on their tender little ant bellies."

He shrugged. "What the hell. The gas is in canisters around the side of the house. Go get it."

I got three gallons of gas and brung it back with me.

"Now, where's the delectable Merry?" I asked. "I wouldn't want to trap her on the wrong side of the fire."

"She's in the house," he said.

"Fixing some vittles, I hope?" I said.

"Nah, just sitting there shaking like a leaf. The thought of being et alive by a bunch of godless insects put her off her feed."

"Well, you can tell her not to worry, now that Lucifer Jones is on the scene."

"*You're* Lucifer Jones?" he said, surprised. "I heard about a Lucifer Jones while I was in Rio, but I guess you can't be the same one."

"Why not?"

"You ain't been lynched yet."

I figgered I'd explain all them misunderstandings later, but the main thing now was to get the war underway, so I walked about half a mile south and parceled out the gasoline, spreading it as far as I could. Then I sat down and waited, and it wasn't too long before the enemy showed up in force just atop the next rise, so I lit a match and tossed it onto the ground, and two seconds later there was a blaze you could have roasted half a dozen dinosaurs in.

I went back to the house and reported that I'd saved the day, and once Merry realized we were going to live and confessed her love to me, maybe she could rustle up some grub.

To celebrate I opened my canteen and took a swig.

"The water around here ain't safe to drink til you boil it," said Harvey.

"Really?" I said. "I been drinking it since I left Rio and I ain't noticed a thing."

"I could get you some boiled water from the house."

"This ain't water," I said. "It's beer."

"Where'd you come by beer out here?" he asked.

"I been carrying it for maybe three weeks now. I been saving it for the proper moment."

"Ain't it a little warm and a little flat?"

"Yeah," I admitted. "But it's better than water."

He couldn't argue with that, so in my great-heartedness I let him take a couple of swallows. He'd just handed the canteen back to me and was wiping his mouth off with his shirtsleeve when he froze. At first I thunk the beer was disagreeing with him, but then he pointed off in the distance.

"They've split into two groups, and they're flanking the fire!" he said.

Until that moment, I had no idea ants was that smart.

So I figgered if one fire didn't discourage the *marabunta* two certainly would, and I waited until the columns joined again about half a mile from the house and used the rest of the gas to set another one. But while it was burning away, Harvey looked across the battlefield through his binoculars and announced that it was just a feint, that the real attack was coming from the west.

"You got any dams on that stream?" I asked him.

"A couple," he answered. "Why?"

"Give me a stick of dynamite," I said. "If I can blow up one of them dams, we can flood the plain between the ants and the house."

"I only got one stick of dynamite on the whole estate," he said. "Are you sure this is going to work?"

"I can't see no reason why it won't."

He went into the house for a few seconds and came out with a stick of dynamite.

"You're positive, now?" he insisted.

"Trust me, Harvey," I said, and he tossed the dynamite to me. I caught it and raced off to the first dam I could find, stuck the dynamite into it, lit the fuse, and put my fingers in my ears. It blew about ten seconds later, and tons of water rushed out across the land.

And started sinking in.

And vanished.

"When's the last time you had any rain?" I asked.

He shrugged. "You're in the dry season. Maybe a couple of months, maybe a little more."

"You might have told me that before I blew up the dam. All the water's sunk into the ground."

"Let me see if I've got this straight," he said. "You set a fire off to the south, and all the ants did was march around it. Then you set another one, using up the last of our gasoline, and it turned out that the real threat was coming from the west. Then you blew up a dam, not a single ant got wet, and now we're plumb out of water as well as gas. Does that pretty much sum it up?"

"I have just begun to fight!" I said with fierce masculine pride.

"God help us all," muttered Harvey.

"I don't suppose we can send away for any anteaters?" I said.

"I don't know," he said, still kind of bitter. "You on a first-name basis with any?"

"I meant from a zoo," I said.

"If you can find a zoo within three hundred miles of here, be my guest," he replied.

"You ain't being too all-fired helpful, Dad Harvey," I said.

"I told you what I'd do the next time you called me that!" he said, picking up his shotgun.

"Come on, Harvey!" I said, backing away from him. I climbed down from the porch onto the ground, and pointed to the ants. "The enemy's out there!"

"You choose your enemy and I'll choose mine!" he said, lifting the shotgun to his shoulder.

"You can't shoot me!" I said. "I'm a preacher!"

"All the more reason," he growled, lining up his sights.

"Think about it, Harvey," I said, still backing away. "If you shoot me, who's going to be left to defeat the ants?"

I couldn't tell whether that got him laughing or choking, but he did so much of whichever it was that he tripped on the edge of the porch and the gun went off as he tumbled to the ground.

I started counting all my limbs, got up to four, and figgered he'd missed me. Still, I knew he'd hit *something,* because I heard this kind of buzzing sound in my ears. I raised my hands to my head and made sure both my ears were still attached. I couldn't figger out what had happened, but I saw that he was getting to his feet, and I didn't plan to just stand there until he finally shot me, so I turned to the east and prepared to take off like a bat out of someplace that smelled a lot worse than Heaven, when I saw that the sky was black with angry hornets, and I realized that Harvey's buckshot had accidentally blown half a dozen hornets' nests off a nearby tree.

The hornets looked around for someone to get mad at, and as it happens, they were closer to the ants than to Harvey and me, so a bunch of them started dive-bombing the ants while them what was left went around to recruit all their friends and relations.

Harvey was just standing there kind of dumbfounded, and I figgered since he wasn't aiming the shotgun no more I was safer on the porch than out here in the middle of the battlefield, so I went back there, and we pulled up a couple of chairs, and spent the next three hours watching the war. For a while it looked like the ants was going to pull it out, but this was one time that air power prevailed over boots on the ground. Both sides took a ton of casualties, and in the end the ants were in full retreat and the hornets had carried the day.

"Well, I can't say you were any help," announced Harvey when the battle was over, "but you didn't desert us, and that's worth a little something. Come into the house with me."

I followed him into the living room, where there was a couch and a couple of chairs and a huge strongbox, which he walked over to and unlocked. I tried not to look too eager to see what I was going to inherit when the old gentleman went the way of all flesh, but I couldn't help but lean forward and take a peek, and what I saw was a box full of shells.

"I collect them," he said, handing me something that looked like it had once played house to a clam. "This one's the treasure of my collection. It's yours, Lucifer."

I realized I'd been flim-flammed but good, that there wasn't nothing in his strongbox but a bunch of seashells. Still, he was the father of the woman I was going to spend the rest of my life with, and I didn't want to hurt his feelings, so I just handed it back and explained that I couldn't take such a treasured item, and if he had some gold or diamonds lying around I'd be happy to settle for some of them instead, and he laughed like I was making a joke and slapped my back and allowed that maybe my parents shouldn't have drowned me at birth after all.

And then I heard dainty little footsteps behind me, and I turned and saw Merry Bunta in all her radiant beauty, and I decided that coming all this way out from Rio was still a worthwhile undertaking, and that Merry without no riches was better than no Merry without no riches.

"Miss Merry Bunta, ma'am," I said, bowing low, "I'm the Right Reverend Honorable Doctor Lucifer Jones, here to pledge my heart to you."

"I think I fell in love with you the first time I saw you back in Rio," she replied, "standing there outside Madame Sarcosa's den of scarlet women. Once we got back home, I prayed night and day that I might somehow be able to see you again."

"And here I am," I said, "the answer to your prayers. Do you want to get hitched here or back in Rio?"

A look of sadness spread over her face. "I watched you this afternoon, Lucifer, and no one can doubt your bravery or your loyalty."

"Two of my lesser virtues," I said modestly.

"But the fact remains that if I marry you, you will be the father of my children, and you were outsmarted by a bunch of ants on three different occasions." She sighed deeply. "I will always love you, Lucifer, but for the sake of my unborn children, I can't marry you."

I explained that the ants had all year to plan their campaign and I'd just stumbled into the fray on a moment's notice, and that I'd be happy to stick around until the next time they were on the march and have a rematch, but she just kept shaking her head and saying that it just wasn't meant to happen, and it was when I asked her *what* wasn't meant to happen, the marriage or the rematch, that she just turned and went back to whatever room she'd come out of.

And that was the end of my tragic romance with Merry Bunta. I began walking north, hoping I'd run into a city sometime before I hit the Arctic Circle. But what I ran into was an old friend and a passel of trouble, and I'll tell you about it just as soon as I hunt up a little drinkin' stuff and refresh my artistic sensibilities.

A JAGUAR NEVER CHANGES ITS SPOTS

'm a city boy at heart. I've heard others sing the praises and charms of living in the wide open spaces, but games of chance and obliging women of quality just ain't in abundance out in the wilderness, and of course my calling—bringing the Word of the Lord to all the unwashed and godless heathen of the world—requires me to go to where the sinners all congregate.

Which is why I find it puzzling that I spent so much of my young manhood being lost in the bush. There are glittering capitols on every land mass I ever been on, just filled to overflowing with works of art, many of which are called Fifi and Bubbles, but it seems that for every hour of heavenly rapture I could snatch with one of 'em I spent days and weeks getting et alive by six-legged critters and sharing my lunch with no-legged ones.

So I probably shouldn't have been too surprised that a couple of days after taking my leave of old Harvey Bunta, his daughter Merry, and a couple of trillion army ants, I decided I was about as thoroughly lost as I'd ever been, and that is mighty thorough.

My sense of direction has stopped me from ever wandering as far as Mars or Venus, but beyond that it ain't been all that much of a help. The only things I'd seen in two days besides them what flies and them what slithers were a pair of lovelorn tapirs what was absolutely shameless and had the kind of stamina you could only wish for in a horse what runs in them super-long six-day races across the desert. I couldn't remember which fruits were good eating and which turned you into wormfood, so I settled for eating grass, which is kind of like eating salad without the tomatoes and the dressing.

Finally I came upon a river. I figgered at least I'd finally have some fish for dinner, but the alligators and anacondas what lived there weren't real keen on sharing. Every time I'd reach into the water to grab a fish, up would come an alligator intent on grabbing a preacher. Finally I found a rope some native had left lying around, and I attached a thorn to serve as a hook, and I stuck a worm on the end of it and tossed it in the water, and sure enough, a twenty-foot anaconda swum by and grabbed it. Well, I pulled on my end and he pulled on his, and long about the time he'd drug me waist-deep into the water and a bunch of his friends and relations starting heading our way I figgered that raw anaconda probably didn't taste as good to me as raw person did to him, and since he had the better motivation on his side I let go of the rope and climbed ashore just before his ladyfriend could give me a great big hug.

I sat on the shore for a few hours, trying to figger out how to con one the alligators out of a fish dinner when suddenly a small canoe came around a bend of the river and a little guy wearing nothing but a loincloth and a couple of bones in his hair paddled up to the shore and shot me a friendly smile and signaled me to hop in. I figgered I couldn't be no hungrier and no loster anywhere else than I was here, so I accepted his invite and a minute later we were floating down the middle of the river.

We'd gone a couple of miles, and the river widened out some, and suddenly he stopped paddling and looked over the side of the boat, and then quick as lightning he reached into the water and pulled out a fish, which he tossed onto the floor of the boat. It started flopping around, and he cracked it on the head with his paddle, and then it just lay there, all quiet and peaceful-like.

I waited until he was busy paddling again, and then grabbed the fish and took a few bites, spitting out a couple of bones and swallowing the rest for some much-needed roughage. I didn't forget my new-found benefactor neither, and left him the head, the tail, and one dorsal fin.

I never did learn his name, but we traveled north along the river for three days, and he was so good at nabbing fish that I didn't feel guilty about gobbling half of them while he was hunting for *his* dinner, and the only problem I had during that whole journey was when he plucked a pirhana out of the water what was even hungrier than I was. We rassled to a draw, and I finally tossed him back after promising to come looking for him again when I was a little better equipped, like with a twelve-gauge shotgun.

Then one day my companion headed for shore. We clambered out, pulled the boat up out of the water, and then he jabbered at me in some foreign tongue, and I blessed him and forguv him for his sins and asked if he had any romantically inclined sisters, and finally he went his way and I went mine.

I was still lost, but at least I was lost on a full stomach, and I began walking north along the river. There was the same fruits and berries that I hadn't eaten a week ago, but I figgered if a bunch of raw fish, scales and all, hadn't killed me, probably nothing growing on a tree could neither, always excepting poisonous centipedes with bad attitudes.

I was munching on something soft and almost tasty, and wondering how many years it would be before I hooked up with civilization again, when civilization manifested itself in the distance with the sound of a gunshot. This was followed by thirty or forty more shots in quick succession, and I realized that I'd stumbled into one of them revolutions what are even more popular in South America than baseball.

Now, I know some people would have run the other direction when they heard all them shots, but I'd *been* in the other direction for close to two weeks and I couldn't find nothing to recommend it, so I began walking toward the sound of the gunfire, ready to sell my services to the first side that would make me a general and promise me three squares a day.

The gunfire became louder and louder, but as near as I could tell it was all coming from one side, and if that meant the enemy was out of ammunition, or better still all dead, then I knew which side I planned to join up with. I got to within maybe two hundred yards of it and was just passing a big shade tree when a voice rang out:

"Duck, Lucifer!"

I figured it was God Himself shouting at me, because none of these here revolutionaries could have known my name, and I took my Silent Partner at His word, diving head-first to the ground.

A couple of seconds later I heard a *thud!* just off to my right.

"What the hell are you doing out here in the Motto Grasso?" said that same voice, and suddenly it sounded mighty familiar and a lot less Godlike, and I lifted my head up and sure enough, there was my old friend Capturin' Clyde Calhoun and maybe eight or nine of his gunbearers.

"Well, howdy, Clyde," I said, getting up and brushing myself off. "Why in tarnation were you shooting at me?"

"Not *you*," he said, walking forward. "Take a look."

He pointed to where I'd heard the thud, and there, sprawled out on the ground where it had fallen from an overhead branch, was a jaguar with a hole right betwixt its eyes.

"Well, that's one you ain't bringin' back alive," I said.

He pulled out a flask, took a swig, and handed it to me. "You still ain't told me what you're doing here," said Clyde.

"Mostly I been concentrating on being lost and starving to death," I admitted.

"For a minute there I thunk we might be working for the same side," he said.

"I don't want to appear unduly ignorant, Clyde," I said, "but who's on the jaguar's side?"

"Come on back to my camp and I'll tell you all about it," he said. "Dinner should be just about through cooking by the time we get there."

"What kind of grub you got? I asked.

"Deer, tapir, alligator, and sloth," said Clyde.

"You traveling with an ice box?"

"Shot 'em all this morning," he replied. "Takes a lot of meat to feed a safari with five trackers, ten gunbearers and twenty skinners."

"Twenty skinners?" I repeated.

"Well, nineteen. One up and run off with a headhunter's daughter."

"Should I presume from the fact that you're traveling with nineteen skinners and no veterinarians that you ain't capturing nothing for zoos and circuses on this safari?" I said.

He nodded. "This time I'm after jaguars."

"I think they're an endangered species."

"Pretty much so," he agreed.

"Ain't it against the law to hunt endangered species?" I asked.

"They wasn't endangered when I got here," he said with more than a little trace of pride.

"So why are you denuding the countryside of jaguars?" I asked. "Have they been killing all the livestock?"

He laughed. "You see any farms around here, Lucifer?"

"Then what leads you to come all the way out here to hell and gone, just to shoot jaguars?"

"It's political," he said.

"Jaguars got the vote?" I asked.

"It's really complicated," he said. "I'll tell you while we eat. In the meantime, what have you been doing with yourself? I ain't seen you since we hunted that Yeti in the Himalayas."

I didn't have the heart to tell him that it wasn't no Yeti but just a eight-foot-tall basketball player on the lam from the mob for not shaving points, so I told him everything I'd experienced since then, covering such heroic adventures as the Clubfoot of Notre Dame, the Island of Annoyed Souls, my six hours as President of San Palmero, and many other such exploits, which I've writ about before and won't thrill you with again (or at least not right this moment), and Clyde, for his part, told me about the mountain gorillas and pandas and blue whales he brung back—them few what was still alive and feebly kicking—after his veterinarians nursed 'em back to health, which he assured me was the very safest way to bring 'em back alive. I told him of the fifteen or twenty times I'd fallen passionately and eternally in love, and he told me about the eighty-three times he'd fallen passionately and briefly in lust—well, eighty-one if you don't count the gorilla and the orangutan—and when we'd caught each other up on the past few years we went to work on dinner. I don't know what it was, but it didn't have no scales, and that was enough for me. And then, as we shared his flask and lit a couple of cigars, just to keep the insects away, Clyde decided to tell me why he was decimating the jaguar population of the Motto Grasso, which I didn't even know we was in until he mentioned it.

"It happened about two months ago," he said. "I was back in the States, peaceably blowing away spotted owls and turning the survivors over to some local zoos, when I got a request from down here for three hundred jaguar skins. I made sure that the jaguars didn't still have to be in 'em, we hit upon a price, and I put together a safari and came down here on the double, figgering them what I only winged could be shipped back home to the Capturin' Clyde Calhoun Circus."

"Why does some guy want three hundred jaguar skins?" I said. "And what's all this got to do with politics?"

"My very questions," replied Clyde. "Well, after my first question, which was what did the job pay?"

"And what's the answer?"

"Well, it's kind of complex," said Clyde. "Maybe not for a sophisticated preacher like yourself, but for a simple world-traveling sportsman like me. You ever hear of the Leopard Men?"

I shook my head. "Sounds like a bunch of men what picked up some disease that left 'em covered with spots."

"Funny," said Clyde. "That was my first thought, too. But the Leopard Men are a cult back in Africa, and the way you can tell they're Leopard Men is that each of 'em wears a mask and cloak made of leopard skins."

"What do they do once they get decked out in their leopard skins?" I asked.

He shrugged. "Beats me. Probably engage in a bunch of fun and fascinatin' acts against God and Nature."

"So you're killing all these jaguars so some local tribe can indulge in some obscene sexual orgy?" I said, and then added: "Can we join in?"

"T'ain't that simple, Lucifer," said Clyde. "Near as I can tell, this particular tribe of Injuns plans on overthrowing the government and grabbing political power."

"And they don't want to share it with no jaguars?" I said, trying to follow his line of reasoning.

"They don't want no one to identify 'em, so they're going to wear these here skins as a disguise and call themselves the Jaguar Men."

"That don't make no sense at all, Clyde," I said. "If I was the government, I'd just shoot anyone wearing a jaguar skin. I think they'd be better off dressing like any other savage out here."

"Well, I ain't privy to their plans, except of course for supplying their wardrobes," he answered, "but I figger the reason they want the skins is so no one can finger 'em in case they got an informer in the group."

"And how big is this government they plan to overthrow with just three hundred Jaguar Men?" I asked.

"It better not be much more then two hundred," opined Clyde. "I mean, hell, if they can't kill their own jaguars, it don't say much about their ability to kill the enemy, does it?"

"Sounds like you better make sure you get your money before the revolution gets out of the starting gate," I agreed.

"Yeah, that's been my thinking on the matter too," said Clyde. "In fact, payday's coming up pretty soon." He turned to one of his trackers. "How many did we bag today?"

"Sixteen," said the man.

"We're getting close," said Clyde. "I figger we're gonna run out of jaguars just about the time I run out of bullets." He turned back to me. "You want to see what one of these here Jaguar Men is gonna look like?"

"Why not?" I said.

"Then follow me," he said, getting up and walking to one of the tents his men had pitched.

We entered it, and there, laid out in near piles, were a few hundred jaguar skins.

"The heads are still attached," I said. "Come to think of it, so are the claws."

"The heads are the masks," said Clyde. "The claws are just for show, though I imagine you could scratch your back with 'em." He picked one of the skins up and handed it to me. "Here, try one on. You'll see how comfortable it is."

I picked up a skin, gathered it around my shoulder, slid my arms into the little loops that his skinners had attached, and then I fitted the head over my face.

"Can you see okay?" asked Clyde.

"Plain as day," I said. "You know, if they decide to cancel the revolution, you could cart these here things to Paris and start a new fashion trend."

"Or export 'em to Africa for when they run out of leopards to skin," added Clyde.

"Yeah," I agreed. "I'm beginning to see that there's no end

of things you can do with three hundred jaguar skins—except breed more jaguars."

Suddenly we heard a commotion from the center of camp, and we left the tent and walked over to see what was going on.

There were a couple of dozen armed natives, who Clyde kept calling Injuns though they didn't look nothing like the drawings of Geronimo and Crazy Horse I'd seen on dime novels when I was growing up. They were little guys in loincloths who obviously weren't on speaking terms with the local barber, and they were carrying spears and knives.

"What's the problem here?" demanded Clyde, signaling five or six of his gunbearers to get some weapons loaded and ready.

"We hear you have gone to work for Mudapa!" said one of the Injuns accusingly.

"Ain't a word of truth to it," said Clyde. "I'm working for some half-naked little guy with bad breath and rotten teeth."

"That *is* Mudapa!" said the Injun. "He is the enemy of our blood."

Which guv me a new respect for these little fellers. I mean, most of us just choose an enemy and that's that—but here were these guys saying that their blood chose its own enemies, and that led me to wonder if their kidneys and livers and spleens also took dislikes to certain folk, and if so, what they were inclined to do about it.

"Not to worry," said Clyde. "He's just out to overthrow the government, not to make war with ugly little runts like you."

"We *are* the government!" yelled the Injun.

"You don't say," replied Clyde, and I could tell he was surprised. "I didn't figger you Injuns had evolved enough to develop greed and corruption. Just goes to show you."

"We are here to destroy the skins," said the Injun. "Where are they?"

"You leave the skins alone, I'll leave you alone, and we'll all be happy," said Clyde.

"Grab him!" said the Injun, and a bunch of his companions grabbed hold of Clyde before he could reach for one of his guns.

"I haven't tortured a white man in weeks," said the head Injun. "This is going to be fun."

Well, I'd been standing in the shadows during all this, but I figured it was time to come to Clyde's aid, so I stepped out into the light of the campfire.

"Unhand that man!" I said. "I, the king of the Jaguar Men, have spoke!"

Everyone turned to me and just kind of stared for awhile.

"Who are you?" demanded the head Injun.

"I just told you," I said.

"You must have a name," he said.

I was thinking of telling him it was Tarzan, or maybe Teddy Roosevelt, but then I realized that I was in South America and I ought to give him a name that would be appreciated down here, so I looked him in the eye and said, "I'm Simon de Bolivar, and that there man you're about to torture is my friend."

"Simon de Bolivar?" he repeated.

"No need to be formal," I said. "You can call me Simon de."

"This man has made a pact with our enemies," said the Injun. "Our laws demand that we torture him."

"*I* make the laws around here," I said. "Unhand him."

"Unhand him?"

"You heard me," I said.

He shrugged, pulled out a knife, and was about to set to work sawing off Clyde's left hand when I told him to stop.

"We got a little communication problem here," I explained.

"You want the other hand?" he asked. "No problem."

"I don't want neither hand," I said.

"Maybe an ear?" he suggested.

"Set him loose," I ordered.

"Why should we listen to you?" demanded another Injun. "You're one of the Jaguar Men."

"That's true," I said. "But you guys ain't thinking this through. There ain't no reason why I shouldn't be one of *your* Jaguar Men."

The head Injun frowned, like he was struggling with the concept. "I don't like dealing with people who have no loyalties."

"I got loyalties, and to spare," I told him. "They just happen to be for rent."

"Explain," he said.

"Can you see my face under this here mask?" I said.

"No," he answered.

"Then the only reason you know I'm a white man instead of one of you godless brown heathen, meaning no offense, is because I sound so cultured, right?"

"We'll come back to that," he said. "Continue."

"What if my friend Clyde here was to tell the illiterate savages he killed the jaguars for that he'd shot out the area and only came up with a hundred and fifty skins?" I said. "And what if he gave the other hundred and fifty to *your* illiterate savages? How would anyone know that one of your guys wasn't a real Jaguar Man? Think of the confusion you could cause and the orders you could contradict."

The head Injun stared at me kind of thoughtfully. "You interest me, white man," he said at last.

"I don't blame you, me being the good-looking young buck that I am," I said, "but I got to warn you that us men of the cloth don't do nothing degenerate, except on special occasions and then only with partners of the female persuasion."

"You misunderstand me," he said.

"Well, *that's* a relief," I said. "So what do you say, Tonto. Have we got a deal?"

"What do you want for the skins, and my name isn't Tonto."

"Tonto's a perfectly good Injun name, and it's probably easier to remember than whatever you call yourself. And now that we're going to be partners, you can stop calling me Simon de Bolivar and start calling me Kemosabe."

"What does it mean?" he asked.

"Great white preacher who speaks for God," I told him.

Tonto made a face. "What do you want for half the skins?"

"First, you got to let my friend go," I said.

He nodded to his men, and they released their grip on Clyde.

"Second, have you got a high priest or a chief medicine man or anything like that?"

"Yes."

"He's fired and I'm the new one."

He considered it for a minute, then nodded his agreement.

"And third, my friend Clyde here gets a free lifetime hunting license."

"Lucifer, they ain't *got* no hunting licenses in the Matto Grasso," said Clyde.

"Okay," I said. "Fire your top general and put Clyde in charge of your army."

"Has he had any experience?" asked Tonto.

"He's sent more men and beasts to the Happy Hunting Grounds than any ten warriors you can name," I said.

"What does that have to do with fighting a war?"

"Same principle," said Clyde. "Anything what's moving within rifle range soon finds out that moving ain't no permanent condition."

"Have you any more conditions?" asked Tonto.

"I ain't sure," I said. "Your temple got any good-looking virgin handmaidens?"

"No."

"Then I got no more conditions."

"I agree to your terms," said Tonto.

"Now that we're all going to be friends and partners," said Clyde, "let's pull out a bottle of fine drinkin' stuff and seal the deal."

I could tell Tonto didn't know quite what Clyde was talking about, and my explaining that it was heap good firewater and much beloved by us palefaces didn't seem to add much to his understanding, but when Clyde actually produced the bottle he smiled and took a healthy swig.

We drank and shot the breeze for half an hour, and then all the Injuns staggered off to their camp, swearing eternal friendship and promising to come back the next morning to pick up the skins and make plans for putting down the revolution.

"That was quick thinking, Lucifer," said Clyde after they'd gone. "And don't think I ain't grateful. But I can't meet expenses if I only sell a hundred and fifty of the skins."

"You ain't thinking this through, Clyde," I said.

"Enlighten me."

"We're going to war with Mudapa's tribe, right?" I said. "And we're the only side what's got guns. After we win, we'll keep the spoils of war, which means the skins."

"I never thought of that," said Clyde. "I feel much better now. You got a real head on your shoulders, Lucifer."

It was certainly a better head than Clyde's, because I'd already figgered out that even if we won he was going to be stuck with three hundred skins and no buyers, but I didn't want to trouble his sleep none, so I decided not to mention it as he was dozing off.

As for me, I wasn't quite sure about all the angles and intricacies of being the high priest out here in the middle of nowhere, but once I arranged a steady flow of good-looking handmaidens and tributes from all the neighboring tribes, I figgered I'd send Clyde off to civilization to sell his skins and while he was gone I'd find some way to confiscate all the money that Mudapa's tribe was going to pay him, which was another thing I was pretty sure

Clyde hadn't thunk of, as a lifetime of having his ears just inches from the explosions of his rifles had kind of dulled his brain, which in truth didn't have a lot of sharp edges to begin with.

Well, morning came, and with it came about a hundred little fellers in loincloths. I expected 'em all to have big toothy grins, since we'd made our deal and they knew all the guns were on their side of the fence, so to speak, but this group looked mighty sour, like something they'd et disagreed with 'em.

I could hear 'em mumbling and grumbling to themselves, and I looked around for Tonto to tell me what the problem was, but I couldn't spot him nowhere, and as I stared at these Injuns it dawned on me that they was wearing different ornaments on their almost-naked little bodies than Tonto's warriors, and I realized that these had to be Mudapa's men, and you didn't have to be no brighter than Clyde to take a look and figger out that at least one of 'em had had a little pow-wow with at least one of Tonto's braves, and the cat was out of the bag. Or in this case, three hundred cats, all of 'em recently deceased and ready to wear.

Clyde burst out of his tent when he heard the commotion, and found himself facing a few dozen spears.

"You have betrayed us!" yelled the leader, who I took to be Mudapa. "You have dealt with the enemy!"

"T'ain't so!" said Clyde. "Do I look like a double-dealing back-stabbing traitor to you?" Then he added, right quickly: "Don't answer that question. Ain't important nohow. I got all your skins over in this tent here. You got your money?"

Which was the first time I wondered where they carried their wallets, since no one was wearing any pants.

Mudapa signaled for one of his warriors to step forward, and the feller handed Mudapa a little bag which he help up in front of Clyde.

"Twenty-five flawless emeralds from the mines of Columbia," announced Mudapa. "Now where are the skins? And if you are lying to me, I will be wearing a Calhoun skin before noon."

I figgered they wouldn't welcome no distractions at that particular moment, so I just stayed in my tent. I noticed that I still had the jaguar skin I'd wore the night before, but I couldn't imagine Mudapa would get too riled over Clyde's total being one short, and besides I thunk it might come in handy before long, so I just tucked it under my cot, and I sat down and listened.

There was a lot of excited jabbering in some strange language that was even more incomprehensible than French, and I figured that was Mudapa and his men talking back and forth. Finally I heard Clyde say, "Now how about my emeralds?" and suddenly there was some wild laughter, but one voice drowned it out, and that was Clyde cursing a blue streak.

I heard Mudapa and his men all leave, and I came out of the tent. Clyde looked up, and I don't think I'd ever seen him so mad, even that time back in Africa when his gun jammed right before he could set a record for the most innocent elephants slaughtered in an afternoon.

"That dirty bastard!" he growled.

"Mudapa?" I asked.

He held out his fist and opened it, and I saw he was holding a bunch of stones like you find on the bottoms of rivers, especially when you're walking barefooted. "Do these look like emeralds to you?" he demanded.

"No," I admitted. "But there's a lot I don't know about emeralds. Maybe you should leave 'em out in the sun to ripen."

"Bah!" said Calhoun, tossing the strange-looking emeralds into the bush. "Nobody flim-flams Capturin' Clyde Calhoun! I'm going to war!"

"Before breakfast?" I said.

"What's more important to you?" he demanded. "My emeralds or your stomach?"

"Do you want a frank answer or a friendly one?" I replied.

"All right, all right," he muttered, "we'll put some grub on. I might as well enlist Tonto and his men in our cause."

"Tonto and his men might be just a tad riled that you guv away their half of the skins to Mudapa and *his* men," I noted.

Well, Tonto showed up just when the eggs were frying, and *riled* is an understatement. They had Clyde staked out spread-eagled and naked on the ground inside of a minute, and while I often thought fondly of coming upon Fatima Malone or some other genteel young lady of my acquaintance in just such a position, somehow seeing Clyde stretched out like that killed my appetite, and I didn't even bother pulling the eggs out of the frying pan.

"You have betrayed our trust," said Tonto, "and for that you must die, slowly and painfully."

"If you really want me to die slowly," suggested Clyde, "why not come back next year and strike the first blow then?"

"We are not going to strike you at all," said Tonto.

"That's a comfort," Clyde allowed. "Now how's about letting me up?"

"No," continued Tonto. "We are going to pour honey all over your body and then leave you to the mercy of all the ants and scavengers of the bush."

"I got a better idea," said Clyde. "How's about you and me squaring off, *mano a mano*? If I win, I ain't no traitor and I get to go free; if you win, *then* you can feed me to the beasts of the jungle."

Tonto looked like he was considering it, but Clyde had him by maybe five inches and seventy pounds, and in the end he didn't like the odds, so he finally rejected the offer.

"Okay," said Clyde, undeterred. "I got a better idea…"

"No more talk," said Tonto. "Time to die."

I figgered if they killed Clyde they might not want to stop at just one foreign devil, so I took the bull by the horns, or the Injun by the loincloth, and stepped out of my tent, wrapped in my jaguar skin.

"Hold your horses, Brother Tonto," I said. "I got something to say before you torture poor old Clyde to death."

"It better be *'don't!'*" muttered Clyde.

"What are horses?" asked Tonto, looking around.

"Okay, hold your tree sloths," I amended. "Just hang on a minute and listen to me."

He shut up and turned to me with an *It better be good* expression on his face.

"I know it appears on the surface that Clyde was dealing with the enemy, but actually that's all part of our secret plan."

"Your secret plan to betray us, or your secret plan to grow rich?" he demanded.

"Clyde ain't made one penny off them skins, and that's a fact," I said. "May the Good Lord smite me dead on the spot if I'm lying to you." The closer Injuns backed away, just in case God decided to exercise His option. "He just guv 'em to Mudapa to gain his confidence and lower his guard," I concluded.

"Right!" Clyde chimed in.

"And what was supposed to happen once his guard was down?" asked Tonto suspiciously.

Clyde seemed stuck for an answer. "You tell him, Lucifer," he said at last.

"It was all your idea, Clyde," I said, equally stuck, "so you should tell him."

"But you thunk of a lot of the most important details," said Clyde desperately, "so you get the honor of laying the plan out for him."

"No," I said. "Credit where credit's due. You tell him, Clyde."

"I'd like to," he said, "but I can't think when I'm staked out like this. Maybe if someone would let me up...?"

"Not until I am convinced you have not betrayed us," said Tonto.

"All right," I said, thinking about three words ahead of where I was speaking. "Our plan was to have Clyde disguise himself as a Jaguar Man with this here skin I'm holding, join Mudapa's army, find out their plans, and then report back to you so you'll be ready for them when they attack. And the reason we let all but one skin go was because we figgered he'd be harder to spot in the middle of three hundred Jaguar Men than one hundred and fifty of 'em."

Tonto was one surprised Injun. "You know," he said, "it makes sense."

"Good," said Clyde. "Cut me loose and let me get on with being a Master Spy."

"It *sounds* logical," continued Tonto, "but we need a hostage, just in case you were lying to us again." Tonto pointed a finger at me. "*You* will infiltrate the enemy. We will hold your friend here until you return with the information we want."

"At least cover me up enough to make me decent in case any ladies wander by," said Clyde. "I don't want my proud masculine appurtenance to be the object of prying eyes."

"If I were you," said Tonto, "I'd be more worried about it being the object of prying teeth, but then, I never did understand white men."

"Lucifer," said Clyde, "why are you still hanging around here?"

"It ain't been thirty seconds since I told Tonto our plan," I answered.

"Then you been loafing for twenty-eight seconds," said Clyde bitterly. "Being staked out naked in the tropical sun is mighty difficult work. The sooner you come back, the sooner they'll cut me loose and I can pour myself a beer."

"You got any beer here?" I asked.

"Damn it, just go!" he bellowed.

I could see there wasn't no sense arguing with him when he was in that kind of mood, so I took my leave of the camp and started walking north and east, which was the direction I'd seen Mudapa and his men heading when he'd swiped all the skins.

It took about two hours to catch up with 'em, as they wasn't in no hurry, and in fact they was all sitting around swapping jokes and smoking little native cigars when I arrived. I waited until they got up and started walking again, slipped on my Jaguar Man duds, and joined 'em. No one paid me no never-mind until lunchtime, when the chef made the rounds and asked each warrior what he wanted. When he came to me, I told him I'd settle for a sandwich, and he said he hadn't never heard of a sandwich and how many legs did it have, and I figgered I'd better start speaking Injun mighty quick or I'd give myself away, so I said, "Ugh. Me heap hungry warrior. Me take-um whatever you got-um."

Well, that's what I *planned* to say, but all I got out was the "Ugh" and he started cussing a blue streak and jumping up and down, and finally Mudapa came by to see what was the matter.

"He insulted my cooking!" said the chef. "He called it 'Ugh'! I will not cook anymore until he apologizes."

Mudapa nudged me with his spear. "You heard him. Apologize."

"Heap sorry," I said. "Me make-um no more trouble."

Mudapa stared at me kind of funny-like. "I've never heard a member of my village speak like that," he said suspiciously.

"I'm from out-of-state, here to visit my cousin," I said.

Suddenly he reached out and ripped the jaguar skin off me. "I knew it!" he said. "A spy in our midst!"

"I ain't no spy," I said. "I'm the Right Reverend Honorable Doctor Lucifer Jones, here to bring enlightenment and the word of the Lord to you poor ignorant heathen."

"You came here with Calhoun to rob us!" he said, pointing the tip of his spear right at my neck.

"Not so," I said. "I heard all that shooting, and I thunk it was a Fourth of July celebration, so I moseyed over and stumbled onto his camp."

"You are working with him!" accused Mudapa.

"No such a thing!" I said.

"You must prove it to me, or your life is forfeit."

Now, truth to tell, I didn't know what forfeit was, except that it probably came between threefeit and fivefeit, but he looked pretty serious, and his spear looked even more serious, so I knew I had to come up with some way to prove I wasn't Clyde's partner mighty fast, and finally my Silent Partner smote me right betwixt the eyes with one of His heavenly suggestions, and I put it right into action.

"You're all wrong about this," I said to Mudapa with all the sincerity I could muster on the spur of the moment. "Clyde Calhoun ain't my friend. He's a crook and a thief, and I spit on him." And to emphasize it, I spat at the ground—and so help me, it wasn't my fault that a wind come up just then and blew it in Mudapa's face.

"That's it!" he cried. "You're a dead man!"

He came at me with a knife in one hand and a spear in the other, and Lord knows what else he'd have been pointing at me if he'd had a third hand. I started backing away, and then he guv out a war cry what would have woke such dead as weren't otherwise occupied and charged at me, but when he was maybe five feet away he tripped over a root or a rock or something, and he fell down to the ground and guv another scream, a little more pained than angry this time, and he rolled over on his back, and we could see that he'd accidentally driven the knife all the way into his chest.

"I just hate it when things like this happen!" he mumbled, and died.

I figgered I was going to have to take all his warriors on at once then, but when I turned to face them they was all kneeling on the ground, looking for all the world like they was getting ready for a hot game of craps, but since they didn't have no dice and they all started bowing in my direction I realized they was worshipping me, or at least waiting for their Chief Justice to inaugurate me as their president.

Finally one of 'em stepped forward, laid his hand on my shoulder, and said, "Lucifer Jones, you have defeated Mudapa in mortal combat. You are now our king and we will follow you into battle whenever and wherever you say."

"Well, I'm sure glad to know you fellers don't hold no grudges," I said. "And for my first official act, I think we'll go rescue Clyde Calhoun, who was in a bad way when last I saw him. And if he's still alive, remember to avert your eyes, as he's kind of sensitive about people staring at the south end of him." Then I got to thinking, and I added, "By the way, do you guys have any of the emeralds you promised him?"

One of 'em nodded. "They are back in our village."

"And if the king wants 'em, they're his, and nobody objects?" I asked.

"Of course."

"Well," I said, "that being the case, I guess saving Clyde moves back to the top of the list."

And since my word was law, we started walking back to Clyde's camp. When we'd covered about half the distance, we bumped into Clyde's trackers and gunbearers and such, who were heading away from camp in a mighty big hurry.

"Why did you desert your boss?" I demanded when they saw us and came to a stop.

"Why did *you*?" one of 'em shot back.

"I'd be mighty careful if I was you, Brother," I said. "Us kings don't tolerate no backtalk. Now, why are you all running hell for leather away from camp?"

"Another tribe showed up and chased Tonto's warriors away," said one of the trackers.

"They're headhunters," said a second.

"Worse," said a third. "They're head *collectors*."

"Is Clyde still mildly alive and twitching?" I asked.

"He's still cursing," said a gunbearer.

"That's how you tell he's alive," I said. "When he stops shooting and he stops cursing, he's dead."

"Are we still going to rescue him?" asked one of my loyal worshippers.

"Yeah, I think we'd better," I said. "If we don't nip this collecting tendency in the bud, they might turn their attention to us next."

So we kept walking, and I noticed that the guys what was pulling the wagon that held all the skins was still with us, since they figured if they tried to make it all the way back home alone they stood a fair chance of being robbed, and I decided we might as well give the jaguar heads and skins a field test, so when we were maybe a mile outside of camp I had everyone slip into them. I'd kind of hoped we'd look awesome and imposing, but actually, when you get right down to cases, a bunch of half-naked Injuns dressed up as Jaguar Men look pretty damned silly.

Still, we'd gone to all the trouble to bring the skins back with us, so I figgered we might as well wear 'em and break 'em in, and a couple of minutes later we marched into camp, which was occupied by all these guys wearing shrunken heads on necklaces and belts. They looked at us, and we looked at them, and suddenly one of them yelled: "It is the ghosts of all the beasts we have slain, come to take their revenge upon us!"

Now, truth to tell, I didn't know if they were talking about all the jaguars they had killed or all the men they had killed, but it didn't make no difference, because ten seconds later they'd all cleared out and were high-tailing back to wherever they'd come from.

Clyde was still staked out, and looking a lot more uncomfortable than he had when I'd left him.

"Man, you're a sight for sore eyes!" he said. "It's nice to see them skins didn't go to waste." He looked around as best he could. "Where's Mudapa?"

"I'm the new king," I told him.

"There's only one way you get to be a king in these here parts," said Clyde. "How did you manage to kill him?"

"I'm a natural athlete," I said with becoming modesty.

"Son of a bitch deserved to die!" muttered Clyde. "Serves him right for getting me down here under false pretexts and lying about having a bunch of emeralds."

"He wasn't lying, Clyde," I said. "He just wasn't much for sharing."

"So I'm getting my emeralds after all!" said Clyde with a great big smile. "It almost makes being staked out here in the blazing sun worth it. Cut me loose, Lucifer, and let's go get my loot."

"That's something we got to discuss, Clyde," I said. "It's *my* loot now."

"What are you talking about?" he demanded. "I honored the contract. Them emeralds is mine!"

"Well, yeah," I allowed, "I suppose at one time you could have laid claim to all of 'em. But that was before I pulled off this fearless and daring rescue."

"What fearless and daring rescue?" he bellowed. "A bunch of superstitious headhunters thunk the ghosts of all the jaguars they'd killed was coming after 'em!"

"Well," I said, taking a couple of steps back, "if that's the way you feel about it, I can take my army home and call the headhunters back."

"Hah!" he snorted. "You don't frighten me none. Them head-hunters ain't gonna slow down til they get back to their village."

"You got a point," I admitted. Then I added: "I suppose we can send word to Tonto that the coast is clear."

"All right!" he grumbled. "Cut me loose and we'll split the emeralds fifty-fifty."

I knelt down and pulled out my pocket knife. "One third, one third, and one third," I said.

"What are you talking about?" he demanded.

"One third for you, one third for me, and one third for the Lord," I said. "I'll hang onto His third until such time as He shows up to claim it."

"Never!" screamed Clyde.

A mighty hungry-looking snake suddenly started slithering up his leg.

"Okay, it's a deal!" he said kind of frantically.

I cut the ropes, and he reached out, grabbed the snake, and flang it into the bush. Then he kind of glared at me in my Jaguar Man duds. "That's a fitting outfit for you, Lucifer," he said bitterly. "Them cats always was a vicious and surly race, and just because a human's borrowed their skins, a jaguar don't never change its stripes."

"Aw, come on, Clyde," I said. "I could have gone off and picked up the emeralds first." That didn't seem to assuage him, so I then pointed out that I could have gone off and picked up the emeralds *only*, and suddenly he allowed that maybe I wasn't quite as selfish as he'd first thunk, even if I was never going to be in a class with them philathrosaurs that people keep reading about in the papers.

Next morning we headed off to the village where they kept all the emeralds, and where I planned to take my rightful place as king and maybe elevate a dozen of the prettier womenfolk to queenhood after field-testing their potential royalty, so to speak, but when we finally got there the whole place was deserted.

Clyde's trackers got busy reading all the signs, and they reported back that a jaguar with an irritable demeanor and a big appetite had paid the village a visit and dined on a couple of its prominent citizens, and the rest had just hightailed it, emeralds and all, to parts unknown.

"If that don't beat all," said Clyde. "Here I kill three hundred jaguars, and I overlook the only one that counts."

He announced that he was cutting his losses and going on his next assignment, which had something to do with koala bears. As for me, a noble king without no noble country, I figured that if emeralds were growing on trees (or wherever emeralds grew) in Columbia, well, the sinners in Columbia were probably as much in need of saving and spiritual uplifting as any others, and besides green was always one of my six or seven favorite colors, so I headed north to make my fortune and build my tabernacle.

But that's a whole other story, and writing can be mighty thirsty work.

CONNOISSEURS

Some people are connoisseurs of art. Some are connoisseurs of fine wines. More than a few are connoisseurs of exotic women.

Me, I seem to have inadvertently become a connoisseur of jails.

The best grub is in the Cape Town hoosegow. The friendliest jailer was in the Hong Kong lock-up, though there's a lot to be said for the guards at the Sylvania calaboose. The most comfortable bunk was probably in the jail at San Palmero. The hottest and stuffiest is the Nairobi jail, though the one in Beria, over in Mozambique, runs it a close second. Probably the friendliest crowd to share a cell with was back in Moline, Illinois, though you find the best card games in the Cairo jail and there ain't no fairer craps game than the one they play in the Madrid lock-up.

Now, when this here story begins, I'd just been introduced to the jail at Bogota, which was on the shore of the Hackensack River in Colombia, though it wasn't nowhere near the White House and the Congress, which I'm told are also in Colombia, but it must be one of the suburbs because they weren't within a few thousand miles of Bogota, which was kind of hiding up in the mountains.

I'd wandered north from the Matto Grasso after serving a brief term as King of the Jaguar Men (I think it was forty hours, but it might have been forty-two), and having spent an inordinate amount of time lately with jaguars, anacondas, alligators, and safari ants (who are just like army ants, only smarter), I figgered it was time to replenish my fortune so's that I could finally get around to building the Tabernacle of Saint Luke, and when I heard that there were emeralds to be found in Colombia, I just naturally migrated up that way.

Truth to tell, I didn't know much about emeralds, except that they're mostly green and womenfolk love 'em, and men what love womenfolk and want to impress 'em will spend tons of money for 'em.

Well, I'd only been in Colombia for a couple of days when I realized that there was more to emerald farming than met the eye. By noon of the first day I knew that they didn't grow wild, and by sundown I'd pretty much determined that they wasn't to be found in no rivers or streams, not even the Hackensack, which must be a mighty long river since I'd crossed it in New Jersey once when I was taking my rather hurried leave of a house of excellent repute in Passaic. Took another day to learn that they didn't grow on trees, and when nightfall came I was pretty sure you weren't likely to trip over 'em in the bush, which is what we adventurous sorts call the wild country, probably because it's covered with bushes.

Anyway, I figured I'd better hie myself to a city and see if someone could shed any light on where all these here emeralds were hiding, and I got to say that Colombians are the greediest folk I ever ran into, because they kept saying "Mine" before I'd even got around to asking them to share.

So I figgered, well, greed is one of the eleven deadly sins, so Bogota seemed as good a place to raise a grubstake and build my tabernacle as any, which was when the trouble started. I had just given some of the locals a lesson in statistical probabilities dealing with the number twenty-one when I had a little mishap with the number three, which is how many cards I had tucked away in the sleeve of my go-to-meeting frock coat, and before I had a chance to point out the humor of the situation I'd been carted off to jail, which just goes to show that preaching has got a lot more hazards to it than most people think.

The grub was pretty good if you liked charred rodent with greens, and pretty awful if you didn't. I tried to interest a couple of guards in a friendly game of chance, but I guess my reputation as a card player of skill and sagacity had proceeded me because they just laughed like I'd told 'em the one about the bishop and the dancing girl, and then I was left on my own, except for the fat old guy who snored louder than most locomotives and the young boy who claimed he was really a butterfly and would fly out through the bars as soon as he unloaded his chrysalis, which he kept trying to sell to the guys in the next cell.

I spent three whole days there, and then one of the guards came by and unlocked the door.

"Which one of you is Lucifer Jones?" he asked.

"I'm the Right Reverend Honorable Doctor Lucifer Jones," I said, getting to my feet.

"Well, come on out, Right Reverend," he said. "Your bail's been made."

"Son of a gun," I said. "I didn't think anybody know I was in town."

"Guy claims to be an old friend of yours," said the guard.

"He did?" I said. "What's his name."

"Vander-something," he replied. "Maybe Vanderhorst?"

I stood stock-still. "Von Horst, perhaps?"

"Could be."

"Erich von Horst?"

"Yeah, that's the one."

I pushed him out of the cell and slammed the door shut. "I'm happy right where I am," I said.

"But your bail's been paid."

"Give it back to him," I said. "I'm safer here."

"He says you're old friends," said the guard.

"He's got a peculiar notion of friendship," I said. "Leave me alone. Come back in five years."

The guard scratched his balding head. "I don't know what to do. No one's ever refused bail before."

"No one's ever had a choice between Erich von Horst and jail before," I told him. "Tell him I died of a disfiguring social disease and anyone who comes in contact with my body will catch it."

"He seems like a friendly sort," said the guard.

"I'll bet Eve said that about the scorpion."

"Wasn't it a snake?" he asked.

"Only in the King Henry edition," I said. "Now go tell von Horst that Greta Garbo and I both want to be left alone."

He peeked into the darkened corners of the cell. "Is Greta here?" he asked. "Why wasn't I told about this?"

"Get rid of von Horst and I'll get you a date with her," I promised him.

"I don't know," he said, shaking his head. "This is too confusing for me." He unlocked the door. "Come. I'll take you to the magistrate."

So he handcuffed me, and led me through a maze of corridors until suddenly we were in a courtroom. The judge was a pudgy, balding man with a bushy mustache, wearing a black robe and keeping a deathgrip on a gavel. There was no one else in the courtroom except for Erich von Horst, natty as ever, sitting in the first row and smiling like a cat what was dining on a slew of canaries.

"Here he is, your honor," said the guard. "He refuses to be bailed out."

"This is most unusual," said the judge. He turned to me. "You understand that Mr. von Horst here has generously agreed to pay your bail?"

"I'm happy where I am," I said.

"You are?" said the judge, surprised. "I've never visited the jail myself, but I am given to understand that it is filthy, foul-smelling, and infested with vermin."

"I've seen worse," I said. "I'll just serve out my thirty days or whatever the sentence is, and be on my way."

"The sentence is ten years," said the judge.

I glanced over at von Horst, who seemed to be enjoying himself immensely. "Make it five years," I said, "and I'll plead *nolo compadre.*"

"Come, come, Doctor Jones," said the judge. "What can you possibly have against this angel of mercy who has offered to save you from durance vile?"

"Nothing," I said.

"Well, then?" he said.

"Judge, this here angel of mercy has flim-flammed his way across the whole wide world," I said. "And when I said I had nothing against him, it's because nothing is what I've been left with every time I've run into him."

"Unlike someone else in this courtroom, Mr. von Horst has not broken any laws in Colombia," said the judge. "Now make your decision, Doctor Jones: allow him to pay your bail, or prepare to spend the next ten years in your cell."

It was a tough decision, but I mulled it over for a couple of minutes, while the judge kept urging me to make up my mind, and I finally figgered that von Horst was the lesser of two admittedly unpalatable alternatives.

"All right," I said at last. "He can make my bail."

"I've never seen such a lack of gratitude in my life," muttered the judge as they led me away to pick up my goods, which consisted of three dollars, two decks of cards, a fishhook, a pair of dice, and my well-worn copy of the Good Book. I didn't see von Horst nowhere, but I knew my luck wouldn't hold, and sure enough, as I walked out the front door, a free man, he walked up to greet me and I felt a little less free already.

"My dear Doctor Jones," he said, "how nice to see you once again."

"Get a good eyeful," I said, "because I'm on the next train, bus, car or mule out of here."

"Really?" he said. "Where are you going?"

"Anywhere you're not," I said.

"Well, I certainly wouldn't dream of stopping you," he said. "It's a pity, though. You could have traveled in luxury with fifty thousand dollars in your pocket."

"I don't want to hear this," I said.

"Certainly," he said. "After all, you have three dollars. That should get you from here all the way to the next block."

"That three dollars will get me a cross and some garlic," I said. "If you don't leave me alone now, you will then."

"Come, come, Doctor Jones," he said, "what have I ever done to you?"

"You mean beside robbing me in Dar es Salaam and Casablanca and Greece and Mozambique and London and Rio?"

"Youthful impetuosity," he said.

"You ain't been youthful nor impetuous since your permanent teeth grew in," I said. "Leave me alone."

"But I wish to make amends, my dear Doctor Jones."

"Do I look that dumb?" I said. I saw he was seriously considering it, so I added, "Don't answer that question."

"As you wish," he said, sighing deeply.

"What I wish is to see the last of you, and the sooner the better," I said.

"Too bad," he said. "The fifty thousand was just a down payment against your share of the emeralds."

"Emeralds?" I said.

"It's all right," said von Horst. "I've no wish to offend you further. I'll just have to find someone else who is more interested in instant wealth."

"It always starts out being *our* instant wealth," I said, "and it always winds up being *your* instant wealth."

"If that's the way you feel, say no more," answered von Horst. "After all, how hard can it be to find someone who wants half a million dollars' worth of emeralds? I would have preferred rewarding you for our continued association, but I will simply have to find someone else."

"Fine," I said. "Go find someone else."

"Fine," he said. "I shall."

"How many emeralds are there in half a million dollars?" I asked.

"It depends on the size and quality of the emeralds," he said.

"I don't want to hear about it," I said.

"Whatever you say," he replied.

"How soon could we get our hands of them?" I asked.

"On what?" said von Horst.

"On the emeralds."

"I thought we weren't talking about them."

"We ain't," I said. "I just got an epidermal curiosity about them."

"You mean an academic curiosity," said von Horst.

"That too," I said.

"Why don't you come back with my to my hotel, and I'll lay the details out for you?"

I shook my head. "Not a chance."

"My dear fellow, it's a four-star hotel, which is about as elegant as one gets in Bogota in this day and age."

"Someplace else," I insisted. "I want neutral ground."

"Well," he said, "I suppose we could always go back to your jail cell."

Which is how I came to be sitting on a chair in his suite at the Casa Medina.

"These here are mighty nice surroundings you've bought yourself with what was supposed to be *my* money," was how I opened the conversation.

"You really should try to control your residual bitterness," he said. "If you hadn't tried to swindle me on each occasion..."

"But it never worked, so it doesn't count!" I yelled.

"We'll let bygones be bygones," he said. "You'll feel better when we're dividing up the emeralds in Medellin."

"Correct me if I'm wrong, but ain't Medellin about a hundred miles from here, give or take?"

"That's right."

"Then are you saying the emeralds are in Medellin?"

"No, they're right here in Bogota."

I frowned. "Then what in tarnation has Medellin got to do with anything?"

"I see I shall have to put my cards on the table, Doctor Jones," he said. "Just as well. There should be no secrets between partners."

I tried to count how many times I'd heard von Horst say that in the past, but I ran out of fingers first.

"Doctor Jones," he continued, "I will be blunt: I am almost in possession of at least a million dollars worth of emeralds."

"Almost," I repeated. "You mean they're in the next room?"

"No."

"The hotel safe, then?"

"I'm afraid not."

"I could play guessing games all night," I said. "Why don't you just tell me?"

"Well, there's the rub," said von Horst with a grimace. "I *can't* tell you, for the simple reason that I don't know."

"In a long lifetime of hearing whoppers," I said, "I ain't never heard one bigger'n that."

"But it's the truth," he insisted.

"Erich von Horst," I said, "you are a lot of things good and bad, mostly bad, but I ain't never known you to be so careless that you misplaced a million dollars worth of emeralds, or any other kind of gem now as I come to think on it."

"I guess I'd better tell you the whole story," he said.

"I reckon you had," I said. "Or I'm out the door and making a beeline for the nearest border. I've had my fill of this country."

"I thought all you'd seen of it was the jail and my hotel suite," he said.

"One's got vermin and the other's got you," I said. "Just stick to the subject, and tell me about the emeralds."

He lit a cigarette and learned forward. "Have you ever heard of the Pebbles of Jupiter?"

"Ain't that a resort in the Caribbean?" I said.

He shook his head. "It is the most magnificent emerald necklace ever created. Twenty-six perfect stones, each of them worth a minimum of fifty thousand dollars. Together, who knows?"

"Okay, now I've heard of it," I said. "So what?"

"Every stone came from a Colombian mine, and it is the property of the government of Colombia. It was on display in Bogota until two nights ago."

"Until you stole it," I suggested.

"That is such an ugly word," said von Horst. "We *emancipated* it."

"That's an even uglier word," I said.

"Emancipated?" he asked.

"No—'we'," I said. "Who is this 'we' what emasculated it?"

"Emancipated," he said. "The Pebbles were under extremely heavy guard, so I had to enlist some help."

"How much?"

"There were four of them to begin with."

"You added more?"

He shook his head. "The police subtracted one. Poor Meloshka."

"Meloshka?" I repeated. "Is that a man, a woman, or maybe something else?"

"Meloshka Krympjyntoveitchsk," he replied. "A wonderful man, small, quick, elusive—he would have made a great running back in your American football."

"Forget my American football and tell me about your Colombian Pebbles," I said.

"Well, it was impossible to free the Pebbles from captivity without setting off alarms, and since Meloshka was much the shiftiest of us, we gave the Pebbles to him while we led the police on a wild goose chase. Four wild goose chases, in fact."

"So this Meloshka ran off with your emeralds," I said.

"Absolutely not, Doctor Jones," said von Horst. "He was a man of honor. He knew the Pebbles were too hot to handle right now, so he put them in a safety deposit box, then passed the name of the bank and number of the box on to me." He shook his head. "Poor Meloshka. The police shot and killed him not ten minutes later."

"So you've got the information?" I said.

"Yes."

"Well, then, you know where the Pebbles of Jupiter are."

"Generically," he replied.

"What's this generically nonsense?" I said. "Either you know or you don't."

"I know they're in Bogota, and I know they're in a safety deposit box," he said. "But I don't know what bank, and I don't know what box."

"When did you forget how to read?" I said.

He turned his lounge chair over on its side, reached into a hole he'd slit in the bottom of it, and pulled out a piece of paper. "Here," he said, handing it to me. "*You* read it."

I took a look at it. There were two or three letters I recognized, but I sure as hell couldn't make no sense out of the rest of them.

"All right," I said. "You've had your joke. Now tell me where the Pebbles of Jupiter are, or I'm leaving."

"I don't know," he said. "This was written in Meloshka's native tongue—but I don't know what country he came from or what language he speaks."

"Why don't you just take it to the local college?" I said. "They got to have someone who speaks languages what's got hardly any vowels in 'em."

"Because I would rather split the emeralds two ways with you than four ways with my partners," he said, which certainly seemed in keeping with my own thoughts on the matter. "They know Meloshka was shot near the Casa Medina. They suspect that he saw me before he died, but they don't know it for a fact, so they are watching my every movement, waiting for me to retrieve the jewels. "

"So you want me to go to the college for you and get this thing translated into something resembling English?" I said.

He shook his head. "At least one of them will follow anyone who leaves my room. If they see you heading to the university they'll know you have the paper with you, and your life won't be worth a plugged nickel."

"Well," I said, "suppose you tell me how I can get 'em if I don't know where they are?"

"They're perfectly safe wherever they are," said von Horst. "No one can retrieve them without knowing the bank, the box number, and the name under which the box is registered, and that's all on this piece of paper and nowhere else."

"Okay," I said, trying to follow his line of reasoning. "Your partners don't know where they are, I don't know where they are, you don't know where they are, and you don't want me to go over to the college. What am I missing here?"

"I have a friend in Medellin, a Professor Jablonovitch, who is an expert in Eastern European languages. We will mail the paper to him, and for a small fee he will translate it for us. Then, at our leisure, perhaps four or five months from now, when the heat is off, we'll liberate the Pebbles of Jupiter."

"I'm still missing something," I said. "You got the paper, and you know this professor. So where do I come in?"

"I'm being watched day and night by my partners," said von Horst. "The instant I leave the building they will accost and strip-search me." Suddenly he grimaced. "I *hate* being strip-searched, especially by Pedro el Flor."

"Pedro the Flower?" I said.

He nodded. "They searched me on my way to the jail, and they will search me every time I leave this hotel."

"So you're stuck here forever," I said. "Or until they die of old age."

He shook his head. "I'm leaving for Buenos Aires next week. They will search me one last time, and conclude that I do not have the paper with me. Then, after Professor Jablonovitch receives it and has had time to translate it, I'll stop by his house in a few months, get the translation, and eventually send you back for the emeralds, since they'll still be watching for me." He walked to a desk, pulled out an envelope that was already stamped and addressed to Jablonovitch, put Meloshka's note in it, and sealed it. "Can I trust you to take this to the post office and mail it for me?"

"Why not just leave it at the hotel desk and let them do it?"

"I can't be sure my partners haven't gotten to them. But once it's mailed, it's safe. I've used a phony return address, so that once it's mixed in with the other mail they'll never be able to spot it." He held the envelope up for me to see. "One or more of them will follow you when you leave here, but if you don't head toward a bank or the university, they'll wait to see what you're up to. All you have to do is drop this off, and then just go about your daily life, such as it is, until we're ready to move."

"And we split fifty-fifty?" I said.

"Of course."

"Okay," I said. "Give me the envelope."

He handed it over. "Take great care with it. It contains our future."

"I'll be back to let you know the post office has got it," I said, walking to the door.

"I'll be waiting," promised von Horst.

I shoved the letter into a pocket, walked out the door, and climbed down the stairs to the lobby. There was a couple of disreputable-looking characters sitting on the furniture, staring at me, and off in a corner I saw a beautifully-groomed young man wearing a pair of pink satin pants and a matching shirt, scarf and shoes, and I knew he had to be Pedro el Flor.

I walked out the door and headed off down the street, stopping to window-shop just long enough to see that I was being followed. I didn't let on that I'd seen him. Instead I stopped at a local bar and had a few beers, and finally the guy who was tailing me must have figgered if I was in possession of anything valuable I'd be off doing something about it, so he got up and went back to the hotel. I stuck around another half hour, went into the men's room (which was lit by candles) long enough to steam open the envelope, then snuck out the back way and headed off to the university.

It took me an hour to wade through all the red tape the secretaries hurled at me, but finally I wound up in the language department, and I was introduced to a little bitty bald-headed specs-wearing guy named Doctor McGillicuddy. I told anyone who would listen that I felt just fine and didn't need no doctor, and he explained that he wasn't no more of a doctor than I was, that Doctor McGillicuddy was just easier to pronounce than Expert Translator McGillicuddy.

"Now, where is the cipher?" he said, reaching out his hand.

"I ain't got no cipher," I said, pulling out the sheet of paper. "All I got is this here conundrum what nobody seems able to read."

"Let me see it," he said.

I handed it over.

"One of the dead Slavic dialects, I suspect," he said, walking over to his desk, where he plumped himself down and opened up half a dozen big thick books. He looked from one to another, then started scribbling under each word. Finally he looked up at me, frowning.

"Is this some kind of joke?" he demanded.

"Not to the best of my knowledge," I said. "Why?'

"Because this is what it says:

Roses are red,

Violets are blue,

Sugar is sweet

And so are you."

"Are you sure there ain't no address and box number on it?" I said.

"Of course I'm sure!" he snapped. "Now get out of here and stop wasting my time! And take *this*"—he crumpled up the note and flang it at me—"with you!"

I caught it and left the room. On my way out of the building I was about to toss it in the garbage, but then my prodigious brain kicked into high gear, and I figgered that von Horst *knew* I was bright enough to lose his partners and make my way to the university. And *that* meant he knew I'd open the envelope and find someone to translate it. And that's where the old thinking machine ran into a stone wall, because if the letter was a phony, why did he give it to me? After all, unlike his partners, *I* wasn't threatening his life and limb. I'd been peacefully minding my own business in a Bogota jail cell. If he paid my way out, he needed me for *something*. And if it wasn't getting the letter translated, then what was it?

I mulled on it for another half hour, and all that happened was that my head started hurting, so I decided that the thing to do was go back to the Casa Medina and confront von Horst. When I reached the lobby I didn't see Pedro nor his two friends, which gave me a very uneasy feeling, but it wasn't half as uneasy as when I pounded on von Horst's door and didn't get no answer.

I went back down to the front desk and asked when he'd be back, and the clerk just shrugged and said he didn't know, that von Horst had just brung his tab up to date, turned in his key, and walked out the door.

"What about them three guys what was living in the lobby here?" I asked.

"That Pedro was such a cute one," he said with a wistful smile.

"Did they leave with von Horst?"

"Not exactly," he said.

"You want to tell me what that means?"

"He walked out the door, and a moment later they began following him," said the clerk, "but about ten minutes later they came back looking very disgruntled and asked if he had left a forwarding address."

"Did he?" I asked, not surprised that he'd been able to lose them.

He shook his head. "No, Señor."

I walked to the front door.

"Señor?" he called after me.

"Yeah?" I said.

"If you see el Flor, give him my regards."

Then I was out in the street, trying to figure out where von Horst would have gone. If he was staying in town, he could just as easily have stayed right at the Casa Medina, so I figgered he'd flown the coop. I couldn't see him doing any work himself, which meant he didn't drive out of town. And there wasn't more than two flights a day from the airport, and it wasn't much worse than even money that at least one of them would land a little early, like against the side of a mountain. That meant the likeliest place to look was the train station, so I moseyed on over to it and asked if Erich von Horst had bought a ticket earlier that day.

"Erich von Horst?" said the cashier. "No, I would remember such a foreign name."

"You're sure?" I said.

"Absolutely," he said. "In fact, we've had only one foreign traveler all day. He bought a first class ticket to Medellin."

"You *sure* he wasn't named von Horst?" I insisted.

"I am certain of it. He had a long name, very difficult to pronounce."

Suddenly I pulled the envelope out of my pocket and held it up for him to read. "This look familiar?" I said.

"Professor Jablonovitch!" he exclaimed. "That was the man!"

I thanked him, then retired to a bar filled with friendly ladies of quality to do a little serious thinking. If I had any doubts before, now I *knew* there was something about that letter that von Horst needed. I uncrumpled Meloshka's note and held it over a candle to bring out any hidden messages, but there weren't none and all that happened was I accidentally set the cuff of my shirt on fire. Dousing it with tequila just made it blaze all the brighter, but eventually the bartender came over and tossed a bucket of water on me. I was kind of jumping around, wagging my arm like unto a bird preparing for takeoff, but all the time I was thinking, too. Von Horst had to know I'd find someone to translate the note, and he knew I was brilliant enough not to destroy the letter once I'd heard the translation, so as I saw it, this was a chess game between two of the finest intellects on the planet.

I stared at that letter, and stared at it, and then stared at it some more, and for the life of me I couldn't figger out what kind of scam von Horst had in mind. I knew I was holding the secret to the location of the Pebbles of Jupiter, but I kept coming up blank.

Finally I decided to go back to the Casa Medina once more and see if there were any hints in his room. As I walked in, there was a new clerk on duty, and the old one was just heading for the door, resplendent in his tuxedo.

"Got a heavy date?" I asked.

"No," he answered. "I don't think Pedro weighs more than one hundred and forty pounds."

"Well, good luck to you," I said. "Before you leave, tell your pal behind the desk that I left something in von Horst's room and I need to retrieve it."

He told the new clerk to give me a key, and then he was on his way out the door and I started climbing the stairs to von Horst's suite. I let myself in, checked all the surfaces—tables, cabinets, nightstands—and didn't find nothing. All the drawers were empty too. So was the closet. And the medicine cabinet. I was just about to leave when I damned near tripped over a waste basket that was by the front door, and suddenly I saw a crumpled piece of paper in it. I bent over, picked it up, straightened it out, and read it. It was a paid receipt for services rendered, and it came from the Gonzales Brothers Photography Studio over on Avenue La Esperanza.

I stuck it in my pocket, left the suite, walked out the door of the hotel, turned left, and headed on over to the studio. I figgered he'd probably gotten a passport photo with a beard or maybe a third eye or something to make him look totally different, and he was only going to stay in the country long enough to pick up the emeralds and then he was high-tailing it out of here.

When I got there I walked up to the counter, and a minute later what I took to be a Gonzales Brother emerged from a room or studio or something else with a door on it and approached me.

"Greetings, Señor," he said. "May I help you?"

"Yeah," I said. "Did you take a photo of a gent named Erich von Horst in the last couple of days? Probably for a passport?"

He frowned. "We do not do passport photos, Señor."

"Well, no sense my guessing what you did," I said, pulling out his paid receipt. "Can you tell me what this was for?"

He stared at it, frowning. "Just one moment, Señor," he said. Then he turned and called out: "Jorge, can you come to the counter for a moment?"

It took about three moments, and then another Gonzales Brother entered, smelling of developing chemicals.

"Jorge," said the first one, "do you remember this?"

Jorge took a look at the bill. For a moment he seemed puzzled. Then he suddenly smiled. "Oh, of course! The micro-dot!"

"Micro-dot?" I repeated.

"Yes, Señor," he said. "Señor von Horst had me transfer something to a microdot."

"What was it?"

He shrugged. "I do not remember. Some numbers, I think, and maybe a word or two."

"And where is it?" I asked.

"I do not know. It was delivered to his hotel yesterday. Perhaps you should ask him."

"Thank you, my Brothers," I said with a great big grin on my face. "I think that's checkmate."

"I do not understand," said Jorge.

"And von Horst thought *I* wouldn't understand," I said triumphantly. "But I do." I looked around. "You got a room where I can work in private for about half an hour? It's worth three dollars American to you."

"Yes, Señor," said the one who wasn't Jorge.

"I'll need a knife, and a kettle of boiling water, and some glue, and a sheet of blank paper."

"Easily done, Señor."

A couple of minutes later I was alone in the room. I held the envelope over the steam from the kettle for about five minutes, and finally the stamp came loose. I kind of insinuated the knife under it and lifted it very carefully—and there, beneath where it had been, was a micro-dot! I moved the dot to a safe place on the table, then meticulously glued the stamp back on so no one could ever tell it had been removed in the first place.

Then, since I couldn't resist letting von Horst know I'd finally gotten the better of him, I wrote him a little note:

Von Horst:

It was a clever idea, but this isn't just any fool you're dealing with here. I'm on my way to pick up the Pebbles of Jupiter now. If we ever meet again, and I'm going to have some harsh words for the Lord if we do, I'll buy you a drink with your share of the emeralds, because that's the kind of Christian gentleman I am.

Sincerely but no longer yours,

Lucifer Jones

Mighty few letters ever guv me so much satisfaction in the writing of them. I folded it, put it in the envelope, and used the paste to seal it. Then I went back into the main room, and asked Jorge if he had some machine that would let me read the micro-dot.

"Certainly, Señor," he said. "We can cast it on a large screen for you to see."

He took the dot and led me into a small room where he stuck it in some kind of viewer, and then there it was, big as life, on the screen:

National Bank of Bogota. Box 1187. Registered in the name of Don Miguel Cervantes.

I had to give him credit. If he registered it as von Horst, his partners might stumble upon it, but there wouldn't nobody be looking for a made-up name like Cervantes.

I thanked the brothers once more, took my leave of them, and headed off to the bank, stopping only long enough to stick the letter in the first mailbox I came to. Once I got to the bank, I went to the clerk what was in charge of the safety deposit boxes, signed "Don Miguel Cervantes" next to number 1187, got the key, unlocked the box and pulled it out, and took it to a private room where I opened it up, preparing to spend a little time admiring all twenty-six of them perfect emeralds.

But the only thing in the box was a neatly-folded letter in a familiar script. I got a right queasy feeling as I opened it up and began reading it.

My Dear Doctor Jones:

Once again we have come to the end of a remarkable adventure, one that would have been far more difficult without your participation. By now you know, of course, that I did indeed have three partners. The fourth, Meloshka, I discovered in an exceptionally bad Russian novel, and I will him to you.

I knew, of course, that you would open the letter the moment you were out of my sight, and I knew you would find someone who could translate it. (You've no idea how difficult it was to find that nursery rhyme in an extinct Slavic dialect.) And because I also know your deceitful and suspicious nature, I knew you would return to my suite, where I made sure you would stumble across the receipt from the Gonzales Brothers. From there it would have been a matter of no more than an hour before you found the micro-dot, removed it, gloated triumphantly to me in the envelope I provided you, and you are obviously now at the bank.

Doubtless you are wondering why you were essential to this operation. The answer is simple enough. My partners and I did not steal any emeralds, as the market for stolen gemstones is currently depressed and the rewards are not commensurate with the risks. No, what we stole was the incredibly rare Fatima one-cent stamp. You see, José María Campo Serrano was the President of Columbia in the 1880s, and they decided to honor his wife by producing a stamp with her likeness. Due to some confusion, the initial engraving was not of Senora Serrano, but of José Maria's mistress, Fatima. Only six were printed before the mistake was rectified, but each is worth well over a million dollars in mint condition. That, of course, was the stamp you replaced on the envelope that you sent to me. Admittedly it will lose half its value when postmarked, but I will have lost three of my partners, and all of half a million dollars is preferable to one-fourth of a million. As for defacing such a valuable collector's item, all I can say is that I leave the appreciation of such items to connoisseurs of art; as for myself, I am a connoisseur of money.

Doubtless you are wondering about the Pebbles of Jupiter. They really do exist. As you walk along the Hackensack River on the outskirts of town, you will see row upon row of sharp stones lining the bank. Those are the Pebbles of Jupiter, and I am sure the government of Colombia will be happy to let you take away as many as you can carry.

Until next time, I remain Yr. Obdt. Svt.,

Erich von Horst

"Again!" I screamed. "He did it again!"

"Who did what?" asked a guard, but I wasn't listening. I was screaming bloody murder, all the while wondering how I could be so stupid when I'm so smart.

They threw me out of the bank for causing a commotion, and I decided to take my leave of Bogota, so I headed west out of town. I was in such a rage that I didn't look where I was going, and I damned near broke my neck when I slipped on the Pebbles of Jupiter.

If that was his idea of exterior decorating, I just hope Mrs. Jupiter gave him hell for it and made him sleep on the couch.

SPRING
TRAINING

Now you would think on the surface of it that it ain't much of a walk from Bogota to Buenos Aires, but let me tell you, they're a lot closer to each other in the alphabet then they are on foot. I made the trek back in 1937 with a heavy heart, since I'd lost yet another fortune to Erich von Horst, a deep-dyed villain what didn't have no respect at all for an honest, good-natured, trusting man of the cloth like myself.

He had that in common with about eighty trillion insects I encountered along the way, plus more than a few anacondas that wanted to teach me the samba, or at least the part where you shake like you got a case of palsy, and there was a jaguar what wanted to turn my hide into a coat for his missus, and a bunch of half-naked little bitty folks what carried around a bunch of heads that were even littler and bittyer, but eventually I made it to Buenos Aires, which seemed like as good a place as any to set up shop and finally build my tabernacle. The sinners were thick on the ground, there wasn't no civic authorities going around trying to tighten all the loose women, and clearly Erich von Horst had never visited the place, because most of the folks still had their folding money.

The biggest place in town was a joint called the Casa Rosada, but the evening I got there I inquired out front by the massive iron gates about renting a room and putting my tab on the cuff, and they just stared at me like they couldn't understand a word, so I started explaining about vows of poverty—mine had come a few miles north of town when I found out that a flush *does* beat a full house when the guy with the flush is also the guy with the machete—but they didn't answer, and I finally figgered that either they didn't speak no civilized lingo or else the whole hotel was rented out, which could well have been the case considering how many generals I seen coming and going whilst we was talking, or anyway whilst *I* was talking and they was listening.

I asked one of the locals to recommend a good cheap hotel. He just shrugged and said, rather apologetically, "Señor, there are not even any good *expensive* hotels."

I was about to explain to him that we were standing in the central district of one of the great cities of South America, but I had to step out of the way as two llamas and a pig walked by.

"Okay," I said, "just tell me where the foreign folk go."

"Home, Señor," he said.

"Before then."

He shrugged. "The Presidente."

"The President puts 'em up?" I said. "I'd call that uncommonly Christian of him."

He shook his head. "The Hotel Presidente, Señor."

He pointed to de Julio Avenue, and I moseyed over there, but before I could reach the door I chanced upon a little beer garden right in front of it. I'd heard of beer gardens before, but I hadn't never seen one until just then, and to my surprise it didn't have no tables nor chairs nor other conveniences. In fact, all it had was three guys in uniforms I couldn't recognize sitting down on the ground and swilling bottle after bottle of beer and speaking in some tongue that was harsher than Argentinian and made even less sense than French.

"Howdy," I said, stepping over the hedge and trying not to crush an excessive number of flowers. "You gents mind if I join you? Finding a hotel in this town can be mighty thirsty work."

"I didn't know one was missing," said one of 'em in a thick German accent, and the other two threw back their heads and laughed, which guv me a chance to delicately reach over and nab a beer bottle.

"Thanks," I said. "You guys are looking mighty spiffy in them uniforms. Are they doing military exercises in these here parts?"

"We have no idea," he answered.

"Well, you're all decked out in your parade finest, and each of you got a chest full of medals," I said. "So you can understand me thinking you were part of the army."

"We *are*," he said.

"But not *this* army," added another one of 'em.

"Got separated from your outfit, did you?" I asked.

"We are members of the Third Reich!" said the first guy.

"So you're looking for the First and Second Reichs, is that it?" I said.

"Fool!" snapped the one what hadn't spoke up yet. "We are the Master Race!"

Well, I could tell right off that these here officers had been drinking all night and were pretty far gone, because they weren't running the Master Race until Saturday over at Argentine Downs, and besides, to the best of my knowledge it was limited to horses.

"I didn't mean no offense, neighbor," I said. "By the way, I'm the Honorable Right Reverend Doctor Lucifer Jones at your service. Baptisms and holy matrimony done cheap, with a group rate for military funerals."

"I am Colonel Guenther Schnitzel," he said, offering me what would have been a snappy salute if he hadn't poked himself in the eye. "And these are my companions: Colonel Hans Grueber and Colonel Wilhelm Schnabble."

"Pleased to meet you gents," I said. "Where do you hail from?"

"We already told you: we are members of the Third Reich."

"Yeah, but I figger that's some kind of amateur theater group or something like that," I said. "What *country* are you from?"

They exchanged looks, and just when I figgered they was gonna tell me that they'd all forgot, Hans spoke up and said "Germany."

"I don't want to be the bearer of bad tidings," I said, "but you must have tooken a wrong turn." I pointed to the east. "Germany's about seventeen trillion miles that way."

"We are the advance guard," said Wilhelm. "The Fuehrer sent us here to conquer South America while he's preparing to conquer the rest of the world."

"Just the three of you?" I asked.

"Nothing is impossible for the Master Race," he said.

Obviously he hadn't considered the likelihood of a muddy track, but I didn't want to point it out to him, because he was already having trouble staying on topic, which was either conquering the world or finding them missing Reichs.

"He's dubious," said Hans, staring at me.

"No, I'm Lucifer," I said. "You guys got a real head start on the beer, didn't you?"

"I can see we shall have to convert you to *Mein Kampf*," said Wilhelm.

"No, thanks," I said. "I'm trying to give up these spicy foods."

"Where are you heading?" asked Hans.

"Pretty much any place with a cheap bed, and if it's occupied by an obliging lady of quality, so much the better," I answered.

"You sound like a man who is in need of capital," he said.

"The Tabernacle of Saint Luke is always looking for substantial donations," I told him.

"The Tabernacle of Saint Luke?" repeated Guenther, frowning.

"I'm its legal representative here on Earth," I explained.

"And where is this magnificent edifice?" asked Guenther.

"Well, it ain't quite got itself built yet," I said. "We're still collecting for the cornerstone. How much can I put you gents down for?"

"What seems a reasonable amount to you?" he asked.

"I don't want to be greedy or nothing," I told him. "How's about six million apiece?"

"How about five hundred deutschmaks?" he countered.

"How much is that in real money?" I asked,

"Soon it will be the *only* real money," he said.

"Well, I'll have to have a heart-to-heart with God, but He's a pretty agreeable critter about most things," I said, stretching out my open hand, "so why don't you just fork it over and if He's in any way displeased, Him and me'll find some way of getting it back to you."

Guenther pulled a wad out of his wallet and counted out the money.

"You understand," he said, "that in exchange for this donation, we will expect something in return."

"I'll put in a good word for you the next time I'm conferring with Him," I said.

"We have in mind something a little more substantial than that," said Guenther.

"Okay, I'll name a pew after you."

"Why don't you let *us* tell you what our five hundred deutsch-marks are buying?" said Guenther.

"A cornerstone?" I guessed.

"Silence, *schweinhundt*!" snapped Guenther.

"Okay," I said, getting a little hot under the collar, "but just between you, me and the gatepost, I'll lay plenty of eight-to-five that Jesus didn't die for *your* sins."

"Listen to me," said Guenther. "We are here to conquer South America and turn it into a German colony. We do not wish to sully our hands with members of inferior races. Therefore, we need a go-between, someone who will relay our commands to the lower orders of humanity that will be serving the glorious Fatherland."

"Fatherland?" I said. "Where is *that*? I thunk you guys came over from Germany."

"Let's get someone else," complained Hans. "I mean, there's inferior and then—" he glanced at me—"there's *inferior*."

"We are running out of time," noted Wilhelm. "We've been here a whole week and haven't subjugated a single nation. The Fuehrer won't like that."

"This guy's your boss, huh?" I said.

"The Fuehrer is the greatest human being who has ever lived!" said Hans devoutly.

Now me, I'd have voted for Bubbles La Tour, the prima ballerina of the Rialto Burlesque back in Moline, Illinois, but I didn't want to seem rude, so I just agreed that this here furrier was all the rage, and made a note to see if I could pick up a cut-rate mink coat the next time I fell eternally and helplessly in love, which tended to happen about every two or three months, give or take.

"Then," said Hans, "after we have subjugated all of South America, we will return home and take our place at the head of the army as we march across Europe."

"So this is kind of spring training for the main event?" I said.

"In a manner of speaking," agreed Wilhelm.

"Okay," I said, "If I'm gonna lead your army into battle, where are you hiding it?"

"On the outskirts of town," said Hans uncomfortably.

"I come down from the north, and I never seen 'em," I said, "so I figger they're to the south. How many divisions you got waiting, armed and ready?"

They just kind of looked uncomfortable and didn't say nothing.

"Okay, then," I said, "how many regiments?"

Wilhelm immediately started watching a bird what was nesting in a balcony across the street.

"Brigades?" I said.

Hans suddenly noticed his shoelace was untied and leaned over to fix it, which was kind of strange since he was wearing boots.

"Platoons?" I asked.

Guenther pulled a monocle out of his pocket and began polishing it with a dirty handkerchief.

"Squads?" I said.

"I think we have a squad," said Hans.

"A small one," added Wilhelm.

"And you guys want to conquer Argentina with a small squad?" I said.

"We *have* to!" said Hans.

"You don't know what the Fuehrer does to failures!" added Wilhelm with a shudder.

"How many men have you actually got?" I said.

"Seven," said Wilhelm.

"Six," Hans corrected him. "One ran off with the milkmaid."

"So you plan to lead six men into battle again the entire Argentine army?" I asked.

"Certainly not," said Guenther.

"I'm glad at least one of you is talking sense," I said.

"We function best in an advisory capacity," he continued. "*You* are going to lead them."

I was about to object, but then my Silent Partner smote me with another of His timely revelations. "That ain't no problem at all," I announced. "You're down here for spring training before you take on the British and the Russians and all them other inferior races that misleadingly seem identical to you in every way except maybe language. Well, I need some spring training too, so if you'll fork over your money and tell me where to find your army, I'll be more than happy to go conquer Uruguay or Paraguay or one of them other guays for you."

"At least we'd have a triumph to report," said Hans hopefully.

"Besides, the Fuehrer flunked geography," added Wilhelm. "He doesn't know one South American country from another."

Guenther considered it for a minute before nodding his agreement. "What the hell," he said. "If he gets captured, tortured with poisonous snakes and hunger-crazed rats, and then has his eyes gouged out before he is finally killed, we still have enough money left to go hire another go-between." He handed the deutschmarks to me. "We are proud to contribute to the Tabernacle of Saint Luke."

"The Tabernacle of Saint Luke thanks you," I said, stuffing the bills in a shirt pocket. "And my first sermon will be about how even vicious, godless heathen can have moments of generosity."

"Just out of curiosity, who *was* Saint Luke?" asked Hans.

"You're looking at him."

"I thought you were Lucifer?"

"Now what kind of haul do you think our poor box would take in if I was running the Tabernacle of Saint Lucifer?" I asked.

"What did you do to become a saint?" asked Wilhelm.

"What did you do to become a colonel?" I shot back.

"Touché," he said. "The subject is closed."

"But the war is open for business," I said. "You guys care which country we conquer?"

"Not really," admitted Hans. "Which one do you prefer?"

"Whichever's got the cheapest busfare," I said. "No sense fighting a war if you're going to tire yourself out just getting there. Although," I added, "since defeat ain't in our lexicon from this moment on, maybe we ought to consider conquering the country with the friendliest ladies of the evening."

"We will leave it entirely in your hands," said Guenther. "Just tell us when you've won."

"Right," said Hans. "You'd best get started. Don't worry about casualties. They're all inferior specimens anyway."

"Well, if that's the case," I said, "maybe I ought to take some superior specimens with me, just to set a bold and noble example."

Well, I never saw three people go deaf so fast. I figgered it might be contagious, so I took my leave of them. They'd kind of pointed off to the southeast when talking about their six-man army, so I hopped the bus and got off when I seen six fellers just kind of standing around a corner, passing a bottle of tequila amongst themselves.

"Howdy, brethren," I said.

"Greetings," replied one of them.

"Nice night for a war," I said.

"Oh?" said another. "Who are you mad at?"

Well, when I mulled it over, I decided the only two people in the world I was mad at were Erich von Horst, and the sheriff what arrested Bubbles La Tour the last time I saw her, when she was giving a thoughtful demonstration of half a dozen new and unique uses for a broom, not a one of which had anything to do with sweeping the floor, but of course neither of 'em was actually countries, so it didn't hardly seem worth the bother to declare war on 'em.

"I suppose we ought to be democratic about this," I said, since I didn't hold no grudge against Uruguay. "Who would you fellers like to go to war with?"

"My mother-in-law," said one of 'em promptly.

"My boss," said another.

"You don't *have* a boss," said a third.

"Well, I would—if I had a job."

"The man who made this tequila," said another, taking a swig out of the bottle and making a face.

Pretty soon they all had a bunch of people they wanted to do battle with, but the problem was that all of them was local.

"Tell you what," I said at last. "If you guys will pitch in and help me conquer Uruguay for the Third Fatherland, I'll pay bus fare both ways."

"What happened to the first two Fatherlands?" asked the one who didn't have a boss.

"I guess the Motherlands caught 'em playing around and guv 'em the gate."

A beat-up old bus with busted windows, torn seats, and worn tires pulled up just then, and I loaded all six of them onto it, bought seven tickets, and then joined 'em.

"Damned lucky I found you fellows so easy," I said. "I was afraid I was going to have to look for loaded cannons and things like that."

"Why would we have a loaded cannon?"

"Well, you *are* the German army," I said.

"No such thing, Señor. We are the janitors for the buildings on this block. We were on our break when you showed up."

"What happened to the army?" I asked.

"Those other men? They got tired of waiting, so they all went home."

"Well, even though you ain't the regular army, I'm still paying your fare both ways," I said, "and as soon as we conquer Uruguay I'm buying the first round of drinks." Then I thunk a little more, and said, "Ah, what the hell—it ain't *that* small a country: the first *two* rounds."

"What about Madame Fifi's House of Scarlet Pleasures?" said one of 'em.

"I give up," I said. "What *about* Madame Fifi's House of Scarlet Pleasures?"

"If I bring you the Uruguayan president in chains, will you treat us to it?"

"Tell you what," I said. "You bring him in chains, and *he* can treat us *all* to it."

They let out a rousing cheer.

Well, we talked about this and that for the next few hours, mostly concentrating on some of the more unusual features to be found at Madame Fifi's, and then the bus driver announced that we had crossed the border and entered Uruguay.

"Keep your heads down, men," I warned 'em. "We're in enemy territory."

"You're on the 3A Bus Route," corrected the driver in bored tones. "I take it every day of the year."

"Yeah," I said, "but we ain't never declared war on Uruguay before."

"Pablo did once, didn't you?" asked one of them.

"Yes, but I didn't really mean it," explained Pablo. "I was dating a girl from Uruguay and she stood me up."

I turned to the driver. "Where does this here assault vehicle let us off?"

"Montevideo," he said.

"Montevideo to you," I replied politely. "Now, where does it stop?"

"Downtown Montevideo," he said irritably. "That is the capital of Uruguay."

"Not much longer," I said. "We may take the whole town back to Buenos Aires with us."

I pulled out a deck of cards and gave my men a crash course in higher mathematics, all having to do with the number twenty-one, and before we knew it the driver announced that we had reached Montevideo.

I walked up to the front and looked out the window. "Well," I said, "if we're going to conquer Uruguay, this is the place to do it. Pull over at the next corner."

He did as I told him, but then I saw a cop walking his beat.

"Is he carrying a gun?" I asked, peering at him through the glass.

"Yes, I think so," said the driver.

"Go another two or three blocks," I said.

He drove three blocks and stopped.

"See any more cops around?" I asked him.

"No, Señor."

"Fine." I turned to my army. "Men, we're getting out here." As they clambered down onto the sidewalk, I turned to the driver. "Pick us up on your way back."

"That will be in about five minutes, Señor."

"No problem," I said. "It ain't that big a country."

I stepped down onto the pavement, briefly examined the area to make sure there weren't no cops around, and cleared my throat.

"I, Lucifer Jones, hereby declare Uruguay conquered and now the property of the Third Fatherland. If anyone's got any objections, let him speak now or forever hold his peace."

"I have one," said Pablo.

"Shut up," I said. "You're on *our* side." I waited a respectable thirty seconds, and there weren't no more objections. "Man and boy, that was the easiest five hundred deutschmarks I ever made," I announced. "Have we got time for a victory drink?"

"I don't think so," said Pablo mournfully. "Here comes the bus."

"Climb aboard," I said. "We'll get our drink at some little town along the way, where they don't water their liquor and the prices are better."

And a moment later, with Uruguay all wrapped up and ready to be delivered, we boarded the bus and headed back to Argentina. We sang martial songs, especially about oversexed enemy captives named Rosita, and played a little more blackjack, and were all set to stop for a drink in some village near the border (which I suppose didn't officially exist no more), when the bus came to a stop again.

"Out of gas?" I asked.

"Out of courage," said the driver, pointing nervously ahead of us, where there were some fifty uniformed soldiers with guns, and most of them guns were pointed right at us.

I turned to say a word or two of encouragement to my victorious army, but all six of 'em was hiding under the seats, so I just climbed down off the bus and walked forward, with my hands up in the air so everyone could see I didn't have no weapons or hidden aces in 'em.

"Greetings, brothers," I said. "To what do I owe the honor of this here get-together?"

"You are our prisoner," announced an officer, stepping forward.

"I'd love to be your prisoner," I said, "but we'll have to do it some other time. I'm in a hurry to get back to Buenos Aires and report that Uruguay has fallen."

"It has?" he said, turning white as a dirty sheet. "I never heard a shot."

"It was a pretty bloodless victory," I said.

"Miguel!" he hollered. "Did you hear the news?"

"I don't believe it!" said the officer called Miguel.

"Don't take *my* word for it," I said. "Ask the men in the bus."

I indicated my troops, who all nodded their heads vigorously, then ducked back behind the seats again.

"This is tragic!" said the one called Miguel. "What foul fiend perpetrated this heinous sneak attack?"

"'Twasn't no sneak attack," I said. "It was right out there in the open for everyone to see. But in answer to your question, the foul fiends are Colonel Guenther Schnitzel, Colonel Hans Grueber, and Colonel Wilhelm Schnabble, and my understanding is that they're considering packing up the whole country and shipping it to Germany."

"Those bastards!" screamed the first officer. "*We* were going to conquer Uruguay next week!"

"Actually," said the other apologetically, "we were going to conquer it *last* week, but I had a hangnail and his cousin was getting married."

"We're not going to permit them to plunder the treasury *we* were going to plunder!" yelled the first one. He turned to me. "I am Colonel José Marcos of the Uruguayan army, and this is my co-conspirator...ah...my fellow officer, Colonel Miguel Garcia."

"And I'm the Right Reverend Doctor Lucifer Jones," I said, wondering what it was about being colonels that made people so bloodthirsty.

"We will give you one thousand American dollars if you will lead us to these German usurpers," said José. "Half now, half when you deliver them."

"Right," said Miguel. "We will find them, cut them to ribbons, and then Paraguay will be ours."

"Uruguay, Miguel," said José. *"Uruguay."*

"Oh, right," apologized Miguel. "Paraguay is *next* month."

I resisted the urge to say "You go Uruguay and I'll go mine," because they clearly weren't in the mood for highbrow sophisticated witticisms, so I simply allowed that it was a right generous offer, and the sooner they paid it the sooner I could put 'em in touch with the German colonels, who were probably right where I'd left 'em unless they finally found them other two Reichs what went missing and took 'em home.

Well, money changed hands, and in my good-heartedness I told 'em that they'd not only paid for a cornerstone, or at least a corner brick, of the Tabernacle of Saint Luke, but they'd also bought absolution for any sins they committed at Madame Fifi's for the next 72 hours.

I thought Miguel was going to head right off to Madame Fifi's, but José said no, they'd paid for the information and now they wanted it. So I told 'em that the three colonels in question had been sprawled out in the garden of the Hotel Presidente when last I saw 'em, and I couldn't see no reason why they should stray too far from it.

"We don't want to march right down de Julio Avenue," said Miguel. "Who knows what kind of trap they might have set?"

"Right," said José. "We should make them come to *our* trap."

"Do we have one?" asked Miguel.

"You, Reverend Jones," continued José, "will arrange a meeting between Miguel and myself, and your three German officers, in the little border town of Salto. Then, when they arrive, our men will attack and cut them to pieces, and Uruguay will be ours."

I got back on the bus, and then we began driving off to Buenos Aires. Me and the army started swapping risible stories—I especially liked the one about the blind carpenter and the dancing girl—and then almost before I knew it we were pulling up to the Hotel Presidente. The colonels were still in the beer garden, crushing the flowers in between bouts of watering 'em, and I walked over to report that Uruguay had fallen. For some reason this seemed to surprise them, but I assured them we'd done it without no casualties nor even any collateral damage, and finally they offered to walk me inside and buy me a victory drink.

"Well, that's mighty nice of you," I said, "but I got urgent business in Salto."

"Oh?" said Guenther suspiciously. "What's in Salto?"

I'd thunk long and hard about it on the way back, and I figgered if I told 'em a bunch of guys were waiting there to chop them into fishbait they'd probably decide they had urgent business elsewhere, so instead I said that Madame Fifi's House of Scarlet Pleasures had opened up a branch in Salto and was giving out free coupons, and suddenly all three colonels made a beeline for the bus and had the driver gun the gas pedal, even before the conquering army could get off and go back to work.

All they could talk about was Madame Fifi's, though Wilhelm, who was clearly the most sensitive of 'em, kept asking if making love to a member of an inferior species might not constitute bestiality, which was good for ten years in the hoosegow back in Germany.

It began raining about halfway through the trip, and pretty soon it was pouring cats and dogs and other critters that unlike most men got enough brains to come in out of the rain. Finally the bus pulled up in the mud in the middle of Salto, and everyone got out—the Germans, who still hadn't stopped talking about Madame Fifi's, and the army and me and the bus driver, just to stretch our legs and keep clear of the coming slaughter.

Then José and Miguel walked out from a nearby building, and I could see that the rest of their army was hiding behind it. José stopped by the bus long enough to pay me my final five hundred dollars, and then the two Uruguayan colonels walked straight up to the three German colonels.

"You have a lot of nerve, Señors," said José. "Uruguay is *ours*, and I demand that you relinquish it right now."

"We won it fair and square," said Guenther, "and we are not giving it back."

"We'll see about that!" snapped Miguel. "You are outnumbered fifty to one!"

"That's seventeen to one," José corrected him. "With one left over."

"What are you talking about?" demanded Miguel.

"Well, we have fifty armed men, plus ourselves, so that's fifty-two, and there are three of them, so that comes to seventeen-to-one, with one of us left over."

"Who cares?" screamed Miguel. "They're outnumbered and we're going to kill them! That's all that counts!"

"I beg to differ," said Hans calmly. "We are members of the Aryan race. One of us is worth fifteen of you."

"Even if that's true, and I'm not conceding it for an instant," replied José, "then we *still* outumber you one-point-sixteen-to-one!"

"Ah, but it's raining," noted Guenther. "That decreases your mobility by nineteen percent."

"But *you* wear a monocle," said José. "That decreases your field of vision eleven percent even if it wasn't raining."

"But there's also a nine percent chance that your pistol will misfire in the rain," noted Hans.

"Can we just stop talking and kill them, please?" said Miguel wearily.

"Oh, all right," said José. "Anything to make you happy. Let's step out of the way of our bayonet-wielding infantry."

Nobody moved.

"Uh...I can't lift my legs," said Miguel.

"Neither can I," said Guenther, frowning.

And sure enough, all five of 'em had sunk into the muck and mire past their knees, and they were stuck there.

Suddenly I saw the Uruguayan infantry break cover and race over toward the bus.

"Take us back to Montevideo," said one of 'em to the driver.

"Don't you want to save your fearless leaders?" I asked.

"They aren't fearless, and they're not our leaders. We only came with them because they told us Madame Fifi had opened a new branch here."

I turned to my army. "How about you guys?" I said. "You want to save any of these here colonels?"

"No!" they said in unison.

"You sure?" I said. "After all, you won a whole country for 'em. They might want to give you a slice of it."

"They would, too, the bastards!" said Pablo passionately.

"I'm not quite sure I follow that particular line of reasoning," I said.

"It's hard enough just to keep our block clean," he said. "Who wants to be in charge of cleaning a whole country?"

I could see where his sentiments lay, so I didn't try to talk him out of it. Then I took one last look at the combatants. Hans was explaining that the mud wouldn't hamper three guys as much as two, and José was answering that any mathematician would know that two guys were one-third less likely to be hampered, and then Wilhelm said he hadn't eaten all day and Miguel said that as soon as he got loose he'd cut Guenther into pieces and feed him to Wilhelm, and Hans snickered and said that his knife would be so rusty by then that it wouldn't cut through Wilhelm's flesh, and pretty soon they were back to yelling and cursing at each other, and I noticed that all their noise had attracted a bunch of curious spectators, most of which had four legs and long whiskers and were covered with spots, and that seemed like an appropriate time to leave all them would-be conquerors behind, because the real conquerors had just showed up.

We dropped the Uruguayan army off in Montevideo, then turned the nose of the bus back to Buenos Aires. We stopped by Salto, but there wasn't no sign of none of the colonels, though we did see some mighty fat, contented jaguars.

Me and the Argentine army got off in the middle of town, they decided to go back to their jobs and their womenfolk, and as for me, I'd had my fill of conquering countries and decided it was time to start plundering them. I'd heard of some forgotten kingdoms off to the west that were filled to overflowing with priceless gems and liberal-minded high priestesses, and I decided then and there to go grab my share of both. But as you will see, it wasn't quite as easy as it sounds....

A FOUR-SIDED TRIANGLE

T here wasn't a whole lot of white folks in La Paz back in the spring of 1937, but them what was there all remember what happened, all the romantic intrigues and double crosses and blazing guns and the like, and they've codified it in song and story what's come down to their descendants and a bunch of scholars who ain't got nothing better to do with their time, and it's gotten so famous that these days I think they're even talking about making a movie or two about it.

So before you get any further misled, I want to tell you *my* side of the story.

As readers what's been breathlessly following my heroic exploits and encounters in South America will know, I'd just finished waging a secret war of conquest against Uruguay. (In fact, it was so secret that not a single history book even mentions it.) I'd tooken my leave of Buenos Aires and the passenger bus from which me and six street cleaners (well, five active, one unemployed) had launched our lightning strike across the border, and I heard talk of some hidden city called Macho something-or-other up in Peru.

Well, right off I knew it was my kind of place, since the one thing a city named Macho figgered to have in abundance was a bunch of scarlet women what was there to help all the men kind of exert their machoness. I figgered I was less than a thousand miles from it when I ran a little short of funds. Now, I could see that the locals was mostly uneducated peasants and probably couldn't count up to twenty-one if I was to introduce a complex game like blackjack, so instead I taught 'em how to play a sporting game with a pair of six-sided cubes that only required 'em to count up to twelve.

Turn out that at least it was right in theory. To this day I don't know if any of 'em could count to twenty-one unless the Good Lord guv 'em an extra finger or toe, but they sure could count up to three, which was how many dice hit the ground when my spare accidentally tumbled out of my sleeve.

Which is how I came to spend the next six nights in the calaboose at Cochabomba, which sounds like Bubbles La Tour's specialty dance at the Rialto Burlesque back in my home town of Moline, Illinois, but was actually this here village what lay directly between me and paydirt, which is to say Buenos Aires and Macho-whatever-its-name-was.

Still, the grub wasn't all that bad, especially if you had a taste for dirt-flavored salamanders and warm water with stuff floating in it. At least the salamanders was mostly dead and the water was mostly wet, which was better than a lot of hoosegows I've been in.

I was still planning on heading to Peru to find a lost empire or two when I sat down to play a game of checkers through the bars of my cell with Diego, who was the sheriff and cook and janitor all rolled into one fat old man with a droopy mustache. He wasn't no happier hanging around the jailhouse than I was, but he looked a lot better fed.

"You know," he said, as he moved a checker, "this jail has sat empty for three years."

"You don't say," I answered. "No wonder all the snakes and rats are so lonely and rarin' for a little companionship."

"Then," he continued, "all of a sudden, three men in three weeks—and all of them English speakers." He lit a cigar and looked like he was thinking of offering me one, and then decided not to. "It would be bad for your health."

"Ain't it bad for yours, too?" I asked.

"Yes," he said. "But then, I eat a diet that is not guaranteed to kill me, my poor *amigo*."

"Getting back to them two other English speakers..." I said.

"It is most unusual," he said. "Not only that I have had to arrest three in a row, but also that you all practice honorable vocations—a military man, a gentleman farmer, and a minister."

"What in tunket was an English-speaking military man doing here?" I asked.

"He threatened to kill another man," said Diego. "I gather it was an affair of the heart."

It's been my long and interesting experience that affairs of the heart usually start about two feet lower, but I didn't feel like getting into no esoteric philosophical argument, so I just allowed that affairs of the heart could be mighty heartfelt and that I hoped he hadn't been busted a rank or two in his outfit.

"Oh, he is retired," said Diego. He rummaged in his pocket for a minute, pulled out a crumpled business card, straightened it out, and read it: "Major Theodore Dobbins, late of His Majesty's armed forces."

"You want to say that name again?" I asked.

"Major Theodore Dobbins."

"Got a mustache?" I said. "Always dresses in black—shirt, pants, jacket, tie, socks, probably even his shorts?"

"That's the man!" said Diego. "I take it you know him?"

"Truth to tell, I'd kind of wished I was all through knowing him. What's he doing here?"

"He is engaged to marry the Baroness Abigail Walters."

"That don't sound like a name what goes with that title," I noted.

"She uses her maiden name, but in truth she is the widow of the Baron Gruenwald von Schimmelmetz," said Diego. "That makes her the richest woman in Bolivia, and the biggest land-owner as well. They say she is worth eight hundred million American dollars."

"Now ain't that amazing?" I said in wonderment.

"That a woman could be the richest citizen in Bolivia?" he asked.

I shook my head. "That Major Dobbins could sniff her out all the way from South Africa," I told him.

"He is a fortune hunter?" asked Diego.

"He's kind of like Frank Buck," I said. "He finds a rich widow and he brings her back alive. To start with, anyway."

"I strongly disapprove of that," said Diego, with a frown that wrinkled up his big bushy eyebrows. "Perhaps it is just as well that he has a rival for the Baroness's hand."

I was about to ask him how he'd figgered it out so fast, since I hadn't known myself until maybe half a minute ago, but he kept right on talking.

"Yes," he said, "at first I thought the Australian interloper was a fortune hunter himself, just out to make trouble. After all, when I queried Interpol I learned that he'd been a jewel thief in Hong Kong, a gigolo in Rajasthan, and the owner of a house of ill repute in the notorious Reeperbahn district of Hamburg. Still, he behaved with a courtesy befitting a gentleman of his social class while he was my guest here, and I feel he was genuinely sorry for shooting those three men in a fit of pique."

"I don't want to start no argument with you or ruin your high opinion of him," I said, "but most gentlemen of Rupert Cornwall's social class spend their last few minutes on earth dancing at the end of a rope."

"Then you know this Cornwall too?"

"We've run across each other a few times," I allowed. I hoped Diego had confiscated Cornwall's gun, since I couldn't be sure he'd forgotten our last couple of encounters, and he'd never struck me as the kind of man what hankered to be first in line to let bygones be bygones.

"Well, since arriving, he, too, is paying court to the Baroness."

"What does she look like?" I asked, since a man always ought to know that about the woman of his dreams.

"Ah, Señor," he said sadly, "Nature has not been kind to her. Her eyes do not always look in the same direction. Her nose... well, it reminds one of the proboscis monkey. She is missing her two front teeth on the top, and the Baron shot the only dentist in La Paz six years ago."

"And the rest of her?"

He shook his head. "She is hard in all the places a woman should be soft, flat in all the places a woman should be round, and soft in all the places a woman should be hard."

"But besides that, she's okay?" I said.

"I do not believe you have been listening to me," said Diego.

"Eight hundred million dollars buys a lot of make-up and padding and corsets," I said.

"It can't cover the wart on her nose, or the shrillness of her voice or the evil glint in her eyes (whatever direction they happen to be looking)," he said.

"Tread easy, there, Diego," I warned him. "You are speaking of the woman I intend to love."

He just shrugged. "You world-traveling English speakers are all alike. Show you the richest widow in the country, and you descend on her like..."—it was his turn to search for the right word—"like a pack of tarantulas."

"I didn't know they traveled in packs," I said.

"Until recently I didn't know *you* did either," he replied.

"You got it all wrong, Brother Diego," I said. "I'm the only one what's descending on the poor loveless lonely widow woman."

"What about Major Dobbins and Señor Cornwall?" he asked.

"They're belly-crawling scum what would have to *ascend* on her."

"I suppose that makes all the difference," he said without much sincerity.

"Sure it does," I said. "Besides, them two ain't got a chance next to a handsome young buck like me."

"*Young?*" he said, cocking a bushy eyebrow.

I thunk about it for a minute.

"Well, I was young when I started out on this here odyssey," I said. "I was only twenty-two when I was kind of forcibly asked to leave the U.S. of A."

"It took you a long time to get here," said Diego.

"I stopped at a few places along the way," I allowed. "I think I hit fourteen countries in Africa, before I was invited to depart and never come back. I guess I must have been twenty-six then."

"Which country asked you to leave?"

"All of 'em," I said.

"*All* of them?" he repeated.

"I don't play no favorites," I told him. "Anyway, I tried my hand in Asia next. China, India, Japan, all them other foreign places."

"How many?" he asked.

"Oh, maybe seven or eight. Could have been ten. Converted a lot of yellow and brown heathen before I left. Hope they stayed on the straight and narrow path I set 'em on."

"You could always go back and see," said Diego.

"And when eight or nine more judges and a couple of kings and sultans and maybe an emperor or two die, that's just what I plan to do," I said.

"They kicked you off the whole continent again?" he asked in amazement.

"Nobody kicked nobody," I said. "They just guv me a train ticket, pointed a battalion's worth of rifles at me, and wished me Godspeed on my way to Europe."

"How long were you there?"

"Five years."

"So you were thrown off three continents by the time you were thirty-one?" he said. "How about Europe?"

"Nice place," I said. "I was even king of my own country for a few days. I guess I must have visited, oh, maybe eleven or twelve countries. Real nice folk, except for them what wasn't. Most of 'em didn't speak no civilized language, and they were all godless sinners, but except for that we got along right well."

"And you were there for...?"

"Three years."

"It only took them three years this time?" he said, his eyes wide with wonder, and I could tell that even a man of the world like Diego was impressed.

"A series of minor misunderstandings, nothing more," I said. "One of these days I plan to go back and straighten them all out."

"And where have you been in South America?" asked Diego.

"Well, let's see," I said. "I landed in San Palmero in 1934, and then I hit Brazil, and Argentina, and the Pampas (wherever that is), and, let me see now, Uruguay...oh, and Columbia, and the Lost Continent of Moo, and..."

"The Lost Continent of Moo?" he interrupted.

"Well, it ain't as lost as it was," I assured him. "And now here I am in Bolivia, and I was on my way Peru before I heard about the grieving widow woman and my soft Christian heart just went out to her."

"But you haven't been to Chile?"

"Nope. Never felt any inclination to go there."

"You're sure?" he insisted.

"Yeah, I'm sure," I said. "Why?"

He mopped the sweat off his face and leaned back, suddenly all relaxed. "I have family in Chile," he said.

"Well, I suppose me and the bride could take our honeymoon there, if you got any notes or parcels you want me to deliver," I said.

"*NO!*" he shouted. I just kind of looked at him. "I would not want you to go to the trouble, Reverend Jones," he added quickly. "They say that Venezuela is beautiful for honeymoons this time of year."

"That's right generous of you, Brother Diego," I said. "And me and the little lady'll sure consider it. I also want to thank you for this little chat, because if we hadn't had it I'd never have realized I was getting on to thirty-seven, and while there ain't no question that I still look like a twenty-four-year-old movie star in his prime, I figger it's probably time to settle down, build my tabernacle, marry my heart's desire, and spend my next eighty or ninety years managing her money so she's free to do the dishes and wash the clothes and slop the hogs."

"What about your two rivals?" he asked.

"I'm a generous winner," I said magnanimously. "They can help with the hogs. What's the minimum wage in these here parts?"

He told me, but it was so small it didn't translate into dollars and cents, and then we finished our checkers game, and he checked the time—he didn't have no watch, but when the church bell rang fourteen times he knew it was either two in the afternoon or the bellringer was drunk again—and I'd served my time and I was a free man.

"So where is the Baroness's house?" I asked.

He pointed off in the distance. "On the other side of La Paz, Reverend Jones."

"Thanks," I said. "Next time me and the Good Lord are having a pow-wow, I'll put in a good word for you."

"Thank you," he said. "Remember: my name is Alejandro Sanchez."

"I thunk it was Diego something-or-other," I said.

"I changed it," he replied quickly. "Remember, when you are talking about me with God, I am Alejandro."

"Got it, Brother Alejandro," I said. "And good day to you."

I headed off toward La Paz, but we was at about ten thousand feet of altitude, and I found that even though I'm a natural athlete what's in great shape and smack-dab in the middle of his physical prime, I started getting leg-weary.

"Hey, Brother Alejandro!" I called. "I'm exhausted!"

"You have only walked forty paces," he noted.

"Call me a cab," I said.

He shrugged. "All right—you're a cab."

"Me and God don't appreciate no backtalking constabularies," I said. "Get me a horse or a wagon, or you're going to be cooking me meals for the next seventy years."

That got a little action, and a few minutes later I was being carted off to La Paz in the back of a hay wagon. (Well, they *called* it a hay wagon, but I'm pretty sure hay is stiff and grassy and doesn't smell like pig manure.)

We hit La Paz at about nine o'clock at night, and they didn't have no drunken bellringers in their church, because at eleven and a half thousand feet there wasn't nobody with the energy to climb up to the bell. In fact, it's my own guess that church bells grow naturally in Bolivia, like trees and bushes and such, since no one in their right minds would want to carry one that high.

I was more than a little hungry when the wagon dropped me off in town, and I saw from some sogns that I was on Matilde Street, which I planned to change to Lucifer & Abigail Street just as soon as we got hitched, and I walked a few paces, which wasn't no easier in La Paz at night than it was in Cochabomba in the afternoon, but finally, after enormous effort, I came to Bellisima's Ristorante, which was four buildings down from when I got off the wagon and seemed to have wandered over from Italy by mistake. I looked in a window and saw that all the tables were covered by checkered tablecloths, all the chairs were old and rickety, and all the waiters had thick black mustaches.

I figgered I had just enough money to buy myself a meal, and maybe a few quarts of beer to bring out the nuances of its flavor, so I walked through the doorway and who should I see sitting right in front of me but Major Theodore Dobbins, late of His Majesty's armed forces.

I walked right over and pulled up a rickety chair, which was the only kind they had.

"What the devil are *you* doing here?" he demanded.

"I was just passing through," I said. "Small world, ain't it?"

"*Too* damned small," he muttered.

"And how's your lovely wife, the former widow Emily Perrison?" I asked. "I ain't seen her in maybe twelve or thirteen years. Has she changed much?"

"Not in the past decade," answered the Major.

"Give her my regards."

"She's been dead for eleven years," he explained. "It seems she fell off a boat in crocodile-infested waters with no one to save her or pull her out."

"Poor thing," I said. "All alone, was she?"

"Except for me." He shook his head in wonderment. "To this day I don't know how the crocs could stand to get that close to her."

"Ain't you also got an adopted son?"

He nodded his head. "Horace. An ugly, foul-mouthed little brute if ever I saw one. I finally sent him off to military school."

"Back home to Britain?" I asked.

"The Soviet gulags. I figured he'd get the discipline he'd need there."

"You always was the caring sort," I said.

"And right now I care for the Baroness Walters," he said. Suddenly his eyes narrowed. "I don't know how you found out about her, but I won Emily's hand in marriage when you were my rival and I can do it again."

"I was young and immature then," I said. "And let's be honest: we wasn't neither of us interested in her hand except when it was signing checks. Besides, I hear you got another rival for the dear Baroness."

"That scoundrel Cornwall. A man of low moral standing and ill repute."

"Not like us, huh?" I asked.

"Precisely, my dear Doctor Jones," he said. "I am glad to see we understand one another."

"Better than you might think, Major," I said.

"I assume it has come to your attention that I am paying court to the Baroness Walters," he said.

"It ain't exactly escaped my notice," I told him.

"That blaggard Cornwall is trying to horn in on...let me rephrase that. He refuses to acknowledge my squatter's right to...um, that doesn't sound a lot better, does it?" He frowned for a minute. "At any rate, he has no business being here, and as the husband of the wealthiest woman in Bolivia, I would be very generous to any friend who sent that Australian mountebank on his way."

Actually, I was about to make the same offer to him, but I didn't see no sense getting into an argument when poor Miss Abigail was just wasting away with no one to love her, so I told him I'd sure consider it, and that a little down payment would put me in a charitable mood regarding his intentions, and he right away reached into his pocket and guv me a twenty-pound note.

I got up and took my leave of him, since if he was here it meant she was there and doubtless waiting to fall into the arms of any handsome man of the cloth who was ready and willing to sweep her off her feet (always assuming she didn't top out at more than one hundred and thirty pounds.)

I walked out into the street and realized I didn't know where the Baroness lived. I figgered I'd probably have to wait until daylight, and then head off to some house that probably looked a little bigger than the Chrysler Building, but as I was trying to decide whether to spend the night on a park bench or perhaps find an obliging lady of quality what left her mercenary streak in her other dress, I heard a voice calling to me. I turned to see where it was coming from, and it seemed to me that it was emanating from a tavern called *The Gelded Goliath*, what looked like it had been built about the time that David whipped the original Goliath in straight falls. I wandered over and went inside it, and the second I entered a hand grabbed my arm and pulled me aside, and a voice kind of hissed: "What the hell are *you* doing here?"

"You called me over, Brother Cornwall," I said, because the second I heard his voice I knew it was Rupert Cornwall, even though he didn't say "Cobber" or "bloke" or "kangaroo" nor nothing else in Australian.

"I mean, what are you doing in La Paz at all?" he demanded.

"Just enjoying the scenery," I answered.

"It's night out!"

"I was taking a walk and enjoying the cool night air," I said.

"We're at twelve thousand feet and you can barely *find* the air!"

"Would I be correct in assuming you are less than thrilled to see me again, Brother Rupert?" I asked.

"Of the ten people in the world I wanted never to lay eyes on again, you're at least three of them!" he snapped.

"You got to let go of them bygones, Brother Rupert," I said.

"Six of those bygones spent an entire afternoon beating the hell of out me in Hamburg!" he bellowed. "I had Lady Edith Quilton all wrapped up and ninety-eight percent delivered back in Rajasthan when you showed up! And thanks to you, I got to spend an extra four months in the Hong Kong jail!"

"But outside of that we've always been friends," I said.

"Those are the only times in my life I've ever been anywhere near you!"

"What about now?" I asked.

"What *about* now?" he repeated. "What are you doing here, as if I couldn't guess?."

"Actually, I was just having a friendly chat with my old friend Major Theodore Dobbins."

"How much did he offer you?"

"Not one red cent," I said. "I know I seem irresistible, but he hankers after women."

"He hankers after one woman in particular," said Rupert. "He's doomed to be disappointed."

"Must be quite a looker if you both want her," I said.

"I think I can truthfully say that there's not another one like her anywhere in the world," answered Rupert kind of carefully.

"So I've heard," I said.

"Then you know the woman of whom I'm speaking?"

"Not personally," I said. "Not yet, anyway."

"Not *ever*," said Cornwall. "I'm warning you, Lucifer—stay away from her."

"If I was you, I'd be more concerned with warning the Major," I said. "He seems to think he's got a prior claim on her."

"I'll make short work of him," said Rupert. "He thinks he's dazzling her with his credentials, but I happen to know he was cashiered out of His Majesty's armed forces, and he is wanted for dealing in certain perishable commodities in six African countries. What do you think of that?"

"So the other three dropped their charges, did they?" I replied.

"There were nine?" he asked, pulling out a pencil and a small notebook and starting to scribble away in it.

"Of course, he might have told her a little something about you," I said.

"I can explain every one of them!" he snapped. Then he paused and frowned. "Of course, the four underaged girls and the dead chicken might cause a little problem."

"So will the fact that you got the entire Greek and Turkish armies after you," I said. "First time they stopped shooting at each other in thirty years."

"I'll just tell her I made peace between those two warring nations," said Cornwall with a shrug. "Why bother her with unimportant details?"

I agreed that there wasn't no reason for him to recite all them details to the Baroness, since I planned to tell her about 'em first anyway, and we chatted about this and that, and finally he asked me how long I planned to stay in La Paz.

"Well, I'm really just on my way to this Macho place over in Peru..." I began.

"Macchu Pichu?" he asked

"The very spot," I said. "But I'm a little short of funds, so I guess I'm going to have to stick around La Paz until I can raise a grubstake, or maybe find a kind-hearted sponsor."

"Look no farther," said Cornwall. He reached into his pocket and pulled out a crumpled twenty, which he handed to me. "Have a safe trip. Be sure to write. Boy voyage. You might as well start now; there are no jaguars up this high."

"Why, that's right generous of you, Brother Cornwall, and I'd be less than a Christian gentleman of modesty and humility if I waited another second to start my trek to this here not-quite-lost empire."

And with that, I stuffed the bill in a pocket and headed out the door.

Now, it ain't generally known, but your body eventually adjusts to altitude, and after six days in Cochabomba and a night in La Paz, I was back in my vigorous prime and could walk almost a block without getting winded. I spotted a donkey hitched up in front of a bar, with a guy sitting on the wood sidewalk just in front of it, so I moseyed over and asked how much he wanted for the donkey.

"It is not mine to sell, Señor," he said.

"I didn't ask whose it was," I told him. "I asked how much you wanted for it?"

His whole expression changed, and a kind of happy glow came over his face.

"Ten dollars American, Señor?" he said hesitantly.

I shook my head. "It'll have to be twenty. I ain't got nothing smaller." Then I thunk on it for a minute. "For the other ten, you can tell me how to get to Baroness Walters' house."

"You mean her palace, Señor," he said.

"Yeah, that's what I meant," I said. "Slip of the tongue."

He told me where she was, unhitched the donkey and guv me the reins, and held out his hand for the money, and a minute later I was on my way to the biggest farm I ever did see. The fields didn't look like much, just a bunch of bushes with ugly leaves and no flowers nor corn nor anything interesting, but it spread out for miles. It took the donkey a good hour to make it up to the house, which might have been smaller than Buckingham Palace or that big art museum in Paris but I wouldn't bet on it.

A tall young guy with slicked down coal-black hair and matching eyes, and wearing a uniform that didn't seem to belong to no army I'd ever heard of, opened the door.

"Yes?" he said.

"Good morning to you, Brother," I said. "Is the Baroness in?"

"It is the middle of the night," he answered.

"It is?" I said. "How time flies. Especially up here, where it ain't got much air to hold it down."

"Who are you?" he said.

"I'm the Right Reverend Honorable Doctor Lucifer Jones, just back from curing a leper colony in Upper Volta."

"There *are* no lepers in Upper Volta," he said.

"Well, maybe I heard wrong and it was next to a leopard colony," I said. "Whatever it was, they was in a bad way until I comforted 'em with the Word of the Lord."

"What are you doing here?" he asked. "We have no lepers in La Paz."

"That's because they're afraid to come a-callin' when Lucifer Jones is on the job, passing out heavenly amnesty and salvation right and left," I said. "I've come to see the Baroness."

"I don't know if she'll see you," he said.

"She's been struck blind?" I asked. "Then we ain't got no time to waste. I'll recite the Psalm of Fifi over her, and lay my hand on her eyes and she'll be seeing normal again in no time. Well, in six months, anyway."

"The Psalm of Fifi?"

"My own updating of the Psalm of Sheba," I told him.

"I'm afraid you misunderstand, Doctor Jones."

"You mean she *can* see?" I said.

"Yes," he said.

That was a relief, because if she really had been struck blind she'd never be able to see how much better a figure I cut than the Major or Cornwall. In fact, it was such an open and shut contest that they probably should have made me wear a mask or something, the way the best racehorse has to carry extra weights.

"What's your name, son?" I asked him.

"Julio," he said.

"Well, Julio," I said, "why don't you take me to the Baroness right now? All I got's a hundred dollar bill, but if the Baroness can make change I'll catch you on the way out."

He led me to a staircase that could have held the whole London Philharmonic Orchestra, with room left over for the Mormon Tabernacle Choir, and we started climbing it. I had to stop three or four times to rest, but eventually we made it all the way up to the second floor, and we went down a corridor for maybe the length of a football field, and finally we came to a door that probably wasn't no more impressive that anything one of them Henrys or Louies ever hung on the royal bedroom, and Julio stopped and knocked on it.

"Come," said a voice that sounded kind of like a bullfrog in his death throes.

"Wait out here," I said to Julio, walking in and closing the door behind me.

I found myself in a study what had a huge desk and a bunch of fancy furniture with curving legs, all of it painted bright gold, and there was velvet wallpaper, and the kind of curtains you usually see as blankets in certain select New Orleans locations, and a ceiling about forty feet high, and a bunch of chandeliers, and standing by the desk was the Baroness Abigail Walters. I tried to think who she reminded me of, and finally it came to me: she looked exactly like a gorilla I saw in the Congo, right after he'd lost a disagreement with a family of lions. Which ain't exactly true neither, because his eyes stared straight ahead and he didn't have a wart the size of a walnut on his chin. Probably his arms were a little longer and his legs a little straighter, too, but I wouldn't bet serious money on it.

"What can I do for you?" said the Baroness.

"Good evening to you, ma'am," I said. "I'm the Right Reverend Lucifer Jones—"

"If you're here to fix the stove, it's downstairs," she said.

"No, ma'am, I definitely am not," I said.

"The leaky faucet, then?"

"No, ma'am."

"I could play guessing games all night, but I have a business to run," she said. "What *are* you here for?"

I'd come prepared, and I was ready with my fanciest lingo. "I've come to blight my troth, and sweep you away on a sea of passion," I said.

She just stared at me without saying a word.

"I realize you're awestruck, me being a handsome young buck what ain't never come courting before, but when you compare me to Major Dobbins or Rupert Cornwall, why, ma'am, I just know you'll throw yourself in my strong manly arms and beg me to take you away from all this."

"From all *what*?" she asked. I thought she kind of frowned, but with that low forehead of hers I couldn't be sure.

"From all this stuff you're growing. I walked by it on my way here, and you ain't got no corn nor wheat nor barley, just a bunch of stuff with leaves on it. That ain't no way to increase our family fortune, ma'am."

"Those leaves are the basis of *my* fortune," said the Baroness.

"Ma'am, I can tell you like a joke as much as the next Baroness, but I'm being serious here," I told her.

"You're in La Paz, and you *really* don't know what they are?" she said, looking about as surprised as a gorilla that's also an elegant Baroness can look. "Why, we've fought three wars over these leaves in the past five years. The American companies keep trying to drive me off my land."

"For a bunch of leaves?" I said.

"Coca leaves," she said.

"Cocoa?" I repeated. "Are you trying to tell me that all this fighting is over some hot chocolate franchise?"

"No, coca."

"That's what I said."

She shook her head. "You get chocolate from cocoa nuts. You get cocaine from coca leaves."

"Are you sure of that?" I asked her.

She just stared at me.

"And you're only worth eight hundred million dollars?" I continued. "Ma'am, I think it's more important than ever that you marry someone what's qualified to run your business. Being a man of the cloth, I could marry us first thing in the morning, or even tonight if you ain't all-fired anxious to sit down and sew yourself up a wedding gown."

She just kind of stared at me, pretty much the way that gorilla did before he lumbered off into the bush. "I must say that your approach is more novel than my other suitors, Reverend Jones."

"You can just call me Lucifer," I said. "Or Honeybunch, if you've a mind to, now that we're gonna get hitched. I know Rupert and the Major think they're engaged in a love triangle with you, ma'am, but I'm presenting myself as the fourth side of that there triangle."

"Are you always this direct and to the point?" she asked.

"Yes, ma'am, I am," I said. "Sloth is against the Eighth and the Fourteenth Commandments."

"There are only ten in my bible," she said.

"You probably got the condensed version," I told her. "It goes easy on all the begatting, too, but I'll give you the benefit of my vast worldly experience."

"Why do I get the feeling that I should check up on your worldly experience?" she said.

"A sweet young thing like you shouldn't worry your pretty little head over such matters, ma'am," I said. "If you're really concerned, *I'll* check up on me and give you a report."

"Is this the way you sweep them off their feet in America?" she asked.

"Why, ma'am," I said in injured tones, "that implies that I ever lost my heart to anyone else, whereas in truth I've been saving it just for you."

"What about your vast worldly experience?"

"Apples and oranges, ma'am," I explained. "I'm talking about hearts and you're talking about bodies."

"I do believe you are quite the most remarkable suitor I have ever had, Lucifer," she said.

"Why, thank you, Abigail," I said, bowing low, which guv me a chance to inspect the Persian rug I was standing on.

"Baroness," she corrected me.

"And now that we've reached an understanding, Miss Abby—"

"Baroness," she kind of growled.

"Baroness," I corrected myself, "I'll just invite them other two suitors to hit the road and I'll be back for your hand"—I guv her The Look—"and everything that goes with it."

I figgered that ought to at least get a happy little giggle from her, but instead she looked like she's just eaten some bad chili, and I made up my mind to restrict her diet to a couple of fruits and maybe a tomato or two, especially since she'd never miss a quick eighty or ninety pounds and it might even straighten up them legs a bit.

"Julio!" she hollered, and her houseboy showed up in about two seconds, still decked out in a jacket what was covered with braids and them little things what goes on the shoulders—paulettes, I think they call 'em, doubtless after some gorgeous dancer who also shook whenever she moved.

"Yes, Baroness?" said Julio.

"Show this gentleman out, please," she said.

I put my hand over my heart. "Until tomorrow, my love," I said. Then I figgered I ought to say something tender and romantic for her to remember me by, and I recollected a delicate love story Diego guv me to read while I was stuck in the calaboose, and I said, "My loins ache for your hot, pulsating flesh."

"Sounds painful," she said thoughtfully.

"Follow me, please," said Julio, leading me back down all them stairs and out the door. "We fed and watered your donkey," he added when we were outside.

"That's might thoughtful of you," I said, "but he could have just grazed at roadside on the way back to town."

"The last donkey who grazed at *this* roadside attacked and ate a pack of wolves," said Julio.

So, since he was going to be *my* servant too, and I wanted us to get off on the right foot, at least until I could replace him with some French maids in them cute little outfits I used to see in the mail order catalogs before the government shut them down, I thanked him for all his help and courtesy, let him boost me onto the donkey, and in another hour I was back in town.

Now that I'd met the future Mrs. Right Reverend Honorable Doctor Jones, I figured there was no sense sleeping in a park or on a bench, so when I hit Paseo El Prado Street, I pulled the donkey up outside the Sucre Palace Hotel, told the doorman I was donating him to the hotel, and went inside to get a room and charge it to the Baroness.

The lobby has a carpet, which was mighty rare in La Paz, and had been painted since the turn of the century, which was even rarer. A few guests were sitting on chairs and couches, their noses buried in newspapers.

"I thought you were leaving," said a voice with an Australian accent, and I turned to see Rupert Cornwall sipping a glass of something that could have been wine and might have been tequila and was mostly wet. He was sitting on a chair in the lobby, and I walked over to him.

"Howdy, Brother Rupert," I said. "I just came back from meeting the apple of your eye."

"And?" he said suspiciously.

"You've really and truly been smitten by Cupid's capricious arrow," I said. "You made her sound even prettier than she is."

He looked right relieved at that. "So you'll be on your way now?"

"Well, I could be, I suppose," I said. "But I thought you might need a second."

"A second *what*?" he said.

"Major Dobbins has challenged you to a duel to the death," I said.

"Oh, he has, has he?" said Cornwall. "When and where?"

"Sunrise, in that big empty field I crossed on my way here from Cochabomba."

"The one just south of town?" he asked, which was mighty useful information, since I'd been sleeping in the back of the wagon and didn't wake up until it dumped me in the center of town.

"The very one," I said.

"I accept!" he said. "Pistols at dawn!"

"I'll tell the Major the good news," I said. "Do you know where I can find him? I ain't seen him in a few hours now."

"He'll be at the Plaza de Lago, over on Aqua Millagro," said Cornwall.

"Plaza de Lago?" I repeated. "They ain't got no lakes nor plazas in La Paz."

"The restaurant next door advertises edible food," he said. "Signs in this town aren't always held to the highest standard of truth."

I thanked him, wished him good luck, and moseyed over to Aqua Millagro, which didn't have no aqua and no milla-gros that I could see, and hunted up the Plaza de Lago, where the desk clerk directed me to Major Dobbins, who was sitting on a stool in a bar what had seen better days and probably better centuries.

"I'd rather hoped I had seen the last of you," he said glumly.

"I'm just here on an errand of mercy, Major," I said.

"Oh?" he said, kind of suspicious-like.

"Yes. I think it's a good idea for you to leave town pronto, and maybe not stop until you're on a ship bound for Europe or some other big island where you can lose yourself in a crowd."

"What are you talking about?" he demanded.

"It seems that no-good Rupert Cornwall has challenged you to a duel at sunrise in the field south of town," I said. "If I was you, I'd be on the first horse, donkey, or wagon out of here."

"I absolutely will not run from a fight with that scoundrel!" announced the Major.

"I ain't telling you to run," I said. "I think you should ride. You'll make better time."

"Nonsense," he said. "What does he want—guns, swords, or fisticuffs?"

"Pistols at twenty paces, last I heard."

"Tell him I accept," said the Major.

I told him I'd do so, and wandered out into the street, feeling like I'd done a good night's work. I'd met the woman I was going to try to fall in love with at some far future date and marry a lot sooner, I'd tooken care of two sides of the love triangle, leaving just my side and the Baroness's side left, and it wasn't even midnight. I decided I might as well stop at a bar what wasn't frequented by no potential rivals for the Baroness's hand, and I entered the first one I came to, about half a block up from the Major's hotel—and who should I bump into but Diego?

"You're a long way from home," I said. "You after some notorious thief or killer?"

"I'm after some good liquor," he answered. "The stuff we get in Cochabomba is awful, Señor." He paused. "Have you run into your two old friends yet?"

"Funny you should mention it," I said. "They're having a duel to the death at sunrise. Let's spend the rest of night drinking, and then you can go arrest the winner."

Since he'd already gotten a head-start on the whiskey he allowed as to how that was a right practical idea no matter whose jurisdiction they killed each other in, and then he poured me a glass, and we spent a few hours reminiscing over old times, which was kind of strange because we only had six days of old times to reminisce about, but we made do, and finally I heard a rooster cock-a-doodling which either meant that the sun was about to come up or he'd sat on something really cold.

We left the bar and headed off to the field where the big gunfight was going to take place. When we got there, I saw thousands of white crosses planted in even rows.

"What the hell happened here?" I asked.

"This was the battlefield for the Chaco War three years ago," said Diego.

"I never thunk one lone Marx Brother could do so much damage," I said, looking at all the crosses.

"You misunderstand, my friend," said Diego. "This was a war between Bolivia and Paraguay, and…"

He might have droned on about for another hour, but just then the Major approached from the east and a minute later Rupert Cornwall began walking toward us from the west. They stopped about five feet from each other, glaring and snarling.

"All right," said the Major. "We have to set the ground rules."

"Ground rules?" scoffed Cornwall. "There are no ground rules in a duel to the death."

The Major suddenly had a gun in his hand and pointed it between Cornwall's eyes. "What the hell," he said. "Have it your way."

"*Wait!*" shouted Cornwall. "I've just reconsidered! We can have rules!"

"Damn!" muttered the Major, lowering his service revolver. "All right, what are they?"

"We stand back-to-back, walk ten paces, turn, and fire," said Cornwall.

"I agree to your rules," said the Major.

"I'm not done, yet," said Cornwall. "Since this was your challenge, you have to wear a blindfold."

"It was *your* challenge!" snapped the Major.

"Liar!" yelled Cornwall.

"Blackguard!" yelled the Major.

"Take that back!" snapped Cornwall.

"Never!" bellowed the Major.

"I challenge you to a second duel," said Cornwall. "Just in case you live through the first."

"I accept!" said the Major. "And after I kill you with my pistol, I'm going to take great pleasure killing you with my sword."

I turned to Diego. "I seen these guys in action," I whispered. "We'd better move a little farther away."

"They're *that* deadly?" he replied, kind of awestruck.

"None deadlier," I said, increasing my pace until we came to a couple of huge old trees. "We ought to be safe standing behind these." I looked behind me, and saw that the Major and Cornwall were already standing back to back, each holding a pistol in his hand, and I could tell by the bulges under their coats that the Major had two more in criss-crossed shoulder holsters and Cornwall had one in his pants pocket and another tucked in his belt.

They agreed to take ten steps, turn, and fire, but they must have forgot how tired they'd get at this altitude, because the Major stopped at eight paces and turned, his gun blazing. But Cornwall must have got himself winded even sooner because he was already shooting.

Me and Diego hid behind our trees until they'd each emptied all their weapons.

"How can they still be standing?" he whispered to me as the last shots echoed through the thin air.

"Nobody provided 'em with chairs," I said.

"I mean, aren't they riddled with bullets?" he asked.

"Well, *something* must be riddled with bullets," I said. "Let's go take a look."

So we did. The final score was 23 dead llamas, two dead donkeys, eleven dead birds, and a badly crippled tree. Diego arrested them both and carted 'em off to jail until he could wire the S.P.C.A. to pick 'em up for crimes against Nature, which differed from the usual crimes against Nature that make such interesting reading on hot summer nights.

As for me, now that my rivals were out of the way, I hopped the first llama I could find that was still breathing and intact, headed him toward the Baroness's farm, and an hour and a half later I was walking up to her house.

A different young man answered the door.

"Are you here for the celebration?" he asked, and I noticed that there was a ton of cars, horses, and donkeys parked around the side of the house.

"News sure travels fast in these here parts," I said. "So she heard already?"

"You misunderstand, my friend," said the man. "This is her wedding day."

"Right," I said. "And I'm the happy bridegroom."

He threw back his head and laughed. "You Americans have such a wonderful sense of humor!"

"We do?" I said.

"Yes," he said. "She just married Julio half an hour ago."

"Just how the hell many sides did this here triangle have?" I muttered.

"I don't understand," said the man.

But me, I understood all too well. I'd opened my heart to the Baroness, and instead of reciprocating by opening her bank account to me, she'd married this mere child what didn't know nothing about business and was probably preparing to sell her latest crop to some soft drink company instead of certain select families what knew how to treat a negotiation with respect.

Once more the fickle finger of Fate had flang down its gauntlet, and once more geometry had triumphed over love. I stayed just long enough to fill my pockets with grub to last me five or six days, and then I proceeded on my lonely way to the lost kingdom of Macchu Pichu, where I figgered to overcome my broken heart by setting myself up as Emperor, corral a few naked High Priestesses, and plunder the treasury six ways to Sunday.

THE FORGOTTEN KINGDOM

'd been told that it was just a good stretch of the legs from La Paz over in Bolivia to Cusco in Peru. Upon sober reflection, it was probably the same guy what told me that Babe Ruth couldn't hit the ball out of the park, or that Equipoise was just a great big brown milkhorse in disguise.

One of the problems with La Paz, which I related in my last thrilling narrative that I'm sure you've all read fifteen or twenty times by now, is that it's a trillion feet high, even though the guide book claims it's only eleven thousand feet above sea level. What it mostly was was about nine thousand feet above air level, so I didn't make my usual sterling progress. Whenever I'd complain about this to one of the locals, he'd just shrug and make mention of Andy's, as if some guy named Andy had a tavern or a boarding house and was using up all the air, which didn't make a lot of sense to me.

Anyway, I'd come to Peru because I'd heard tell of this here lost city called Macho Something-or-other, which sounded just perfect for a manly man like myself, the kind of place what was filled with men of low character and charming ladies of easy virtue, and if you're in the soul-saving business like I was, why, you got just to have a bunch of sinners to start the day with or you're out of business almost before you begin.

The word on the grapevine was that this Macho city had been discovered by Pizarro. I figgered they was referring to Billy Pizarro, who'd been run out of Deadwood by Doc Holliday back in 1882 and wasn't never seen again, doubtless because no one had thunk to look for him in a South American mountain chain. And if the town was discovered as recent at 1882, which was only 56 years ago, it might very well have indoor plumbing and running water and maybe even a tavern or two, all of which would be right handy when I finally built my tabernacle.

I was about 50 miles across the Bolivian border into Peru when I came upon a little village, so I stopped to see if any of 'em had a Willys Jeepster to trade for advance absolution for a month of serious sinning, but none of 'em had ever heard of one, and they wasn't no better educated about the existence of the Dusenberg. Finally one of 'em offered me a llama. Well, it wasn't no car, of course, but we negotiated a bit, and while I couldn't absolve him of the mortal sin of murder—he was thinking of doing in a matched set of his wife and her mother—I absolved him of a batch of them little venereal sins. The llama was kind of dirty and kind of smelly and kind of foul-tempered, and I decided I wasn't going to waste no good Christian name on him, so I made his first name The and his middle name Dolly.

I rode The Dolly Llama across what passed for the countryside, stopping here and there to grab a few fruits and berries—I knew they was safe because any poison would just naturally have to lose its punch at 94 billion feet of altitude—and finally we stumbled into a sleepy little Spanish-looking town called Cusco that didn't stay sleepy for long, because we hadn't been there two minutes before the bell in the church tower rang six times and because I knew there wasn't enough air for there to be no wind at this altitude it had to mean it was six o'clock, and since I hadn't et since four o'clock I'd worked up a powerful appetite.

I stopped at a restaurant called Rosario's. Now, there'd been a Rosario's back in La Paz, too, so I figgered either there was a pair of twins and the mother couldn't tell 'em apart so she named 'em both Rosario, or else one was really called Russell or Rossellini but flunked spelling in school. It didn't make any difference, though, hungry as I was, so I just sat down at a table and a minute later a little feller wearing a stained white jacket walked up and shot me a great big smile.

"Greetings, Señor," he said. "May I offer you a llama steak on an uncooked potato?"

"I'm more in the mood for a T-bone, or maybe some pork chops," I said. "You got any?"

"Yes," he said. "Provided that you won't mind if it looks and tastes like llama steak."

"I suppose your lobster looks and tastes like llama steak too?" I said.

He smiled and nodded.

"It all costs the same too?" I asked.

"Yes, Señor."

"Then shoot the works!" I said. "I'll have pheasant under glass."

He saluted, went back to the kitchen, and brung out my pheasant about twenty seconds later. It looked exactly like llama steak on an uncooked potato.

"And now for the *pièce de résistance*," he announced, holding an empty beer mug over the plate.

"What in tarnation are you talking about?" I asked him.

"The glass," he answered.

Well, I proceeded to dig in. The pheasant needed to have some of the hair removed from its wings, but I could see where all that dead hair might have been a fire hazard, so it was probably just as well that nobody'd thought to cook it. Finally I'd had my fill—one mouthful pretty much did the trick—and I looked around at the other diners, and I finally spoke up and said: "Anyone here got any notion of where I can find this Macho place?"

Two flighty young men wearing a lot of satin got up and walked out with their noses in the air, but an old geezer at the next table said, "Are you perchance talking about Machu Picchu?"

"My name ain't Perchance," I said, "but beyond that you hit it right on the button."

"Why are you looking for it?" he asked me.

"I hear it's a forgotten kingdom, and that means it ought to be in serious need of spiritual comfort," I told him.

"Are you a preacher man?" he said.

"Sure as hell am," I answered. "And meaning no offense, you don't sound like no Peruvian, or Perimander, or whatever these here people call themselves."

"Actually, my name is Jasper MacCorkle," he said. "Iowa born and bred. And you are...?"

"The Right Reverend Honorable Doctor Lucifer Jones," I replied.

"What religion do you preach?" asked Jasper.

"One me and the Lord worked out betwixt ourselves of a Sunday afternoon back in Moline, Illinois," I told him.

"Why, we're practically neighbors!" he said.

"And what brings you to Peru?" I asked.

"I got word of Machu Picchu back when I was laying tar on a road just outside Jackson, Mississippi, and I figured that if I was ever going to become emperor of my own kingdom, this was as good a time as any," said Jasper.

"So you just dropped everything and came on down?" I said.

"Well, I had to get out of my leg irons first, and to lose that damned striped suit, but yes, as soon as I could I made a beeline for Machu Picchu."

Which was exactly when I knew we were gonna hit it off.

"I can't see no reason why we shouldn't go plunder this here forgotten kingdom together, can you, Brother Jassper?" I said. "I mean, there's got to be more gold and precious stones than one man can carry, no matter how hard he tries."

"I can always use a partner who's got a head on his shoulders," said Jasper. Suddenly he frowned. "But it's got to be understood on the front end that *I* get to be king."

"That don't pose no problem for me at all, Brother Jasper," I told him, which was true, since I figgered that being a white god was probably higher on the employment ladder than being a king, and so long as he didn't try to stake no claims to no gorgeous half-naked High Priestesses we'd get along just fine.

"I suppose we can set out for it right now, if you're done with your"—he stared at my plate—"whatever it is."

"So is Machu Picchu far from here?" I asked him.

"About fifty miles as the crow flies," he replied. "Of course, crows can't fly at this altitude. They mostly crawl and gasp for air a lot."

Now, if we'd been on foot, that would have been a perfect description of us after the first two hundred yards, but I was riding The Dolly Llama, and Jasper was atop a donkey he called Man o' War but which should have been called Equipause, because he paused to nibble every single green thing he could find at roadside, which was a lot of green things since there wasn't hardly no road at all.

"Who lives in this here forgotten kingdom?" I asked as we made our way out of Cusco.

"Mostly a bunch of Indians, and a few professors from Yale," he told me.

"Indians?" I said. "You mean like unto Geronimo and Sitting Bull and that whole crowd? You know, I was wondering why I never ran into them back in Illinois."

"No, you're thinking of the wrong kind of Indian, Lucifer," said Jasper.

"What kind lives here?" I asked.

"Inca."

"You're welcome," I said. "But you didn't answer my question."

"Inca," he said again.

"You got something caught in your throat, Brother Jasper?" I asked.

"That's the name of the tribe," he said. "Inca. They live in the forgotten kingdom."

"Yeah?" I said. "I notice that the Indians around here are little bitty fellers. It shouldn't be no trouble tossing 'em out of our city and all the way back to Cusco. How many of 'em are there?"

He shrugged. "Thousands. Maybe tens of thousands."

I frowned. "You know about it. I know about it. Folks in La Paz know about it. Everyone in Cusco knows about it. A bunch of Yale perfessors know about it. Tens of thousands of Indians know about it. Just who the hell was this kingdom forgotten by?"

"Well, let's hope the answer to that is fortune hunters," said Jasper, and I sure couldn't argue none with that.

We passed the Los Portales Hotel, which was about the only hotel in town back in those days, and he asked me if I wanted to stop and pick up my suitcase and possessions, since we figured to be a few days pulling gold and diamonds and stuff out of Machu Picchu, and he even offered to distract the desk clerk so I didn't cause him no undue consternation by checking out and making him think I disapproved of my room.

"Thanks for the offer, Brother Jasper," I said, "but the truth of the matter is that I ain't got no room yet. Me and The Dolly Llama just blew into town about an hour ago."

"So where's your goods?" he asked.

"Us men of the cloth travel light," I told him.

"So they ran you out of your last town too?" he said with a smile.

I denied it vigorously, mostly because no one could run at this altitude, and we kept heading for the forgotten city, passing a bunch of Indians who were walking to and from it and didn't seem to have no trouble remembering it at all.

Along the way Jasper told me the long, tragic series of events that had ended with him working on a Mississippi chain gang, and

I allowed that his little problems with the bank and the grocery store and all them poor innocent bystanders could clearly be seen as a series of misunderstandings, but even me and the Lord had some trouble buying his excuse about how he wound up with the fourteen-year-old Siamese twins.

Then he asked me about myself, so I briefly told him about my adventures in Africa and my exploits in Asia and my encounters in Europe, adding only a few poetic flourishes.

"That is a *lot* of land masses to be told never to come back to," he said and I could tell, one man of the world to another, that even he was impressed—and that was before I told him he could add North America to the list.

It took us two days of traveling—llamaback and donkeyback ain't the quickest way of getting anywhere—and finally we came to this big river.

"Urubamba," said Jasper.

"I think he used to play right tackle for Notre Dame," I said. "Or maybe I'm remembering the drummer for Xavier Cugat. What about him?"

"No," he said, pointing to the river. "*That* is the Urubamba, and Machu Picchu is on the other side of it."

Now, as far as I could tell, neither The Dolly Llama nor Equipause came equipped with wings or fins, and it sure looked like they were going to need one or the other to get us across the river, but Jasper didn't look distressed. He just pointed about half a mile upstream, and sure enough there was a rope bridge across the Urubamba.

Now, if you ain't never walked across a river on a rope bridge, let me tell you that it ain't the steadiest way to get from one place to another, or even the forty-third steadiest now as I come to think about it. But somehow we managed, and suddenly we stepped around a corner, which Jasper insisted on calling a bend, and there was the forgotten kingdom of Machu Picchu laid out in all its glory.

"See that big building?" said Jasper. "That's the Temple of the Son."

Since I didn't want to sound ignorant, I asked him to point out the Temple of the Daughter, but he just stared at me for a minute and then began pointing out the other sights, like the Room of the Three Windows, which was in what they called the Sacred District. I asked what was so sacred about it, and he explained that that was where they sacrificed warriors and virgins, occasionally at the same time when they caught 'em doing something that I planned to reserve only for gods just as soon as I set the kingdom straight on a few matters.

We moseyed over to the Temple of the Son, which I later found out was really the Temple of the Sun, which sounds alike but has a whole different set of false doctrines attached to it. Nobody paid us much attention, and I didn't see no college types at all, unless they'd shed their clothes and taken to wearing loincloths, which in my broad and vast experience is not something college types are really inclined to do, and then we were inside the Temple, and truth to tell it didn't look a whole lot better from close up.

"These here folk are even more backward than I thunk," I allowed. "What kind of religion ain't got a half-naked High Priestess or two roaming around the temple, or at least some Heavenly Handmaidens what are dressed for extremely warm weather?"

"Keep your mind on business, Lucifer," said Jasper.

"I'm a man of the cloth and half-naked High Priestesses *are* my business," I told him.

Well, we explored every corner of that temple, and couldn't find a single gold nugget, let alone any ten-carat diamonds, or even any paltry little five-carat ones, and I began thinking that maybe there was a reason everyone went out of their way to forget Machu Picchu. By the time we'd examined the Room of the Three Windows I was wondering why anyone would come all the way from Yale just to look at this place. I'd been in a *lot* of rooms what had more than three windows in 'em, and no one was racing to make *them* into national shrines.

"What do you think, Lucifer?" said Jasper. "Should we keep looking or take a rest?"

What I was thinking was that Billy Pizarro could have saved us all a lot of trouble if he'd just stuck around Deadwood and shot it out with Doc Holliday, but before I could say anything something happened that changed my whole view of Machu Picchu, because suddenly I was looking at the most beautiful woman I'd ever seen (at least since the last most beautiful woman I'd ever seen), and far from being a half-naked High Priestess she was a ninety-eight percent naked High Priestess, and the only thing she was wearing besides a smile was a gold headdress with the biggest diamond I'd ever seen in a long lifetime of admiring big diamonds.

"She's mine!" whispered Jasper. "I saw her first!"

"Sorry to disappoint you, Brother Jasper," I said, "but the church has first call on her."

"What church?" he demanded.

"The Tabernacle of Saint Luke," I answered.

"Never heard of it."

"Well, it ain't quite got itself built yet," I said, "but if you'd like to make a donation..."

"I'm not donating anything," he said heatedly. "And who is Saint Luke?"

"You're looking at him," I answered.

"I thought you were Lucifer."

"You've be surprised how few people donate to a tabernacle named Saint Lucifer," I said.

"We're getting off the subject," said Jasper, "said subject being that I got first claim on her."

"You can argue that with the High Priest," I said.

"High Priest?" he repeated. "I don't see any High Priest."

"You're still looking at him," I answered.

"Why don't we leave it up to her?" he said, but I could tell that the second the words left his mouth he started having second thoughts, which figgered for a guy who hadn't shaved all month and hadn't showered since Babe Ruth was still pitching for the Boston Red Sox.

Still, womenfolk can be flighty at best, and a naked High Priestess figured to be even flightier than most, so I wasn't any more eager to let her do the choosing than he was. In fact, I was all set to suggest we avoid a religious war by just cutting a deck of cards for her when she saw us and walked over, which is not exactly right because part of her walked and some of her bounced and the rest kind of undulated.

"I have not seen you here before," she said by way of greeting.

"Hello, ma'am," said Jasper, who didn't have no hat to tip so he reached up and tipped some of his hair, of which he had an awful lot to tip since he clearly wasn't on speaking terms with his barber. "My name's King Jasper, and I'm pleased to make your acquaintance."

"*King* Jasper?" she repeated. "Are you visiting from a distant land?"

"No, ma'am," said Jasper. "I was kidnapped as an infant, and I've come back to claim my rightful throne."

Her face lit up in a great big smile. "Our legends said that one day our vanished king would return and live in our midst! This shall be a day of celebration! What may I call you?"

"A simple Your Highness will do," said Jasper, shooting me a triumphant grin.

She turned to me. "Are you with King Jasper?"

"*With* him?" I said. "I *created* him."

She frowned. "What are you talking about?"

"I'm the god of Machu Picchu, come back to see how all my creations are doing," I said.

She immediately dropped to her knees. "How do I address you?" she asked.

"Lord'll do," I said. Then I thunk about it and said, "Ah, what the hell—since you're my Apprentice Goddess, you can call me Lucifer."

"Apprentice Goddess?" she said, looking half pleased and half scared.

"Just put yourself in my hands and you won't have a thing to worry about," I said, returning Jasper's grin. "You got a name?"

"Don't you know it?" she said. "After all, you made me."

"I got a lot on my mind, what with creating the moon and the stars and trying to get the Chicago White Sox out of last place," I told her. "Why don't you just tell me?"

"I am Culamara," she said.

"You certainly are," I said admiringly. "Especially when you breathe in. But what's your name?"

"Culamara is my name," she said. Suddenly she frowned. "Are you *sure* you're a god?"

"If I ain't, how do I know that Jasper's going to try to convince you to go away with him?"

"Don't you listen to him, Culamara baby," said Jasper. "You're *my* loyal subject."

"But she's *my* Apprentice Goddess," I said. "You give me any of your lip, I'll turn you into an insect and step on you."

"Yeah?" Jasper shot back. "Well, I'll have you arrested for impersonating a god."

"Just you try it," I said. "Anyone touches a god, it means an instant transfer to the fiery pits of hell."

"Then you'd better not touch your Apprentice Goddess," he said.

"Goddesses are a different union," I told him.

"Who says?"

"Me," I answered.

"You don't make the rules, Lucifer!" yelled Jasper.

"Of course I do," I hollered back. "I'm God!"

Well, by this time we'd drawn quite a little crowd. Half of 'em knelt down to worship me, and the other half decided I was a false god, or at least an out-of-town one, and began to threaten me with their spears, with Jasper encouraging them every step of the way.

Finally one of the ones what had been kneeling approached me, being careful never to look me in the eye.

"What are we to do, Inti?" he said.

"I ain't your Auntie," I said.

"*Inti*," he repeated. "You are Inti the Sun God, the greatest god of all."

"I'm glad *someone's* been paying attention," I said.

"What shall we do with this false king?" he asked.

"Well, you know what they say," I told him. "Render under the false Caesar the things what are the false Caesar's, and render unto Inti the things what are mine."

"I don't wish to appear unduly ignorant, O Inti," he said, "but what things are yours?"

"If I'm the Sun God, the Temple of the Sun is mine, ain't it?"

"Yes, Inti."

"Then throw them unbelievers from Yale out of it or start charging them rent."

"It will be done, O Inti. What else is yours?"

"The most beautiful High Priestess I ever saw in a long lifetime of admiring naked High Priestesses," I answered.

"And who is that, Inti?" he asked.

"Culamara," I said.

"Her?" he said contemptuously. "But she is merely the local woman of ill repute."

"Well, her repute is about to get a lot better," I said. "I'm teaching her the goddess trade."

"*Her?*" he repeated incredulously. "But why?"

Which was when I figgered out that the men who'd left may have forgotten the kingdom of Machu Picchu, but them what stuck around had clearly forgotten something even more important.

"She's a goddess and she's mine," I said. "Don't go tempting my heavenly wrath."

"What shall we do with the pretender to the throne, Inti?"

"What's your name?" I asked.

"Giroba, Inti."

"Okay, Giroba," I said. "You guys ever sacrifice any virgins? I mean like on an altar?"

"Of course, Inti," Giroba answered. "Are you not pleased with the ones we select?"

"I got no complaints," I said. "I'm gonna sacrifice 'em in my own unique way from now on. But what I want to know is: where is this here altar at?"

"Why, in the Monumental Mausoleum, Inti," he said, frowning. "But surely you know that."

"Of course I do," I said quickly. "I was just testing you. Why don't you take False King Jasper over there, tie him down good and tight, and I'll be along after I give Culamara her first lesson in the goddess biz and decide what to do next with him?"

"It shall be as you say, Inti," said Giroba. He nodded to all the other men what was busy worshipping me and they all held their spears and bows and knives at the ready.

But nobody moved, and finally he said to me, "Uh...Inti?"

"Yeah?" I responded.

"We have a little problem, Inti."

I turned in the direction he was pointing, and knew immediately that he was dead wrong. What we had was a *big* problem, because them what wasn't worshipping me had been busy pledging their loyalty to Jasper, and suddenly he had as many armed men on his side as I had on mine.

"You are Inti, the Sun God," said one of the men near me. "Wave your hand and wipe them out of existence."

"I'd like to," I said, "I truly would. But I threw my shoulder out of whack hurling all them moons into orbit around Jupiter, and it's so wobbly now that if I tried to wave it I'd be just as likely to miss them and send *you* all straight down to Hades, or maybe Ephrata, Pennsylvania, whichever comes first."

They all backed up and spread out right quick.

"Then curse the False King," said Giroba, who was becoming a real nuisance.

"You sure that's what you want me to do?" I asked.

"Yes, Inti!" said a couple of hundred warriors in unison. "Curse him!"

"Okay," I said. "What god wouldn't answer a heartfelt prayer like that?" I turned and faced the other side. "Jasper MacCorkle," I intoned, "you are a dadgummed ding-dong ribbityflabberting sonuvabitch!"

"Uh...we had in mind something a little more godly," said another of my followers.

"Look," I said, "I'm the Sun God and the sun's behind a cloud right now. Just take what you can get."

"Lucifer," Jasper yelled at me, "you relinquish all claims to Culamara or this means war!"

"Yeah?" I yelled back. "Who elected *you* king?"

"King isn't an office you run for," he said. "I'm king by birth and by the grace of..." He stopped and frowned.

"Go on and finish that sentence," I said. "I dare you!"

"Damn it, Lucifer, I saw her first!"

"Your problem is that she saw me second, so she had something to compare you with," I shot back.

"I'm not kidding, Lucifer," he hollered. "I'm telling you by all that's holy to me, I'm willing to go to war over her."

I turned to my followers. "Did you hear that?" I said. "I ain't holy to him. What do we do with unbelievers in these here parts?"

"Educate them?" said one.

"Forgive them?" offered another.

"Convert them?" suggested a third.

"We kill 'em!" I shouted.

"But they outnumber us," said one.

"On the other hand, we have Inti on our side," Giroba reminded them.

"Hey, that's right!" said another. "Will you lead us into battle, Inti?"

"I'd love to lead you brave men into battle," I said, "but my lumbago has been acting up lately, and besides, us Sun Gods work best in an advisory capacity."

I looked across the temple, and I could see that Jasper wasn't doing no better with his constituency.

"Goddammit!" he was shouting. "I'm your emperor! When I tell you to take up arms, you've got to do what I say!"

"I thought you were just our king," said one of them.

"I promoted myself!" he yelled. "Now go kill that false god!"

"Can't the two of you just talk things over?" said another.

"The time for talking's come and gone," said Jasper. "You're my army. Go kill him!"

"Actually," said a third one, "I never signed any enlistment papers."

"You know these emperors and gods," said another one. "They're never happy unless all us mere mortals are busy killing each other."

"Did you hear that?" I said to my followers. "They're afraid of you!"

"Well, that makes sense," said Giroba. "*We're* afraid of *them*, too."

"Ain't none of you gonna fight when I, Inti, the Sun God, tell you to?"

"It's nothing personal, Inti," said Giroba.

"Right," said another. "We all worship you, and we're thrilled that you've taken human form and come down to pay us a visit, and if you want the harlot with the big...well, you know...you can have her and good luck to you and we hope you live happily ever after—but I don't see why I should kill my brother-in-law because you couldn't find a piece of what you wanted up in heaven."

I looked over at Jasper, and he wasn't having no better luck rallying his troops.

"Hey, Lucifer," he called. "You want to trade armies?"

While I was considering it, I heard my men muttering things like, "Hey, that's a great idea!" and "Yeah, I wouldn't feel so guilty about disobeying a mere emperor."

Finally I faced Jasper's men. "What about it?" I said. "Are you guys willing to fight on the side of Inti, the Sun God?"

"If we come over to your side, who is there left for us to fight?" asked one of 'em.

"Us!" said a bunch of my men.

I could see that swapping armies wasn't going to solve nothing, and then my Silent Partner hit me right betwixt the eyes with one of His timely revelations, and I turned back to my men.

"This is the last time I'm going to ask," I said. "Are you going to destroy the enemy army and kill that pretender to the throne or ain't you?"

"Thank goodness you're all through asking!" said Giroba with a sigh of relief.

"Yeah," said the man standing next to him. "What'll we talk about now?"

"All right," I said. "If you won't fight, you won't fight." Then I played my ace in the hole. "When I tell this to my brother, the God of Impotence, he's gonna want a list of all your names. Giroba, you want to start writing 'em down for me?"

Suddenly every member of my army was waving his weapon and screaming for Jasper's blood.

"If it's war you want, it's war you'll get!" hollered Jasper. He turned to his men. "Anyone who fights for me gets to share in the spoils after we win."

"What spoils?" asked one of them.

"Her!" he said, jerking a thumb in Culamara's direction.

Suddenly his army was screaming for blood even louder than mine was.

The two armies started moving forward, yelling and cursing and brandishing their weapons, when suddenly Culamara stepped between them and held up her hand.

"Stop!" she cried.

Everybody stopped and stared at her, and at least three or four men on each side drooled a little bit too.

"I cannot have all this bloodshed on my behalf," she said. "What if I choose which of these two, your god or your emperor, shall have me?"

I looked at Jasper, and he looked at me, and I could tell he was comparing us feature by feature. I knew I had him beat cold on manly good looks, and I'm sure if I'd had a chance to shave or wash or change my clothes in the past few weeks I'd clean up pretty well, but women are a peculiar bunch, and you have to figure that a woman who walked around naked in the midday sun was a little more peculiar than most, and I decided that I didn't really want to stake my godhood on her ability to make the obvious choice, and I could see that Jasper had pretty much reached the same conclusion.

"Well, that solves everything, doesn't it, Inti?" said Giroba.

"Not really," I said.

"Not at all," Jasper chimed in.

"But why not?" asked Culamara.

"Ma'am," I said, "in the course of my life I've seen two dogs fight over a bone a couple of hundred times, maybe more," I said. "But man and boy, I ain't never seen the bone choose who it wants to win."

"That's a telling point, Miss Culamara," said Jasper. "He's a tricky one, this Lucifer. If you were to vote, he might very well pull the wool over your eyes, and while that would still leave all the good parts in evidence, it would surely hamper your ability to make the right decision, which would otherwise be to choose me."

"The fact of the matter, ma'am," I said, "is that while you are the most perfect creature God—I mean *I*—ever made, when all is said and done you're just a woman, and these matters are better left to gods and emperors."

"Okay," said Jasper to his followers. "The first one to bring me Lucifer's head is the first one to share in the spoils!"

"I still don't know why she can't just choose and settle the war that way," said one of his men.

"I already explained that," said Jasper. "Right, Lucifer?"

"Right, false emperor," I said.

"*I* have an idea," said Giroba. "Since *she* can't choose, why don't *we* all vote?"

"Hey, that's a great idea!" said one of the guys on Jasper's side of the temple. "That way nobody gets killed!"

Jasper and I done our best to talk them out of it, but they were bound and determined to avoid a war by voting, despite the fact that it never did a bit of good in Europe or anywhere else, and pretty soon they were passing out ballots, and then everyone voted and handed the ballots in and then a bunch of men from each side started counting and double-checking while Jasper and I couldn't do nothing but stand around and see which of us had won the election.

"I have the results," announced Giroba, and we all leaned forward to hear. "There were three hundred and eighty-six votes cast"—suddenly he frowned—"and it appears that we have a three-hundred-and-eighty-six-way tie."

"Just a minute," I said. "I ain't voted yet."

"What difference will that make?" demanded Jasper. "I haven't voted either. But you'll vote for you, and I'll vote for me, and nothing will change."

"That's what you think," I said. "I am hereby issuing a heavenly decree. Gods get one and a half votes."

"Then I'm issuing an executive order," declared Jasper. "Emperors get two votes."

"And I'm issuing a commandment," I said. "Thou shalt vote for no other god but me."

"And I'm writing a new constitution," said Jasper. "From this day forward, Machu Picchu is a secular society and our first principle is the separate of church and state."

"What does that mean?" asked one of his followers.

He pointed to me. "See that god?" he said. "He's got a head and he's got a body. Separate 'em!"

The man put one hand over his mouth and clasped his belly with the other. "I think I'm going to be sick!" he whined.

"Well, this has all been a lot of fun," said one of my men. "I can't remember when I've been so amused. But I still have fields to harvest. I'd better be getting back to work."

"Yeah," said another. "Entertainment is all very well, but we have to make a living."

"And I promised my wife I'd pick up some spices at the market," said a third.

"Let's go over to the Urubamba," said a fourth. "The fish should be biting in another half hour."

Jasper's army started saying the same kind of thing, and pretty soon they were all wandering off in twos and threes, and after five minutes the pair of us were alone with Culamara again.

"Well, Miss Culamara, ma'am," I said, "come on along with me and I'll get busy teaching you the white goddess trade."

"He doesn't know the first thing about being a god," said Jasper. "Come with me and I'll make you Executive Vice President and Social Director."

"Ask him what the job pays and where he's gonna get the money," I told her.

"It's an empire, isn't it?" Jasper shot back. "We'll plunder the treasury."

"It's a *forgotten* empire," I pointed out. "It ain't got no treasury."

"How do you know?" demanded Jasper. "Maybe the folks who left forgot to take the money with them."

"They'd have to be mighty forgetful to leave their money behind," I noted.

He pointed to Culamara. "They left *her* behind, didn't they?"

Well, I couldn't come up with no answer to that, so I figured I'd better get my offer in fast.

"You come away with me, Miss Culamara, honey," I said, "and I'll give you the first ten stars you see tonight to practice your goddessness on."

"Looks like rain," said Jasper, staring out one of the Three Windows. "What if she can't see any stars through the clouds?"

"Then she can choose 'em tomorrow night," I said. "Stop complicating the issue."

"If I can quote the false god here," said Jasper, "ask him what the job pays."

"I'm glad he brung that up, Miss Culamara, ma'am," I said, "because if you put yourself in my hands, which is a distracting thought in itself, you'll get ten percent of every poorbox of every church in Machu Picchu."

"Hah!" said Jasper. "There's *aren't* any churches in Machu Picchu!"

"All right, then," I said. "Ten percent of every church in all of Peru. We'll work out the details later."

Culamara looked from one of us to the other, a distressed expression on her face.

"I don't know what to do!" she said plaintively.

"Jasper," I said, "we been rushing this poor girl into making a decision before she was ready to. We ought to be ashamed of ourselves."

"I agree," he said. "Especially the part about you being ashamed of *your*self."

"I ain't even gonna argue with you. Culamara needs time to think and reflect on all the things she's heard today."

"Yeah," he admitted, "that seems fair enough, especially since we've lost our armies."

"Jasper, why don't you go fishing for a couple of hours while the poor girl—make that the poor goddess—considers which of us she's going belong to." I turned to Culamara. "Let's you and me go lay down under some bushes where no one will bother us and contemplate your problem."

"Hey, just a minute!" said Jasper.

"All right, all right," I said. "You don't have to go down to the Urubamba to fish."

"Damned right I don't," he said angrily.

"You can swim," I said. "Just watch out for them pirhanas."

"I'm not leaving the two of you alone!" said Jasper.

"You don't have to leave alone," I said. "You can leave with anybody you want."

"Fine," he said. "I'll leave with *her*!"

"What's come over you, Brother Jasper," I said. "I thought we were friends and partners."

"We were," he said. "Until you got greedy."

"You were the one who claimed you weren't sharing no High Priestesses," I pointed out.

"Well, you don't seem all that anxious to share any white goddesses."

I thunk about it, and finally I reached out my hand. "We can't let a little thing like a voluptuous naked woman come between us," I said.

"Right," he said, shaking my hand. "After all, we've been friends for almost three days."

"Right," I agreed. "Share and share alike?"

"Share and share alike," he said.

"Okay," I said. "You can have her from the waist up."

"Now wait a minute!" yelled Jasper and Culamara at the same instant.

"I hope our high-level negotiations haven't upset you none, Miss Culamara, honey," I said.

"I resent being treated as a piece of property," she said.

"That's not a fair thing to say, ma'am," I told her.

"Why not?"

"Because you're being treated as a piece of *female* property," I said. "That makes all the difference in the world."

"Not to me, it doesn't," she said. "I'm sick of gods *and* emperors!"

"Don't listen to him!" said Jasper desperately. "I'll make you Chief Operating Officer!"

"And what'll you be?" I asked him curiously.

"Chairman of the Board."

"Miss Culamara, ma'am," I said, "if it'll make you feel any better, I'll give you twenty percent of all the poorboxes in South America."

"Animals!" she cried. "You're like animals!"

"Maybe so," I agreed. "But he's like a vicious jungle beast with bad breath what doesn't never wash, while I'm more like a cuddly puppy."

"Bah!" she said, taking off her headdress and throwing it on the ground. "You like to fight over things? Fight over that!"

"You sure you don't want to reconsider?" I said. "I mean, don't you feel kind of naked without it?"

But she just turned on her heel—an eye-catching sight in itself—and walked right out of the Temple of the Sun.

"Well, by Myself!" I said. "What a strange way for a sweet little woman to behave."

"Lucifer," said Jasper, as we both stared at the headdress, "I'm getting a little long in the tooth for battles to the death. What say we split the spoils and go our separate ways?"

"We ain't got no tools for splitting the gold nor the diamond," I pointed out.

"You take one, I'll take the other," he said.

"Okay," I said. "I'll take the diamond."

"I kind of thought *I'd* take the diamond, as a cherished remembrance of our friendship."

"I'm right touched by that, Brother Jasper," I said. "But every time I look at that diamond I'll remember our three days together, and the fact that being men of good will we averted a war at the very last moment."

"It'd help me remember the beautiful virginal Culamara," he said.

"I ain't met that one," I said, "but it'd help me remember the Culamara we *did* meet."

"I'm an old man," said Jasper, "and we're at altitude, and everyone knows gold is one of the heaviest elements. I don't know if I could carry it back."

"You won't have to," I said. "I'll stick it in Equipause's saddle bag for you."

"I just *have* to have that diamond as a remembrance of my time in Machu Picchu!" he said.

He was so adamant that I knew he'd seen the gold flaking off the inside of the headpiece too, so finally I suggested we cut cards for it, and since neither of us had any cards we decided to roll my dice. He shook 'em and said baby needed a new pair of shoes, and I knew he wasn't talking about Culamara because shoes were the least of what she needed when night fell and it started getting chilly out, and he finally rolled a ten.

"Hah!" he said happily. "I've got you, Lucifer!"

Then it was my turn. I shook them dice over my head, whispered a small prayer to myself, and rolled a seventeen.

"I guess you lose after all," I said.

"Wait a minute!" he said. "You can't roll a seventeen!"

"Two sixes and a five," I said. "You got a problem counting?"

"There's three dice there!" he yelled.

"See?" I said. "I *knew* you could count."

Well, we argued back and forth for a few more minutes, and then a lady who could have been Culamara's better-looking and less-dressed sister moseyed through the temple, and Jasper pulled the diamond off the headdress and tossed it to me, then picked up what was left and started walking after the demure young lady.

As for me, I hunted up The Dolly Llama and began retracing our journey. I figgered I'd pull out the diamond and admire it a little before the sun set, so I held it up and stared at it, and I saw what seemed like a little scratch on it, so I looked closer, and what the scratch said was "Manufactured by the Coca Cola Corporation."

I flang that diamond just as far into the bushes as I could, and as I continued riding back to Cusco I joined the long line of folks what were doing their best to forget the kingdom of Machu Picchu.

MOTHER SCORPION'S HOUSE OF FALLEN FLOWERS

After what became known in local history as the Battle of Machu Picchu, I decided the time had come to take my leave of Peru. I took the path of least resistance which, when you're a zillion feet high in the middle of what they call Andy's Mountain Range, means down to the sea, and the sea to the west was a whole lot closer than the sea to the east. (You know, I never did meet this Andy, who either discovered or owned the mountains; I guess he had enough brains to stay down where the air was still thick enough to breathe.)

Anyway, I soon found myself in Chile, which when the sun was high in the sky was anything but, and I stopped in Santiago long enough to engage in a fine old game dealing with pasteboards, statistical probabilities, and the number 21. I even put back the couple of pounds I'd lost in Peru, courtesy of the Santiago constabularies, who were a pretty serious bunch and just couldn't see the humor in them three extra aces what slipped out of my sleeve at an inopportune time, and while I wasn't thrilled with my surroundings for the next five days they saved me the price of fifteen delicious meals, always providing you think moldy bread, brown water, and the occasional salamander or grubworm in one or the other is delicious.

Finally my time in durance vile was up, and as a longtime student of durances I got to say the Santiago calaboose was among the vilest. A team of gendarmes kept walking ten feet behind me, and as you can imagine this put a certain crimp in my style when I was finally freed and looking to negotiate price with one charming lady of quality or another, and finally I figured that their jurisdiction ended at the city line, so I made a beeline to it and crossed it, and found myself with no one to talk to except a herd of llamas, and when the king llama saw some of the lady llamas eyeing me provocatively he started bellowing like a politician at election time and chased me downhill until he ran out of interest and I ran out of hill. I figured as long as he'd chose my direction for me I'd keep walking in it, because there was no question that he knew the lay of the land better than I did.

So I walked, and like all them adventurers say in their books, I existed on a diet of fruits and berries (though I rescued mine from the occasional farmhouse I'd pass by in the dead of night), and once I rescued a beautiful senorita from an evening of boredom because just as things were getting interesting her husband showed up with a shotgun and believe you me *nothing* was boring for the next few hours, and the next day I found an even prettier senorita to remove the buckshot from my backside in exchange for my not singing any love songs beneath her balcony.

Finally I could smell the salt air of the sea, and I hit the town of Valparaiso, which was exactly like Santiago except for the waterfront and the ships and the buildings and the smell and all them churches and the fact that all the signs said "Welcome to Valparaiso" which none of the signs in Santiago had said.

I wandered down to the waterfront and took a room at the Castille de Oro Hotel, promising to pay them just as soon as I converted the eighty-three dollar bill in my wallet into local cash. They kept asking where my luggage was, even after I explained that us men of the cloth didn't have much use for worldly goods, and finally, just to ease their minds, I explained that all my steamer trunks were coming in on the next passenger ship, that there'd been some kind of a mix-up whereby a Lucius Jones had wound up with my baggage and I'd wound up with his pretty blonde wife, and that seemed to please everyone.

I moseyed along the waterfront, getting the feel of the place (which seemed to go hand in glove with the smell of it), and finally came to something called O'Higgins Street, which sounded a little like home, as I used to go courting Lulubelle O'Higgins in Moline, Illinois back when I was fourteen and her husband was working the night shift. Anyway, I came to a restaurant called The Lascivious Llama, which, it turned out, specialized in dead stuff but hadn't yet got around to specializing in cooking it none, and when I was done, which was about two mouthfuls after I started, I decided to go out and see if this was the town where I would decide to finally build my tabernacle. Being a sensitive soul what didn't want to upset the chef by walking out in the middle of a meal, I stuck around until both waiters were in the kitchen before taking my leave and making a mental note to pay them someday and come back for another try just as soon as they bought a stove.

I was strolling down the waterfront when I looked into the window of a bar I was passing and did a double take, because sitting there was the prettiest Oriental lady I ever did see, and this wasn't the first time I'd seen her neither. I could have mistooken them dark eyes and high cheekbones and long coal-black hair, but not the extra pair of lungs, and I knew right off the bat that if the Scorpion Lady was here in Valparaiso then there was money to be had in Valparaiso, and lots of it, and that meant that my Silent Partner had led me to the right spot on the map, and this was His way to telling me that this would be the right place for my tabernacle, because there wasn't likely to be any shortage of money for the poor box.

I walked into the bar, went over to her table, and sat down across from her. And it *was* her, all right; now that I was close up I could see the little gold scorpions on her ring and necklace.

"Howdy, my little exotic flower of the East," I said, flashing her my Number Three smile (the one that showed all the teeth). "Remember me?"

"I never saw you before in my life," she said.

"Siam?" I reminded her. "We was almost lovers and sort of partners?"

"You've mistaken me for someone else," she said. "Now please leave me alone."

"You owned a gambling house, don't you remember?" I said.

"If you don't stop bothering me and go away, I will be forced to call for the police," she said.

"You was gonna teach me all them Oriental love techniques what gets writ up in books no one in the U. S. of A. is allowed you read," I said, standing up to demonstrate. "We were going to start with—"

"Oh, shut up and sit down, Lucifer," she said.

"See?" I said triumphantly. "You *do* remember!"

"What are you doing here, anyway?" she said.

"It's a long story," I told her. "But it's a really *good* story. Why don't we go on back to your place and I'll tell you all about it?"

"You haven't changed," she said.

"No, ma'am," I said. "I'm still the same handsome lovable buck you lost your heart to back in Asia."

"I was referring to your clothes."

"I'll slip out of 'em the second we hit your bedroom and you'll never know the difference," I said.

"You seem to be laboring under a number of delusions," she said.

"It'd be a lot more fun for both of us, Miss Scorpion Lady, ma'am," I said, "if you were laboring under just one: me."

"Is that the way you used to knock them dead in Peoria?" she asked.

"Moline, ma'am," I said. "A big city like Peoria was just for holidays."

"I stand corrected."

"You could lie down corrected anytime you want to leave this den of iniquity," I said.

"I own it," said the Scorpion Lady.

"You do?"

"Yes."

"Then I presume the drinks are on the house?" I said, signaling the waiter over.

She sighed. "If I treat you to one drink, will you leave me alone then?"

I began to get the feeling that she wasn't as glad to see me as I was to see her.

"All right, ma'am," I said. "You cut me to the quick, but I'll take one last drink and one last loving look at you, and then I'll go back to my lonely room at the Castille de Oro."

"*Where?*" she shouted.

"The Castille de Oro," I said. "I know it ain't no luxury retreat like you're probably living in, but it suits a humble man of the cloth just fine."

"Damn it!" she muttered. "I *told* them the front desk was just for appearances! It's impossible to get any competent help in this town!"

"I don't think I follow you at all, Miss Scorpion Lady, honey," I said.

"Shut up!" she said. "I have to think."

"If we're still partners, I could do half of the thinking for you," I offered. "The hard half."

She stared long and hard at me, so I poured a little of her beer on my hands and ran 'em through my hair to slick it down some. Then I guv her another great big smile.

"Don't do that, Lucifer," she said, frowning. "It reminds me of the expression on my mastiff's face just before he tried to breed the hassock."

"I don't remember no mastiff back in Siam," I said.

"Remember that dish you thought was veal?" she said. While I was trying to recall what it tasted like and whether there was any trace of a smile on it, she stood up. "All right," she said. "It will lend verisimilitude."

"What are you talking about?" I asked.

"Come with me, Lucifer," she said. "I have a job for you."

"Sounds good to me, ma'am," I said. "But you should know I don't do no heavy lifting, and I got to have Sundays off for preaching in my tabernacle once I get around to finally building it."

"You were made for this job, Lucifer," she said. "You'll be preaching every day."

"Well, that's right thoughtful of you, ma'am," I said. "I passed about twenty or thirty churches on my way to the waterfront. Which one are we setting up shop in?"

"You'll see," she said, heading out the door, and I fell into step behind her.

We hit the waterfront and turned right, and pretty soon we walked into the lobby of the Castille de Oro. There were two guys behind the desk who snapped to attention when they saw us.

"Which of you rented a room to this man?"

"I did," said the one what did. "We have one room that's not in use, and I figured a preacher man would give us good cover."

"You're fired," she said. She turned to the other man. "Who hired that fool?"

"I did," he said uneasily.

"You're fired, too," said the Scorpion Lady. "I will not have my orders disobeyed."

"Ain't you being a tad harsh on them?" I said.

"Shut up or I'll fire you too," she answered.

"You can't fire me," I pointed out to her. "You ain't hired me yet."

The two men guv her a wide berth and walked out the door.

"Follow me, Lucifer," she said.

She led me down a hall to a wood-paneled room lined with books in some language what wasn't English, and had a podium next to the far wall.

"Well?" she said to me.

"You want me to hire on as a librarian?" I said.

"Idiot!" she muttered. She walked over to the podium and patted it with a delicate little hand what probably hadn't killed more than fifteen or twenty men plus her mastiff. "I want you to preach the word of the Lord right here."

"What's the job pay?"

"Why do you care?" she shot back. "You'll be doing the Lord's work." She paused. "Well, *your* Lord's, anyway."

"I still got to eat," I said.

"We'll fix all your meals right here. You'll never have to leave."

"I got to pay for my room," I continued.

"Gratis," she said.

"Gratis to you too, ma'am, but that still don't tell me how I'm going to pay for the room."

"It's yours for no charge."

"Well, I still need money to—"

"There are perks, Lucifer," she said.

"Oh?" I said.

She walked me to the doorway and pointed down the hall, where a young redheaded lady with a figure like unto Hedy Lamar was just moseying back and forth, dressed for extremely warm weather.

"That's one of them," said the Scorpion Lady.

"One of what, ma'am?" I asked.

"One of the perks."

"Let me make sure I got this straight, ma'am," I said. "She's one of the perks?"

"That's right."

"And the Perks ain't the name of no all-girl band nor women's soccer team what's just passing through and spending the night on its way to Santiago?"

"Would I lie to you, Lucifer?" she said.

Based on my previous experience with her, I was tempted to say only when her lips were moving, but then another perk showed up, wearing even less than the first one.

"I accept the job!" I said. In fact, I must have said it pretty enthusiastically, because three more perks stuck their heads and even nicer things out of the doors lining the corridor to see what the commotion was all about.

"Somehow I knew you would," she said.

"What *is* this place, besides the Castille de Oro?" I asked.

"Mother McCree's House of Fallen Flowers," said the Scorpion Lady.

"Who's Mother McCree?" I said. "Some local benefactor?"

"*I* am," she said.

"Well, now that I think of it, that's probably a pretty good idea," I said, "considering you got warrants out for your address over most of Asia and probably half of Europe and America. You wouldn't want no act of Christian charity ruining your business reputation."

"I'm delighted to see that you are so understanding, Lucifer," she said.

"Well, us men of the cloth are like that," I said. "Always understanding, always forgiving. In fact, I could absolve you right now for any sins you'd like to commit with me in the next couple of hours."

"I'm afraid I'm quite busy this evening," she said. "One of my frail flowers has fallen from the path of virtue...."

"No!" I said in shocked tones.

"I'm afraid so. The police want to deport her, and I have to go down to headquarters and plead on her behalf."

"Would you like me to come along?" I said. "Pleading at police headquarters is one of the very best things I do."

"No, that won't be necessary," she said quickly. "You just stay here, get to learn your way around the place." She shot me a knowing smile. "I'll pass the word to the perks."

"Right," I said. "And look at it this way: if they're with me, they won't have time to fall off the path of virtue with no strangers what's only thinking of their own pleasure."

"How understanding you are, Lucifer," she said.

"I'll bring them spiritual comfort like they ain't never had before," I told her.

"I knew I could count on you," she said.

"It's the least I can do for them poor fallen flowers," I said. "I'll comfort the bejabbers out of 'em!"

"Try to keep your enthusiasm under control," she said. "And remember, this is Mother McCree's House of Fallen Flowers. If any strangers ask about it, be sure to give her the credit."

"Helps with the donations, huh?" I said knowingly.

"Precisely," she said. "And now, if you'll forgive me, I really must be off to the station."

She walked toward the front door, but along the way she stopped to speak to a couple of more fallen flowers, turned an pointed toward me, and then she was gone.

I was torn between examining my new office or my new parishioners, when suddenly a brunette approached me, wearing naught but her unmentionables.

"Hi, Big Boy," she said. "You see anything you like?"

"Ma'am," I said, "I got to tell you that as flowers, fallen and otherwise, go, you got two of the lovelier stems I ever seen—and there ain't nothing wrong with your petals, neither."

"So are you going to introduce your stamen to my pistil?" she said with a wink.

This made me back off a few feet, because if a flower had fallen so far that she was toting a pistol in a nice friendly place like this, who knew what she might do with it? But the more I looked at her, the more I could see that she didn't have enough clothes on to hide no pistol.

"I do believe you're having fun with me, ma'am," I said at last.

"That comes later," she said. "Are you ready for some cross-pollination?"

"I ain't cross at no one, ma'am," I said, "and especially not a frail fallen flower like yourself."

She giggled. "Fifi *likes* you."

I looked around. "Is Fifi joining us, ma'am?" I asked.

"I *am* Fifi," she said.

"And I'm the Right Reverend Honorable Doctor Lucifer Jones, at your service."

She giggled again. "There are so many of you I should charge double."

"Just how many of me do you see, ma'am?" I asked, wondering if there was time to get her to an optician before they all closed up shop for the day.

"Cut the talk, Big Boy," she said. "Time is money."

"Now ain't that interesting?" I said. "I always thunk Time was a measurement of how long it takes to get from one place to another."

Well, I could tell she was a real intellectual what had studied Time and flowers and all kinds of things, and I couldn't wait to see what we'd talk about next, but just then a trio of the local gendarmes arrived, and they flashed their badges, pinched a couple of fallen flowers on the way in, spotted Fifi, and announced that she was under arrest.

"Now hold on just a doggone minute here!" I said, standing between them and the door. "What's this here sweet innocent little frail flower done that you think you got a right to come in here and arrest her?"

I thunk two of them was going fall down, they was laughing so hard. The third just limited himself to six or seven guffaws, and finally caught his breath long enough to talk to me.

"This particular frail flower has been selling her favors all over the city," he said.

"I'm her minister, and I find that difficult to believe," I told him.

The second I said it I heard a bunch of high-pitched giggles from behind closed doors.

"You're the minister to *all* these girls?" he asked.

"That's right," I said.

"It must be an exhausting job," he said.

There was another burst of giggling.

"I'm up to it," I said.

"I have nothing but admiration for you," he said. "Many men might be up to the job at the beginning, but I suspect most of them wouldn't be up to it for long."

He looked mighty smug, like he'd just said something George Bernard Somebody-or-other, that English writer what ain't Shakespeare, would want to swipe for one of his plays.

"Take your low humor and your dirty-minded friends elsewhere," I said. "The women who depend on the Mother McCree House of Fallen Flowers for their sustenance are under the protection of me and the Lord."

"These flowers have fallen a little farther and a little more often than you think, Reverend," he said. "Interpol has been trying to get the goods on the Scorpion Lady for years. It will be a real feather in our caps if we can nail her for running the biggest whorehouse in Chile."

"You got the wrong idea," I told him. "The Scorpion Lady herself hired me to bring the power and the glory to these poor downtrodden women."

"And you've never touched one of them?" he said.

I raised my right hand. "As God is my witness, I ain't never touched a one of 'em in the whole time I been employed here." And while I was invoking my Silent Partner, I also thanked Him for not requiring me to answer that question the next morning.

He shrugged. "Well, you can't say you haven't been warned." He turned to his partners. "Okay, let's take her in."

They drug poor little Fifi off. Just as she reached the door she turned and shot me a great big smile, and flashed some of the girls one of them V-for-victory signs the way politicians do right before they lose an election. For the life of me I couldn't figure out what was so all-fired victorious about getting tossed in the calaboose, but I didn't have no time to worry about it, because it struck me that there were dozens of demure young ladies in need of both clothing and comforting.

But before I could do anything about it, a middle-aged man with dark eyes and some kind of accent walked in the door and said he had a donation for the Mother McCree House of Fallen Flowers, and handed me a package what was maybe a foot on each side. I thanked him and stuck it behind the counter of the desk.

He moseyed back out into the night, and then three more men came in, and each of 'em announced that he'd be making his donation in private to a particular fallen flower, and off they went with the flowers of their choosing, and suddenly the place was bustling with private and public donaters, and the interesting thing was that the public donaters always brought a neatly-wrapped package which I figured contained food or champagne, or, if they was really thoughtful, ladies' clothing for chilly nights, but the private donators all knew which of the frail flowers they wanted to make their donation to and they was an exceptionally shy lot because none of them wanted to do it in public.

The Scorpion Lady wandered in around midnight, and plumped herself down in an easy chair.

"How did it go?" I asked.

"I failed," she said without much show of remorse. "Poor Mitzi is already on a ship bound for Malaya."

"While you was gone, they came by and arrested poor innocent little Fifi," I said.

"Yes, I know," she said. "I saw her there."

"Are you gonna be able to get her off the hook so she can come back here?" I asked.

She shook her head. "I doubt it, Lucifer. I'll try, of course, but it's my guess that she'll be on the next boat to Hong Kong."

"Boy, when the police in these here parts label you an undesirable they don't waste no time doing something about it," I said.

"We just have to put up with it," she said.

"But your Home for Fallen Flowers must be emptying out at record speed," I said.

"I have four more moving in tomorrow," said the Dragon Lady.

"You sure got your ear to the ground to be able to hear that many flowers falling," I said admiringly.

"One does what one can," she said. "And now," she added, getting to her feet, "I think I'll take a hot bath before retiring to my bed."

"I hate to think of you getting lonely all by yourself in that tub, Scorpion Lady sweetie," I said.

"Why don't you avail yourself of one of the perks I mentioned earlier?"

"They're getting deported almost faster than I can avail myself," I replied.

"Then there's no time to waste, is there?"

But then I got to thinking about it, and I realized that there wasn't an endless supply of fallen flowers, and somebody had to do something to make sure that these poor frail critters weren't all shipped off to godless lands, so instead of introducing myself to the rest of the young ladies and helping them ease the terrible tension they must have felt living alone in strange surroundings, I decided that the thing to do was go right down to the police station and plead their case for 'em.

I walked in and asked to speak to the head man. They told me that would be Captain Miguel Rodriguez, and they ushered me into this large office, where I found this gray-haired guy with a captain's uniform sitting behind a desk.

"Howdy," I said. "I'm the Right Reverend Honorable Doctor Lucifer Jones, here on a mission of mercy."

"I gave at the office," he said.

"This *is* the office," I pointed out.

"I gave at home," he amended.

"I ain't after no donation, Captain Rodriquez," I assured him.

"Oh?" he said, leaning forward.

"No, sir," I said. "I'm after something bigger."

"How many tickets do I have to buy?" he asked.

"Don't go understanding me so fast," I said. "I'm here to plead for the young ladies from Mother McCree's House of Fallen Flowers."

"You don't have to negotiate with *me*," he said. "That Oriental villainess is their...shall we say...business manager?"

"But you keep chuckin' 'em onto boats and shipping 'em out of here," I said.

"It's my duty to clean up Valparaiso," he said, "and that's what I intend to do."

"Let's talk man to man, Miguel," I said. "You don't mind if I call you Miguel, do you?"

"Call me Captain Rodriguez," he said.

"Let's talk man to man, Captain Rodriguez," I said. "These frail flowers are bringing in donations to the cause every two or three minutes. I'm sure the Scorpion Lady would be happy to pay you ten or even fifteen percent of them donations if you'd just stop shipping all these poor girls off to other countries."

"You're wasting my time, Padre," he said.

"That's Reverend," I corrected him.

"Whatever the hell you are, leave police business to the police. This interview is over."

Well, I'd done my best, and I'd have let it go at that, the Lord being the understanding critter that He is, but on my way out the door I saw Fifi being led off to the docks, and I knew they were deporting her even before the Scorpion Lady could argue in her defense, and that got my good Christian blood boiling, so instead of going back to the Castille de Oro I walked across the street to the Church of the Ascension where I found some local church ladies' club in progress, and I asked if they'd mind if a visiting man of the cloth spoke to 'em, and they seemed flattered as all get-out.

I got up there, and pointed out that every person deserves a second chance, especially them that publicly admitted their past indiscretions by living in Mother McCree's Home for Fallen Flowers, and there was an enormous injustice going on, because unbeknownst to all the good, God-fearing populace the police force was deporting these poor, sweet, penniless girls at a rate of maybe two a day, forcing them to seek asylum in strange countries what they've never been to before.

I explained and I ranted and I roared and I demanded justice, and before long the outraged ladies of the church marched across the street and started tearing the jail apart. They released all the women prisoners, since it's harder to tell a fallen flower from the outside than you might think, and then they refused to leave until they got a written promise from Captain Rodriguez that he was all through deporting the residents of Mother McCree's.

I went back to the hotel, and figgered the least I could do was make a donation to the nice ladies of the church, so I grabbed a few of the boxes what was behind the front desk and carted them back to the church with my compliments.

Then I returned to the Castille de Oro, woke the Scorpion Lady, and told her the good news.

"Fool!" she screamed. "You've ruined everything!"

"You're letting your joy get the better of you," I told her. "Anyone who didn't know you would think you were mad."

"Idiot!" she yelled.

"What's the matter, my love?" I said. "Have I done something to upset you?"

"Of all the gin joints in all the world, why did you have to choose mine?" she snapped. "Why couldn't you have just kept on walking?"

She pulled a suitcase out from under the bed, went to her closet, and started throwing her clothes in it. She'd just about finished when a squad of police came to the door.

"Madame," said the leader, "I regret to inform you that you are under arrest."

"For running a bawdy house?" I said. "I already explained to your Captain Rodriguez that this is a house for fallen flowers."

"For smuggling," he answered. "And Captain Rodriguez is already in jail."

"Smuggling?" I said, as they cuffed the Scorpion Lady. "What in tarnation are you talking about?"

"It was a fiendishly clever operation, run in tandem with a bawdy house," explained the officer. "We never minded the bawdy house. In fact, the police of Valparaiso were among its best customers. But it was just a front. The *real* business was smuggling jewelry and contraband out of South America." He smiled at the Scorpion Lady. "She was the mastermind, of course, but she required a confederate, and that was Captain Rodriguez. She would run the Home for Fallen Women—"

"Fallen Flowers," I corrected him.

"Whatever," he said. "And he would arrest each willing confederate and ship her off to the country where the contraband had been purchased. The women, who were each allowed to leave with a single bag or package, were actually the delivery agents. And we never would have discovered this foul scheme if it weren't for you, Reverend Jones!"

"Me?" I said, over the sound of the Scorpion Lady gnashing her teeth.

"If you hadn't delivered those packages containing drugs and stolen jewels to the good ladies of the Church of the Ascension, the plot would have gone unnoticed for who knows how long?"

"I guess I *did* break it up, didn't I?" I said. "Do I get a medal for this?"

"I am afraid that if we pin it on you, we shall have to do it in your prison cell. I regret to inform you that you are under arrest too."

"What for?" I demanded.

"I will let the magistrate explain it all to you," he said apologetically. "And now all that remains is to bring the two of you back to headquarters and lock you up."

"Me and the Scorpion Lady are old friends," I said. "I don't suppose you could lock us in the same cell while we're straightening out this little misunderstanding."

The Scorpion Lady walked over to me and spit in my eye.

"Well, maybe not, then," I said.

So they carted us off to jail, and I didn't see the Scorpion Lady no more, but I was across the aisle from Captain Rodriguez, who slept about four hours a day and cursed me for the other twenty. The food could have been better, but at least Valparaiso never had to worry about being overrun by rats and other rodents as long as the jailhouse had a chef what specialized in 'em.

I cooled my heels for close to two weeks, and then finally the jailer came by one morning and shaved me and guv me a haircut and a clean set of prison duds, and told me to get ready, that I'd be seeing the judge that afternoon, and sure enough, right after a meal of dried something on what wasn't rice, they unlocked my door and marched me into the courtroom, where I was brung before the bench.

"Good afternoon, Doctor Jones," said the judge, who seemed like a kindly-looking old geezer—or maybe he was a young geezer who'd had to eat the jailhouse food a little too often. "I am Chief Magistrate Ramon Valenzuela."

"Howdy, Ramon," I said. "I'm pleased to—"

"Call me Chief Magistrate, please," he interrupted me.

"Sure thing, Chief Magistrate," I said. "I keep forgetting what a formal country you run here."

"Have you any idea why you were brought before me today?" he asked.

"The kitchen is running out of rats?" I guessed.

"You have been implicated in the running of a house of prostitution," he said.

"That's a lie!" I said. "I didn't even know they *was* prostitutes."

"I find that difficult to believe," he said.

"Well, when you get right down to it, so do I," I said. "You'd be surprised how them flowers can dazzle you with their innocent smiles."

"I shall have to take your word for it."

"But even so, I had nothing to do with running the place."

"You were employed there, were you not?" he asked.

"Yeah, but as a preacher."

"In a brothel?"

"Nobody told me it was a brothel."

"You seem so sincere I am almost inclined to believe you, Doctor Jones," he said. "But that in no way alters the fact that you were consorting with a known international criminal who goes by the sobriquet of the Scorpion Lady."

"Another false accusation," I said. "I kept asking her to consort with me, and she kept turning me down."

The folks in the gallery started laughing at that one, and the judge had to warn 'em to keep quiet.

"The fact remains that you worked in a bawdy house and associated with a notorious criminal," continued the judge. "Even if I were inclined to believe you, you do not strike me as the kind of person we want setting up shop here in Valparaiso."

"That suits me fine," I said. "I'll just go back to one of the other countries I been to lately."

"Those were my thoughts precisely," said the judge. "So I looked into the matter to see which one might be willing to take you back." He shook his head and made a kind of "tsk-tsk-tsk" sound. "You've been a busy boy, Doctor Jones."

"Well, you know how it is," I said.

"I had no idea how it is," he replied. "But I do now. I made inquiries of the government of Brazil. It seems that you were complicit in the theft of the jewels known as the Pebbles of God, to say nothing of stealing and making ransom demands for a famous race horse."

"That was none of my doing," I said. "I was as innocent as Phar Cry."

"As *who*?" he asked.

"The horse."

"It appears that you were also wanted for hunting jaguars out of season."

"I never shot no jaguars," I said. "I just wore them."

"You wore jaguarskin coats?" he asked. "In the tropical jungle?"

"The heads, mostly," I said. I looked at his face. "I guess that'll take some explaining."

"The government of Brazil doesn't wish to hear your explanations," said the judge. "Next on my list was the government of Equador, which has issued a warrant for your arrest for participating in crimes against Nature with a mysterious Doctor Mirbeau."

"Was the Island of Annoyed Souls in Equador?" I said.

He ignored my question and kept right on talking. "The nation of San Palmero has issued an arrest warrant in your name for overthrowing the president and robbing the treasury."

"Which president was that?" I asked. "They got so many of 'em."

"The nation of Columbia claims that you stole the world's most valuable postage stamp," said the judge.

"Erich von Horst stole it," I said. "I just kind of mailed it for him."

"Argentina wants you for disrupting a religious retreat, as well as creating and leading an army on behalf of German war criminals."

"Now I can explain that," I said.

"I should love to hear it."

"First, it wasn't no army," I said. "It was me and six street cleaners, and it ain't our fault we conquered a whole country without firing a shot. And the religious retreat was actually a lost continent what I discovered, though I guess it ain't as lost as it was."

"What a cogent explanation," he said. "Moving right along, I find that the nation of Uruguay wants to question you for possible complicity in the disappearance of Colonels Marcos and Garcia."

"Which government of Uruguay?" I asked.

"I beg your pardon?"

"Well, there's the old one, that I secretly conquered, and the new one, that probably ain't tooken office yet."

The judge sighed heavily. "Bolivia wants to question you about conspiring with a pair of known international criminals, a Major Theodore Dobbins, late of His Majesty's armed forces, and an Australian named Rupert Cornwall." He looked up from the list he'd been reading. "You *do* have the most interesting friends, Doctor Jones."

"Is that everything?" I asked.

"If only it were," he replied. "It seems that our neighbor to the north, Peru, wants to question you about allegedly fomenting a religious war in the forgotten city of Machu Picchu." He paused and stared at me. "I am aware that Americans are known for their energy and industry, but isn't this carrying it just a little too far?"

"A series of easily explained misunderstandings, nothing more."

"I find you a most fascinating man, Doctor Jones," he said.

"Yeah?"

He nodded his head emphatically. "So much so, in fact, that I went back even further in your records. It would appear you have been forbidden ever to return to North America, Africa, Asia and Europe."

I just knew what was coming next.

"I have come to the conclusion that the authorities on those continents knew what they were doing." He suddenly looked troubled. "I have nothing against the continent of Australia," he continued. "Indeed, I find their constitution exemplary, and I have personally never met an Australian I didn't like. They seem like a God-fearing, law-abiding, happy, decent people. I almost hate what I am about to do to them." He paused and stared at me. "Doctor Jones, I have conferred with all the governments I mentioned, and it is our unanimous decision that you are forthwith barred from the continent of South America. You will be placed on a ship heading west into the Pacific later this evening, and never allowed to return."

They marched me back to my cell while they were doing the paperwork for my release, and the judge came by for a minute on his way home.

"You are quite the most remarkable man I have ever met," he said.

"Thanks, I guess," I replied.

"I hope you turn over a new leaf and behave yourself in Australia," he said. "That is the last habitable land mass in the world that hasn't yet barred you from its surface. If they should fall in line with all the others, where else can you go? I mean, *The Man Without a Country* was bad enough—but the Man Without a Continent?"

Then he was gone, and in another couple of hours so was I, heading west across the Pacific to points unknown. Over the next five years I had my share of adventures there, what with naked pagan goddesses and tribal wars and hunting in the Outfront or whatever they call it, and no matter what General MacArthur and General Tojo say I wasn't responsible for Pearl Harbor, and I got every intention of telling you my side of the story, plus everything else I experienced during the next few years, but I been writing for a couple of hours now and its time to go renew my artistic sensibilities with an understanding lady of quality.